$\dfrac{\$10-}{5}$

1st
32078
Myst

THE ALLAH CONSPIRACY

THE ALLAH CONSPIRACY

Christopher Warren

BEAUFORT BOOKS, INC.
New York / Toronto

Copyright © 1981 by William F. Brown

Library of Congress Cataloging in Publication Data

Warren, Christopher.
  The Allah conspiracy.
  I. Title.
PS3573.A7713A78 1981 813'.54 80-27097
ISBN 0-8253-0052-5

Published in the United States by Beaufort Books, Inc., New York.
Published simultaneously in Canada by Nelson, Foster and Scott Ltd.

Printed in the U.S.A.   First Edition

10 9 8 7 6 5 4 3 2 1

To my patient wife

THE ALLAH CONSPIRACY

PART 1

LEBANON
APRIL, 1981

1

" . . . and in news from the Middle East, tensions are still running high in Israel following last Thursday's bombing of a civilian bus. The brutal terrorist attack killed the driver and all nineteen of his passengers. With the PLO High Command now claiming credit, even President Bannon's personal appeal to the Israeli government for restraint isn't expected to have much effect. Sources in Jerusalem say some retaliatory action will undoubtedly be ordered.

"Jack will be back with TV Three's sports and weather right after this brief message. . . . "

In his lead plane, Major Lehrmann banked gently to the right. The rest of his Phantoms followed as they began the final leg of their approach. High over the Mediterranean, they were now pointed straight at the Lebanese coast and the small fishing village of Ras Awwali. They'd be there in less than three minutes, Lehrmann thought as he glanced at his instruments.

Ras Awwali was just one of the three bases the Fatah commandos used to launch their vicious attack six days ago. They were about to be repaid in kind. At that same moment, many other squadron commanders were headed for Ras al Ayn, Ras al Abyad, Qana, and dozens of inland targets that dotted the map of southern Lebanon.

"Major, I've got so many planes on my scope, we ought to have a traffic cop up here," his navigator cracked.

As Lehrmann looked up through his canopy, he saw the white contrails of a squadron of sleek, twin-tailed F–15 Eagles flying high cover above them. They were the only cops he needed. The F–15s ruled the skies of the Mideast, allowing his lumbering bombers to have a quiet morning without worrying about being disturbed. There simply weren't any Arab planes or pilots with the skills to challenge them. Lehrmann had seen the burned scars on the hills of Lebanon that marked the fate of the foolish ones who'd tried.

A milk run wasn't so bad, though. Low-level precision bombing with a heavily loaded jet takes years of practice and all your concentration, he thought. The weight of the bombs makes the controls slow and sluggish. Your eyes had to keep darting over the instruments while the target rushed up toward you, and a third eye had to be kept on the spacing and alignment of the rest of your birds. Who needs excitement?

It had happened to him before. His eyes had been riveted on the target when his navigator had shouted, "Unidentified aircraft! Coming in at . . ." Breaking formation, evading, scattering, climbing, diving, and screwing up the mission. No thanks! The Syrians can sleep in. We'll all have a nicer day.

The coast came up fast now. Squinting, he focused his eyes ahead. A thin, dark line appeared through the dawn mist. He dropped the nose a little, putting the plane into a shallow dive. The line rose higher and stretched across the canopy. Closer now, it slowly puffed out, widened, and separated into a series of different lines. One by one, he could tell them apart as the first rays of the bright morning sun back-lit the jagged line of hills. The distant mountains grew taller and popped up above the shallow coastal hills, the cliffs that lined the shore itself, and the white puff of the surf. Each grew larger, rapidly. Looking inland to the plain, he could see the lines and patterns of small fields, orchards, trees, and finally the village.

Seen through the bomb sight, the target was shades of gray upon gray. Indistinct. Formless. Then he saw shapes, lines, rectangles, squares. The shapes became buildings, walls, roofs, streets, windows. The colors changed from gray to black and white, and finally to browns,

12

reds, and greens. The curved line of the breakwater flashed by. The blue of the harbor, the white strand of beach, houses, windows, movement, figures, people running, looking up. All rushing by through the sight. Quickly. Toward him. Under him.

His thumb rested firmly on the button of the bomb release.

Slowly. Pressing.

Six nights before, Ras Awwali had unleashed a violent force of its own.

Two small boats full of their best young men, hand-picked, had set out on a desperate assault against the coast of Israel. They'd trained and prepared for months and were honed to a keen fighting edge. When the day finally came, the whole village teemed with activity. Every detail would be decisive and must be attended to, checked, and double-checked.

But this target was well worth the price, thought Jamil Rashid as he looked down at the maps and photos spread across the table. It was a glittering new high-rise apartment complex perched above the beach at Haifa.

His group of six was only one part of the total force of eighteen commandos who'd put out from three bases. It was the largest seaborne attack they'd ever tried.

The boats would travel in widely separated pairs. The attack could succeed if even one of the pairs, or even one boat, reached the target. Strapped tightly under the gunnels were neatly wrapped packages of plastic explosive. When they were placed by experts, two or three of these would bring one of the tall buildings crashing down in rubble along with its screaming occupants.

Yes, it is worth it, Jamil thought.

Like the others, he'd been chosen from only the best volunteers in the unit. None of them had any real combat experience, but they were well trained, eager, and intense. With the keen mind and quiet leadership he'd shown throughout his training, Jamil had been given the added honor of being chosen for boat commander. He could feel the sense of mission weigh down even heavier upon him as he reviewed the plans.

As their officers watched closely, the young commandos carefully cleaned, oiled, checked, and reloaded their automatic rifles. Once again they examined the ammunition, the wrappings on the explosives, the grenades, detonators, food, water, maps, gasoline, and heavily muffled boat motors.

As the last light of a gloomy sunset faded away, Jamil and the other boat commander ducked into the operations center to meet with their captain and go over the route, defenses, and escape roads.

"The night's going to be overcast, which is perfect," he said. "But that makes it all the harder for you to navigate and keep together. There's no help for you out there, so stay close. Use your compasses often and follow the lights down the coast. If you fall behind schedule and are still out there when the sun comes up, you know what will happen! You can't be too early, or late. Everyone has to go ashore at five A.M. precisely."

As his eyes bore into each of them he added, "The whole mission depends on surprise. Evade their patrols, and no gunfire until you get ashore. If you have no other choice, then you'll have to fight. Use maximum firepower."

Jamil could remember the sign that hung in the small mess hall at the training camp in Iraq. It was their most important rule. "They don't take prisoners! Kill them or they'll surely kill you."

All commandos knew it was a dangerous mission, despite their outward swagger and bravado. Taking a small boat at night through thirty miles of rough open water that was constantly patrolled by a cruel enemy was a risky job for skilled sailors, which they weren't. Most had been raised in towns or on small farms. Once they got to Haifa they had to land and attack with converging forces against an alert defense they didn't know much about; that was if they were still in keen fighting shape when they got there.

"Remember," the captain concluded, "you've drilled and practiced this over and over. You have the edge. They don't know you are coming, much less where or when. You cannot fail. Allah is with you."

To Jamil this wasn't a suicide mission despite the odds. He was ready to die for the cause he fought for, but others had succeeded and he would too. If they struck quickly and got away to the hills, they knew where to find refuge with the PLO underground inside Israel. Then they'd work their way back and be greeted as heroes. Like Carlos and the others.

Standing on the dark jetty, he and Ahmed said good-bye to Kadri. His little sister and Ahmed's bride, she'd pray hard for them both.

Their captain gave them his last words of inspiration. "For a generation of our young men, you are the hope. You have the honor to strike at the oppressor that weighs them down. You go where they cannot go. You strike where they cannot strike. You carry the strength of a thousand who wait for your return!"

He steadied the boat as Ahmed and Haidar climbed down to join him. As he looked at them and over at those in the other boat, Jamil thought tomorrow the world would see they were not all a bunch of cartoon characters—the fat Bedouin lounging on his pillows under a tent in a desert oasis, or the oil sheik in his spotless white robes and sunglasses driving a big black Cadillac, or the unwashed mob of pickpockets in a Cairo market. No, we are fighters for a free Palestine.

"Palestine!" Jamil shouted, and the others shouted back.

A homeland few of them had ever even seen, or if they had, couldn't remember. It had become a mystical place nonetheless. A land of verdant green fields, lush rolling hills, flowing streams, ripe orchards, and small idyllic villages full of peaceful, happy families. A land they only knew from stories told over and over in crowded refugee camps. But it was theirs.

The mission they set out on was very special. Code-named "Day of Redemption," it was to take place precisely in the early morning hours of April 9, the thirty-third anniversary of the Dier Yassin massacre. To Jamil and the others, that was inspiration enough and a symbol of infamy to all Palestinian Arabs.

On April 9, 1948, the radical troops of the Stern Gang annihilated the Palestinian village of Dier Yassin. Only a handful of its 250 men, women, and children had lived to tell of the slaughter. It led to the first mass exodus of over 500,000 Palestinians from areas of Israeli control.

Jamil wasn't even born until years later, but he could remember old women breaking into tears at a mention of the name. Men spitting on the ground, curses, angry voices, threats, clenched fists.

"What are they mad about, Haleem?" Jamil had asked, looking up.

"About Dier Yassin . . . You'll learn about it soon enough," his older brother replied, stroking Jamil's hair. "Soon enough."

They all knew that the Israeli government had denounced the

attack, but it was little consolation. Like the bombing of the King David Hotel—the Jews had elected the man responsible, Begin, as their last Prime Minister.

It had become a rallying cry to action. Like Kfar Etzion on the other side; or at another time and place, the Bataan death march, Malmady, Lidice, Dunkirk, Wounded Knee, and a thousand more. Every nation had a sordid page in its history that it tried to forget. But this one would not be forgotten.

Trapped in this caldron of violence was the small fishing village of Ras Awwali, indistinguishable from hundreds of others like it that dot the shore of the eastern Mediterranean. For centuries the lives and customs of its people had changed very little. Their concerns didn't go much further than the sea they fished and the small farm plots and orchards they tended.

They were Lebanese. An ancient and proud people, their roots went back to the Phoenicians who had settled the land before Moses led his flock from bondage in Egypt. Their empire rose in the tenth century B.C., built on trade, the arts, and manufacture, not conquest and war. Being men of the sea, they spread colonies as far as Cyprus, Sicily, Sardinia, the coast of Africa, and Spain. Their ships explored the coast of Celtic Britain before the armies of Rome had even crossed the Alps.

Phoenicia was the Land of the Deep Purple, so called for the radiant blue dye they produced and exported that became the badge of royalty across the Mediterranean. Like all nations of that period, their boundaries were vague, but stretched out from the capital at Sidon to far up the present-day coast of Syria. To the south was Tyre, and Phoenicia stretched beyond it to Mount Carmel, well within twentieth-century Israel.

Just to the south of Tyre lay Ras Awwali. It was a tightly packed semicircle of fifty buildings pressed against the shore. In between the buildings wound narrow streets and alleyways that opened out into a small market square. Here could be found the few public buildings, a small church, and an inn. All of the buildings were made of a fairly uniform gray-beige stone dug many years before out of the nearby hills. The thick stone walls kept out the worst of the summer heat and winter cold. By local custom, the windows in the buildings were tall and narrow with a distinctive round arch at the top. Giving vivid accent to the dull stone and dark streets were the bright red tile roofs, which could be seen from miles away in the morning sun.

At the water's edge a stone seawall curved out to make a small harbor for the village's fishing fleet, which consisted of perhaps two dozen wooden sailboats. Each was a little over twenty feet long with a shallow draft, wide beam, high curving bow, one lone mast, and a tiny cabin near the aft end. They were very old and weathered, but well maintained.

Each morning the men of the village sailed out to fish while the women, children, and elders mended nets, cooked, or worked the fields and orchards nearby. After breakfast, the old black-garbed grandmothers took their tattered straw brooms and swept the stoops of the houses and the surrounding streets. The children helped to harvest the dates, citrus fruit, wheat, and bananas. Late in the afternoon, the whole village would gather at the seawall to help haul in the day's catch. When it was good they sold the surplus on the docks in Tyre. Even when it wasn't, the sea and the land would provide.

They were scrupulously honest in their dealings with each other, but were known to do a little smuggling or grow a little hashish from time to time. These were ancient and honorable forms of creative commerce and none of anyone else's business.

But time and outside forces began to fray and tear this regular social fabric into ever smaller pieces. By the late 1960's Ras Awwali and its neighboring villages across southern Lebanon were dragged deeper and deeper into conflicts they weren't part of and didn't understand.

Waves of Palestinian refugees were driven into their land seeking sanctuary, bringing their own passions and causes. Many sought a refuge from war, but others sought a base from which to continue it. It was home to none. The migration brought attacks, reprisals, civil war, invasion, and destruction. It tore apart the long-standing accords between Lebanese Christians and Lebanese Muslims, and a way of life.

Beginning in 1960, Fatah commando bases were established in the south. The guerrillas struck at Israel and Israel struck back. This cycle continued with increasing violence, but the Lebanese government and her small, weak army were powerless to stop either side. Finally they just abandoned the whole region to the terrorists and Israeli bombs.

The rest of the Lebanese came to ignore the bloodshed far to the south and lived their own lives in peace. But it was not to be, as a new and deadlier force was unleashed on them in 1970. Jordan had been one of the few Arab nations to open its borders and try to resettle the Palestinians after each war. But, like Lebanon, the Palestinians only used Jordan as a military base, triggering Israeli reprisals. Unlike Lebanon, Hussein had a well-trained army and the determination that he alone would rule in his land. That September—Black September—he launched his Bedouin tank corps to disarm the PLO. He routed them and forced them to shift their base to the one remaining country they couldn't be thrown out of: Lebanon. Soon, 400,000 Palestinian refugees followed.

They engulfed Lebanon as they spread far to the north. By 1977 Beirut symbolized the nation itself, with boundaries, barbed wire, burned-out buildings, checkpoints, no-man's-lands, bodies in the streets, and gunfire in the night. It had been called the jewel of the Mediterranean. Now it lay like a pile of opaque powder, shattered by the crazed blow of a steel hammer.

Like most others, the Lebanese villagers of Ras Awwali finally fled north to find safety. The Lebanon which was is no more.

As Jamil's boat pulled away from the seawall that night it was a far different Ras Awwali he left behind. Now a base camp for a PLO commando detachment, they and their families were its only occupants. The larger homes in the village were their barracks. The public buildings served as a command center, field hospital, training rooms, armory, and storerooms.

The buildings were battered from a decade of artillery, bomb, and rocket attacks. Walls were scarred and pitted. There were gaping holes in many of the roofs. Stones, bricks, crumbled plaster, and broken roof tiles littered the narrow streets along with an old assortment of trash and garbage, making them all but impassable. What was still intact suffered from painful neglect.

In the harbor could still be seen a few badly leaking and seldom-used fishing boats riding sluggishly at anchor. The rotting hulks of a few more lay half-buried on the beach or rested on the bottom in shallow water. The protecting seawall had several large gaps where stones had been dislodged by the water or pried up to reinforce nearby gun emplacements.

18

The fields at the edge of the village were trampled and barren. The trees in the orchard were untended and spoiled fruit lay on the ground beneath them, the even rows of trees broken by open spaces where many had been cut down for firewood.

It was an unpleasant place. It had a past and a present, but no future.

The six commandos in the raiding party had trained together for many months, but knew little of each other. They used code names taken from hometowns, Muslim heroes, or their own first names. They were forbidden to discuss their pasts. This was to protect family and friends from reprisal but it also lent an aura of adventure to the group.

An exception was Jamil and his brother-in-law, Ahmed Saed. They'd met and become close friends in the harsh mountain training camps in Iraq. Hot days and freezing nights of assault drill, rifle practice, infiltration, demolition, and indoctrination drew them together as it screened out the willing but unfit.

Jamil, like the rest of the trainees, hated the ''Pit'' worse than any other part of the camp. This was the crude ring where a stocky Syrian taught them his own special brand of hand-to-hand killing. His favorite sport was to match recruits against each other. If they weren't quite aggressive enough to please him, or if one of them needed a little discipline, he'd jump down and demonstrate.

The Syrian only tried to demonstrate on Jamil once. He threw Jamil around the ring, but not without effort, and he saw enough to know not to keep trying as Jamil got better. Circling him in the dirt, he knew he hadn't paid enough attention when he had watched from the stands. Jamil had a natural grace, deceptive speed, quick mind, and calculated viciousness. His technique was still crude, but his black eyes darted back and forth, looking for an opening. The Syrian missed as often as he connected, and he noticed that although his best blows might knock Jamil flat, they didn't break his concentration or slap that damn grin off his face.

Ahmed was the complete opposite—short, muscular, and with exceptional power in his arms and legs. To the Syrian it was like looking in a mirror. When he fought Ahmed there was no guile or strategy, just brute strength that had to be stomped senseless before it stopped. Ahmed never spoke and never changed his blank expression. With his huge neck, round face, and hooded sleepy eyes, he was like a rock with legs.

Jamil remembered their first very rugged forced march. Afterward, he and the other recruits collapsed on the rough wood floor of the barracks in total exhaustion. Lying on his back with his eyes closed, he kept trying to block out the agony of the present, but with no success. A metallic clicking and rattling kept disturbing his reverie. Slowly turning his head, he opened one eye and looked over to the corner by the window. In the square of bright sunlight sat Ahmed slowly and methodically cleaning his rifle. He looked up at Jamil with an embarrassed shrug and said, "Take a nap. I'll clean yours when I'm done."

Totally dissimilar, they began to rely on each other and became a team. During a field exercise they lay next to each other on their blankets under the stars.

"Ahmed, if you could be anywhere else, at any other time, where would you like to be right now?" Jamil asked quietly.

"I . . . I don't know . . . I never thought much about it. . . . I'm here. The rest doesn't matter much, I guess."

"Well, I know what I'd like to be doing. I'd like to be on a beautiful, white Arabian stallion. A desert horse. Galloping across the hills at the head of a troop of cavalry in the army of the Great Saladin. In flowing white robes. A black harness with silver studs. In one hand I'd hold my small round shield and the reins. In the other would be my curving, razor-sharp scimitar. I'd ride with him as we took Damascus, Aleppo, Antioch, Tyre, and even Jerusalem. Fighting the Templars and Crusaders, man to man. The Holy War. The *jihad*!" he said as his voice rose and his eyes flashed.

Ahmed lay silent for a while. "You have too much imagination, Jamil. I guess I'd be happy if I could just tend our old farm in Galilee. Work hard. Sweat. Till the fields. Not have to kill people . . . That's what I'd like."

Ahmed met Kadri while he and Jamil were on leave in Damascus. She was being trained as a PLO nurse. As the months passed they corresponded and saw each other more and more often. Finally, Ahmed came to Jamil in the traditional way to ask his permission for them to marry.

"You know, Ahmed, our older brother Haleem should be doing this, but God knows where he is. I guess the duty has fallen to me. He'd be as pleased as I am to give our blessing to you. The three of us are very close. Kadri hasn't had a happy life and I know you'll take care of her.''

As they rode back to camp, he told Ahmed, ''The biggest joke about this whole thing is that we really aren't even Palestinians.''

''Wait a minute—you told me you were born in Nablus.''

''Oh, we were, but our parents were Jordanian. Our father was a captain in the Fortieth Jordanian Armored Brigade stationed there. He was killed on the first day of the '67 War when the area was overrun by Israeli tanks. Haleem got us out that night. I can still remember walking along the dark road holding Kadri's hand on one side and our mother's on the other. We had to leave the road and go through the dark fields. We hid in an orange grove for a while as some tanks went by. I don't even know whose they were. We were very young. But I remember the gunfire and explosions. And crossing over the bridge on the Jordan River before it fell,'' he said, staring quietly out the window of the bus.

''Something like that is very hard to forget, but why did you end up in the camps if you were Jordanian? Didn't you have relatives to go to?''

''Our mother was sick, so we stopped the first place we came to. She died a few weeks later. She just couldn't adjust. . . . Besides, many of our friends were there. People took care of us as best they could. We thought of ourselves as Palestinians. It was the only land we knew, and the Jordanians did nothing to help us, so we stayed.''

Jamil's memory of his father dimmed over the years. He remembered him in his light beige uniform with the ribbons and shiny tanker boots, but his strongest memory was of him at prayer. He was a devout Muslim and five times each day he'd heed the muezzin's call, face Mecca, and kneel down on his mat to pray.

''*Laa ilaaha illa llaah!* There is no God but God! *Allahu akbar!* God is great!'' On his forehead was the pale, proud mark left by years of supplication on the rough mat.

''Father,'' he asked one day, ''our teacher said that in the eyes of God, all men are equal. . . . ''

''Yes, Jamil, that goes for the king or the poorest man in the country. To God they are all equal.''

''But what about the Jews, are they our equal?''

''Ah,'' his father laughed. ''Well, yes, to God. We are both the children of Adam and Eve. And of Abraham. But you remember Cain killed Abel, his brother, just as they have killed many of our people. And God punished Cain as he will punish them—because we are equal in his eyes.''

"But you are a soldier. And you have killed Jews.''

"Only to defend our land and our people. It is God's place to punish, not mine!''

The older Jamil grew, the less a belief such as that gave him the answers he needed.

He heard a more powerful voice in the refugee camps. It was the voice of the first PLO organizer he heard speak. The organizer's piercing eyes and fiery rhetoric caught the imagination and attention of his young listeners. Here, Jamil thought, was a belief that offered hope and self-respect to offset the squalor of the camps.

"We are Palestinians and our land has been stolen by a foreign invader. The British and Americans salved their consciences and solved their problems by giving away our land to the Zionists. But it will not be! Palestine belongs to the Palestinians. We will be free men in our own land.

"Look around you . . . Are there any here who can see his mother or sister living in this filth and degradation and do nothing? Can he still call himself a man?'' Pausing to look at each of them, he continued, "We must bring forth a new elite of only the most dedicated and strong among you who will lead us back to cleanse our land with blood and fire!''

Over the years that followed, the cause provided the only sense of purpose that was strong enough to fill the vacuum of the camps.

The Rashid children grew and matured along with the PLO. After years of infighting, the ten major Palestinian organizations set aside their differences at the Palestinian National Congress in Arab Jerusalem in 1964. It was not an easy task, since they spanned the spectrum from Muslim to nationalist to communist. But they set up a joint military command and bases. The small but militant PFLP of George Habash never did join and launched the majority of the most savage raids of the late 1960's and 1970's. In 1969, Yassir Arafat became the head of the gangly PLO.

The morning of Kadri's wedding at the camp, Jamil was hurriedly summoned to the commandant's office by a breathless runner. As he knocked on the headquarter door, he knew it had to be important and quickly dusted off his well-worn fatigues. Young recruits always feared an order to appear like this. Even trivial infractions of the strict rules would produce severe punishment. God, he thought, what did I do wrong, especially today!

"Enter," he heard a stern voice say.

With strictest military precision he opened it, marched into the room, and came to rigid attention three paces in front of the large desk.

Staring straight ahead he said crisply, "Sir, Recruit Jamil reporting as ordered." He was dimly aware of two other figures seated in the deep armchairs off to the side. As one of them slowly turned toward him, Jamil's eyes involuntarily looked back. In shock he sputtered, "Haleem!... What on..." Oh, Lord, he thought, what have I done. "Excuse me, Commandant."

"Relax, Jamil. At ease. I can understand your surprise." The commandant laughed with a touch of nervousness. "We are very pleased that your brother... Colonel Rashid, could join us for the wedding today. He's told me that he hasn't seen much of you for a number of years, so I can understand."

Haleem rose and smiled broadly at his little brother. "It's good to see you again. It looks like the camp life has been good to you.... I would have let you know I was coming, but your letter took weeks to catch up with me, and I wasn't able to swing a trip back until last week. But I wouldn't miss it!"

"Colonel," the commandant asked with great deference, "can I provide you with anything?"

"No, Captain. This is a social visit. But if you would, my aide Lieutenant Arazi needs to use your radio to call Beirut. And if you don't mind, perhaps my brother could be excused to show me around. I doubt that much has changed since I was here and your people have better things to do."

As they walked out into the dusty compound, Jamil was still stunned. A colonel, he thought. No wonder the commandant acted so odd. As he looked at Haleem, he saw the years had changed him. Older, more filled out, and with a casual self-confidence in his eyes and mannerisms. His clean, well-tailored fatigues were out of place here. He noticed they had no rank or insignia, but Haleem carried himself like a man who didn't need them.

"Now, little brother," Haleem said, throwing a rough arm around

Jamil's shoulder. "Let's go see Kadri . . . and this Ahmed fellow you are about to let her marry. If I don't like him, I'll break his neck . . . then yours!"

Grinning, Jamil replied, "So long as you do him first."

Haleem gave him a questioning look. "Oh, by the way, the commandant had some pleasant things to say about you. I was very proud. He said a few of the older cadre here remembered me and said you were just like me when I came through here. They think you'll be a fine officer soon. I used a little influence with him and I think he'll assign the three of you together if he can. You and Ahmed have good records, and they always need nurses. I'd like to see as much of our small family together as possible. He's going to be sending a group to a detachment in Lebanon soon." With a knowing smile he added, "I think he'll find a way to do what I ask."

Jamil stared at Haleem with a puzzled expression.

Haleem just laughed and said, "Don't ask. I can't tell you any more, and you really don't want to know anyway."

2

The two small boats disappeared from sight as soon as they passed the breakwater and reached the open sea beyond. With dark faces, dark clothes, and dark-painted boats, they blended into the night. Outside the shelter of the harbor they were greeted by the fresh ocean breeze. Small swells chopped and slapped the side of the boat, spraying them with a fine mist of salt water. The overcast sky and gloomy sea were one.

Like all the others, Jamil was tense and nervous with the responsibility he bore. It was his one chance to repay all the pain and suffering of his youth, the deaths of his parents, the frustrating years in the camps, and the months of hard training. Each of these had become a lens that provided a cruel focus for his life, driving him to this time and place.

His small squad was a highly destructive projectile. It had been patiently crafted, aimed, and fired at a distant target. Those who'd lit the fuse so expectantly could now only sit and wait through the long hours of the night. Their jobs were done. They were now mere spectators. Success was in the hands of fate and forces far beyond their control. It would be many hours before their ears picked up the first faint echo.

But intense young commandos are not insensitive machines. With the cheers of their comrades still fading into the night, each of them felt the heady electricity that all new soldiers feel on the eve of their first battle. Hours later, after interminable rolling and buffeting in small open boats on a cold, dark sea, the first tinges of doubt would begin to creep in. Imperceptibly at first, the faint shivers would soon mount in intensity. Each minute of their journey etched itself out so very slowly. Gradually, the first tiny fissures appeared and spread across the thin veneer of their self-confidence. With no support from below, the surface cracked, broke away, and fell in large pieces into the deep pit of fear below.

The significance of April 9 was not lost on the Israeli Coastal Command Headquarters at Haifa. The date hadn't been marked by major incidents for some years, but it remained one of those dozen or so days in the year that called for increased alerts, extra guards, and intense patrolling. It was now a quiet routine and only the most senior officers fully appreciated the meaning of the date.

That evening as Captain Yitzak Navon prepared for his 5:00 P.M. briefing of the patrol boat commanders, he had a formidable array of weapons at his disposal. As operations officer for the "hot corner" from Haifa to the Lebanese border, he needed every one of them. "When they come at us from the sea, this is the area of our greatest danger. There are too many targets and too many enemy bases nearby. The sea is an open highway and we are the only forces standing in their way," he often told his men.

Navon had joined the navy soon after Israel gained her independence. They had grown and matured together through four wars and four uneasy peaces. Each improvement they made was barely enough to match a more skilled, more numerous, and better equipped enemy. The early days when the navy consisted of one cast-off American pre-World War II destroyer and several battered PT boats were long gone. Their navy's priority was still a distant third behind the air force and army, but they were respectable. And now that there was peace with Egypt, the Northern Command had the luxury of most of the better equipment available.

As Navon looked down his order of battle chart for the evening, he noted that he had the old Yarkon, one of the large 96-ton Israeli-built patrol boats commissioned in 1957. Just back from repairs, it would serve as his forward command post because of its range, size, heavier armament, and electronic gear. He also had five of the 35-ton Dabur class boats armed with two 20 mm. and two .50 cal. guns each. Finally, he had three of the fast, new American Mark Is. Any of these nine boats could easily outgun an intruder.

But, Navon thought, the problem wasn't blowing an enemy out of the water, the problem was finding him. They must patrol over three hundred square miles of dark ocean. On an overcast night like this, you could hide the whole Seventh Fleet out there. He was responsible for the ten miles from Haifa to the Lebanese border plus the first ten miles of Lebanon itself. From the ragged coast he went fifteen miles out into the sea. They must watch for rubber rafts being put over the side of passing freighters, raiders disguised as fishermen, and even small rowboats hugging the coast.

But with starlight scopes, infrared scanners, motion-sensitive radar, and complex night optical gear on his ships and planes they were able to do a reasonable job of filling in the gaps, he thought.

"We have six good shots at stopping the bastards," he told his officers. "We've got to do each as if there are no others. We watch their coastal bases and keep hitting them so they can't even put an attack together. Then we dog their shore and try to catch them when they just come out. We must constantly block all of their likely approach courses. We have to watch the line of the border so they can't cross over. Toward morning, we watch all the approaches to our own shore. Finally . . . God forbid . . . the army must stop them on the shore. When they get that far, you and I have failed."

But Navon had a few other aces up his sleeve—his specially equipped search planes. He had salvaged two World War II PBY Catalina seaplanes from the scrap heap. Too slow for any other use, they were ideal for him. Modified with night optical gear, larger fuel tanks, flare chutes, and muffled engines, they were reliable and durable. Their large, round plexiglass waist bubbles were perfect for observers. He also had probably the last remaining Lockheed YO–3A still flying. They'd been built for the United States to spot enemy troop movement at night and were so incredibly quiet they could pass within a few hundred feet of a target without making a sound. Navon thought they must have been useless in Vietnam. What's the sense of not being heard in jungle you can't see through? Leave it to the Americans. He laughed. But on the open sea, now that was a different story.

Navon was immensely proud of his men. As he'd told a visiting

United States senator the week before, "We don't usually have the best equipment, but like our sister services we use what we have with economy, skill, and daring."

"You certainly have some brave young men, Captain."

"It isn't a matter of being brave, Senator. The Egyptian and Jordanian troops, and even the Fatah, are just as brave as our boys."

"Then how do you account for the shellackings you gave 'em in '48, '56, '67, and '73?"

"Well, believe me, the Arab troops can stand and fight and die when they are well led. Or when they can get us one on one. But they can't match our system of war or match armies in a fast-moving modern battle. We are a technological society with a citizen army. We are highly educated and trained so that even a private can understand complex weapon systems, tactics, and the employment of combined arms at the lowest tactical level. There are too few of us to shed our blood needlessly. We use the air force to locate, contain and isolate. Our armored columns then slice through and flank. The infantry closes in and holds. And then the artillery pounds them to pieces. Together it is a well-drilled machine, a system of firepower, movement, and economy of large forces at the right time and place."

"But you are so outnumbered; it must take large numbers of troops to hold the thin borders you have."

"We could never afford that. We have a small hard core of regulars whose job it is to block the well-known invasion points. They are hand-picked and constantly trained. Their job is to jump into the breach and hold it against huge numbers of enemy troops. The first twelve to twenty-four hours they're on their own except for the air support we can send them. They buy us the time for our large reserve units to mobilize and dash to their aid. Like on the Golan in '73."

"I guess that isn't much help against terrorists, though."

"No. It is impossible to completely defend against a terrorist who is willing to die. One can always manage to get through if they send enough. We hate them and are very glad when we get the opportunity to kill them. But it doesn't console the relatives of the people they kill. It is a senseless way for men to die, but I suppose you must admire their courage."

As they gathered around the table, Navon asked, "Everyone

here?'' Unfolding his large area map, he continued, ''I hope you all got some sleep. I think you're going to need it. The reports from the Lebanese coast don't look good, and we are long overdue. If you see anything at all tonight, check it out and call in some backup. Keep the base informed and monitor your radios. Here are your assignments on the map, so look them over closely.''

God, he thought, pausing to light his pipe, they are all so young and sure of themselves. They're much better than we were. Better trained. Better equipped. But they don't know how close it was. They don't know a day when we were not a nation. Or a day when it was almost lost. 1948. We hung by a thread. We had nothing. Almost pushed into the sea. The ringing blood oaths from all around us. From King Saud, the Grand Mufti, Nuri Pasha. Even in the heart of the Jewish Quarter a massive bomb shattered all of Ben Yehuda Street. There were no front lines then. Every village, every farm, every city block was the front line. Our convoys massacred at Bab el Wad. The mutilated dead at Kfar Etzion. Fresh immigrants right off the boat thrown against the legion at Latrun. We bent and we bled, but we did not break. We bought time, but at a price. It was ever so close.

''As you see, I want the pattern to be a little different tonight. The Yarkon will be up on the border in a good position to coordinate. The rest of you keep Dror informed. I want no holes in the coverage. Not tonight. Here's your lists of the call signs and frequencies.''

They could never understand those heady days of May. What it meant to us back then. A Jewish city of Jerusalem. A Nation of Israel, for the first time in two thousand years. Only three years out of the stench of the death camps, a Nation of Israel raising its head to the world. May 14. Ben-Gurion speaking aloud the prayer mumbled during the nineteen centuries of the Diaspora. We are home. Not for us but for them, those who were not there with us. Old prophesies on fragile parchment now fulfilled. The lands of the seven tribes at last united. The land of Abraham, David, Solomon. Ours. We had returned. Our land again. The *hatikvah*—the hope. A Nation of Israel.

''Ghory, Kunz, your boats go up on the Lebanese coast. Bottle it up. The other three Dabur boats go from the border south, five to ten miles out. I want the Mark Is in the same area but only one to three miles out. Watch close in to the shore. At midnight, everyone drops south of the border. At three A.M., begin to fall in toward the shore. I want the

Mark Is to be sure to watch the Bay of Haifa and the shore around Nahariya. If we have problems, I'm positive that's where we'll find them."

Relighting his pipe, he laid the wooden match on the edge of the bowl. The added stability made the tremble in his hands less noticeable. "Okay, any last questions?" Looking around from face to face, he added, "Then go crank 'em up. Good hunting!"

He watched them gather up their papers and leave in small groups. Talking among themselves, they laughed and sauntered down the hall. It was the banter of young officers under pressure. They could only relax and communicate with others in the same circumstance.

Navon dimmed the overhead lights, poured a fresh cup of coffee, and sat down in his armchair across the room from the large back-lit sector map mounted on the wall. Alone in the room, he lit another match but did not try to control the wavering flame. When he couldn't light the pipe on one match, he knew it would be time to get out. He wasn't there yet.

In the long hours that followed, the tension slowly mounted in the operations room. Navon knew the odds were heavily in his favor, but this game didn't respond to mathematical rules. Human error, weather, and just plain bad luck made an eventual failure inevitable. It was rare, but the result was always the same—a frightful toll of dead and maimed civilians.

Whenever there was a successful boat action and they'd stopped a commando raiding party, his junior officers would come in jubilant and invite him to go to the club with them to celebrate. He always declined and they had finally stopped asking. He had always said, "Thanks, you men go on and have a good time. You earned it." What he always wanted to say but never did was, "I've learned that these victories are hollow. You see, each victory only brings the odds of failure one step closer." But as they rose up the ladder of command, they'd see this themselves. Then they'd finally understand.

Navon realized long ago that he was just another example of how the daily year-in and year-out responsibility wore down and occasionally broke even the strongest Israeli commanders and political leaders. It also explained why they were so inflexible at the bargaining table. It was a tense and nervous fatalism. The sure knowledge of their responsibility for failure. They were like old men on a bomb squad. Waiting.

Years before, Navon could still remember the parting words of the operations officer he replaced. The man stared out the window for several long minutes and finally said nervously, "... You know, Yitzak ... I was the kind of deck officer who always grieved the loss of one of my men in battle. But that was their job, a risk that went with the uniform.... But when I failed here ... in this room ... I knew for certain that it was women, children, unarmed civilians that paid every time for my mistake.... The responsibility just became enormous ... I ... " He turned slowly to face Navon. He had the eyes of a whipped dog. Silently, he twisted his cap in his hands and then walked out of the room.

Navon didn't understand then, but he grew to clearly understand the message over the years. The relentless pressure, slow agony, wrenching frustration, and fear of failure was the occupational hazard that he and all other senior Israeli leaders bore. He could now see why so many filled their spare time as skilled archaeologists, watch repairmen, built ships in bottles, or retired to the life of a simple farmer on a small, remote kibbutz. It was a search for order and sanity, to find things that have been lost, to put things together, to build, to grow, to find something real that you can anchor to.

"No," Navon thought, looking at the large operations map on the wall, "I'm not quite there yet."

Jamil's two boats quickly pushed five miles out into the dark ocean before he put the tiller into its looping arc southward into Israeli waters.

He remembered the words of the mission planners, who told them, "Your greatest areas of danger will be getting out to sea from the coast, crossing the frontier, and going ashore. Do these quickly. It is where they'll have the most eyes looking for you. Stay very low in the boats." Several times he heard boats and planes pass nearby. They quickly turned off the small motor and lay nervously in the bottom of the boat until the searchers had passed. But the two boats were cut low to the water and blended into the dark swells of the rolling sea.

The night was very dark and cold. Bobbing, pitching, and rolling hour after hour, they had only the dim coastal lights and the fading glow of two luminous compasses to keep them on course. The slow steady swells came in on them from the right rear quarter, putting them on an angular, sharply tilting roller-coaster ride that went on and on. The waves often slapped against the hard wood of the boat, splashing them with spray and mist. Gradually their clothes were soaked through with cold, pungent salt water. The hours passed with agonizing slowness as they sat chilled, wet, and sick in the small, cramped boat. Much of the glory and romance had long since faded away.

Jamil couldn't see the other four boats. Although he knew it was a good sign, the company would have been reassuring. They had all left at the same time, but from different points and on slightly different courses. Still, he knew they were out there somewhere.

The two boats from Ras al Ayn were only a mile away from Jamil when they ran into their first problem. At midnight one of their motors began to run rough. By 1:00 A.M., it coughed and sputtered and finally gave out completely. Its crew tried over and over to restart the hot, muffled engine. They checked the propeller, added more gasoline, blew out the fuel line, and put in another can of oil. Even cursing it and kicking it produced nothing. Its frustrated crew finally abandoned the boat and climbed in with their companions, who had stayed nearby.

At 2:00 A.M., the wind began to rise from the northwest. The previously gentle roll of the swells took on a more ominous tone as they tattooed the side of the boat. They rose higher and higher with an ever more jarring chop. They pitched and rolled and took in more water so that the bailing became constant for one man, then two.

The remaining boat from Ras al Ayn was overloaded and labored along in the rising seas. Now too heavy to ride with any grace on top of the swells, it wallowed too long in the deep troughs and could never quite make it to the top of the next crest. The cramped crew bailed faster and faster as they shipped more water, but they only bumped into each other and fell further behind as the minutes passed. The boat turned and tossed off course and lost all headway in the rough seas. Helplessly its crew looked up to see one of the larger waves rise up and break over the low starboard gunnel. The boat rolled over and threw them and their equipment into the sea as it capsized.

Weighted down by their water-logged clothing, the end came quickly for the six tired and sick men.

At 3:30 A.M., Lieutenant Baer's Catalina had just finished another low sweep down the coast. After crossing through the Bay of Haifa he turned the plane in a low bank out to sea. It was sweaty, nervous work demanding all of his concentration. Powered down to less than one hundred knots an hour, he continuously scanned the instruments and the faint line of the horizon. The search required that he fly low, eighty to one hundred twenty feet above the dark waves. He and his copilot would alternate flying every twenty minutes because concentrating very hard on an overcast night could easily disorient the most skilled flyer over a longer period of time. He'd heard too many stories of pilots who went into the sea without even knowing they were near it. It became hypnotic.

When he turned back to the northwest his intercom suddenly crackled. "Lieutenant . . . port bubble here. I think I saw something out my side. . . . There . . . ah, I lost it again. . . . "

"Okay, what was it?" Baer replied, taking a quick check of his instruments.

"I'm really not sure, but it looked like a low, dark shape against the waves. It was a straight line and I thought I saw a small wake, but it was too quick to really tell. It was out maybe two hundred yards or so. . . . "

"We'll check it," the pilot said. "Hang on, folks, I'm going back around to get some altitude. We can use a break anyway." Turning to his copilot, he added, "Jani, radio in to base that we are checking out a possible. Nothing definite, but if they have a boat nearby tell them we'll illuminate to see what we've got. You have our position?"

"Roger. I've got us on a bearing of three hundred fifty degrees from Haifa. Maybe four miles out." The copilot switched his set over to the command net and relayed the message to the plotters on the Yarkon.

Baer took them rapidly up to fifteen hundred feet, then flicked on the intercom once more. "Hey, Crew Chief, get ready to poop out some flares on my command. One every thirty seconds. You guys in the bubbles keep an eye out back there. Maybe we can ruin somebody's day."

On orders from the Yarkon, Commander Lashov's Dabur class patrol boat sped into the area from the southwest as the first flares popped and lit up the sky with their eerie, cold, white glare. It blinded him for a few minutes until his eyes could recover. Trying to focus in the unnatural pale light always added to the tension. He was still squinting out over the bow when his topside lookout shouted, "Boat in the water. Dead ahead, sir!"

Lashov quickly focused in on the dark shape as he saw a second; no, three small boats pinned under the harsh light of the slowly descending parachute flares. Two were dead ahead beyond his bow. The third was off by itself farther back and to starboard.

"Forward gun crews, bring the two lead targets to bear!" Lashov shouted into his microphone. "Order them to heave to!"

His radioman activated the loudspeaker and spoke alternately in Arabic and Hebrew for the boats to halt immediately.

Over the command net he heard the PBY calling in the sighting. Swinging his glasses to the right he saw the crashing bow wave of one of the Mark Is closing in from the east. "We've got 'em in the box now," he yelled in anticipation.

The small black targets lay naked in overlapping circles of bright light as more flares dropped down over them. Less than two hundred yards away, the crew of the lead boat suddenly opened fire on Lashov's Dabur.

Lashov could barely hear the dull chatter of the AK–47s above the low throb of his powerful engine and the crash and clatter of his crew going to battle stations. As the bullets from the commandos splashed in the water nearby and tore into his high bow, Lashov's gunners eagerly responded without further invitation. The even thumping of the heavy 20 mm. cannon in the bow dotted a path to the lead boat. The powerful shells slammed into its low hull, pounding it with a long steady burst for several moments before traversing over to engage the second dark craft. As Lashov steered over to starboard, cutting across the front of the two raiders, his .50 cal. machine guns on the port side came to bear.

From the high vantage point on the bridge, Lashov watched in fascination as the explosive 20 mm. shells tore the second boat apart, sending large chunks of wood, metal, equipment, and bodies flying out to splash into the water nearby.

The first boat had been severely riddled by the heavy cannon when the rapid chatter of twin 50s joined in with their long bursts. The streaking red lines of tracers held the boat in their grasp when it suddenly erupted into a fiery red ball of flame. Less than fifty yards off his port side, the exploding gasoline cans on the small boat ignited like bombs, showering the deck and bridge of the patrol boat with flying debris.

The Mark I finally joined in the deadly light show as its 50s tore into the third target to the rear. Several long bursts riddled the low hull and the panicked figures huddled behind it. The impact of the bullets and falling bodies flipped the small, low boat over backward, throwing men and equipment into the black sea. Dead or dying, the crew was quickly dragged under by the weight of their heavy gear.

The tumult of gunfire suddenly stopped as quickly as it had started. The only sound to be heard was the rumbling idle of their own boats as the Israeli crews were frozen in place in stunned silence. After several long seconds they slowly began to rise up from behind their heavy armor plate to stare out at the scene. It had all taken less than a minute or two, but the deafening crash of battle heightened the deathly silence that followed. It was like a vacuum. After hundreds of loud gunshots, sharp muzzle flashes, streaking tracers, the smell of cordite, the billowing black cloud from the burning gasoline, the shock wave from the exploding boat, and the searing flames, their senses were overloaded and exhausted. They could only stand and gape.

The drone of the approaching PBY high above them in the blackness snapped Lashov back into sharp awareness. Its new string of flares replaced those about to extinguish themselves in the sea. Below their high cones of light, all he could see was one upside down and badly holed boat and two large circles of floating debris.

Groping for his microphone, Lashov pressed the button and said quietly, "Clear from action. All sections report casualties and damage." He stopped to wipe the sleeve of his blue jacket across his sweating forehead. "Put out the boat and search for survivors or any equipment. Keep your eyes open out there. Well done, men, well done."

Lashov slowly turned around and leaned against the bulkhead. He became aware of himself as the mental numbness drifted away. His subconscious was about finished taking inventory of the various parts of his body. He now felt his heart pound. His muscles were tense and sore. The sea breeze chilled the cold sweat on his legs and back. He could feel the tight quivering in the back of his knees. His right hand was still on the railing. Slowly uncurling his white knuckles, he realized he must have been clenching it in a vise grip throughout the short firefight.

He composed himself and looked around at the other men on the bridge, then realized he was bareheaded. Glancing around nonchalantly, he saw his cap lying against the far door on the floor. His legs were very unsteady as he walked over to pick the cap up, and shook worse when he bent down. I feel like I've just boxed ten rounds, he thought.

35

Lashov was an experienced combat officer, and he knew that the feeling of leading in a deadly, violent battle could never be forgotten no matter how many times you do it. As had happened to him before, once he got over the physical and emotional exhaustion, every split second of detail would be replayed over and over in his mind for the rest of his life in a slow and never-changing or fading motion. It was already like that with the few battles he had gone through.

To Lashov it was a terrifying experience to be in war, but also an incredible high. Each time it took him to a sensual and emotional peak that nothing else in life could come close to. It was electric. It was why he stayed in and craved sea duty. It was why there was an instant bond between combat veterans, an understanding. That peak gave a perspective on all other subsequent experience.

Those who were no longer part of the game could only press their noses against the glass and look in. They could only get it on again in their minds. Those who stuck with it like Lashov were like drug addicts. They knew the beast might kill them too one day, but they chased after it because they must.

Lashov's men found no survivors. He didn't expect them to. These were the rules both sides played by in this desperate game of cat and mouse.

3

A half mile back, Jamil watched the short, sharp battle in stunned silence. With the boat bobbing and rolling, they could only catch brief glimpses. They had become separated from the other Ras Awwali boat over an hour ago, and when they saw three boats come under the merciless fire, they knew its fate.

As the firing and explosions faded out in the night, Jamil realized he and his two companions represented the last hopes of a rapidly failing mission. There were two other boats out there somewhere, but the odds were getting longer.

A new string of flares came down far ahead, and Jamil could hear planes and boats approaching rapidly from several directions.

"Quick, Ahmed," he whispered, "turn the boat around. We've got to get as much water between us and them as we can. They'll be expanding the search area any minute now. . . . Get down low!"

Turning northward, Ahmed opened up the throttle as far as it would go.

Several nervous minutes later, Haidar began to whisper angrily, "What are we going to do? You can't just take us back to Lebanon. . . . I won't go! We'll be disgraced." His voice grew louder and trembled as he looked up at Jamil in rage.

"Oh, shut up, you fool," Ahmed hissed. "We aren't going back to Lebanon. Don't be so stupid!"

"Relax . . . both of you," Jamil said calmly as he looked toward the shore. "Haidar, we couldn't go back if we wanted to. There isn't enough gas or darkness to make it even halfway to the border. Use your head! The sun will be up in an hour or two. But it's obvious we can't get through to Haifa now, either. Not with all those planes and ships sitting in our way. We wouldn't have a chance."

"Then . . . what are we going to do?" Haidar pleaded.

"Well . . . one thing's for sure, the plan is dead," Jamil replied as he turned his eyes toward the dark coastline. "We're just going to come up with a new one! Not that we have much choice, since time's running out. We'll head in to shore and find a new target. We aren't finished yet!"

"But all our plans are for Haifa," Haidar sputtered. "We'll be going in blind . . . no contacts, no target, no escape routes. . . . "

"Have you got a better idea?" Ahmed snarled. "I came here to kill Jews, and I don't care which ones. Jamil's right! If you don't want to come along, then get out and swim. Otherwise shut up and do what he says!'

"Haidar," Jamil said, trying to smooth things out, "we're stuck. Remember, they don't know we're here, so the idea isn't all that bad. If we move quickly and get ashore, we can find a good target and be away into the hills before dawn. That's Acre," he pointed off to some lights. "We can go in there from the south—they'll be less likely to be looking from that direction." He smiled and punched Haidar lightly on the shoulder. "It's going to take all three of us to pull this off successfully, and I need you . . . so are you with us?"

Haidar looked away and nodded.

"I've still got my Kalashnikov rifle and a lot of explosives," Ahmed said contemptuously. From the tone, Jamil could tell that Ahmed couldn't care less whether Haidar came or not.

Jamil looked back over his shoulder toward the open sea. "It looks like only three of the boats got caught. The others are probably sitting somewhere just like we are trying to figure out what to do. Or, they might have gotten farther and are heading in toward Haifa right now while we are still debating. Just think," he grinned. "If we can get in two or three attacks at different places, their security will be racing around in all directions thinking they've been invaded!''

"Pick a spot, Jamil . . . where do you want me to steer?" Ahmed asked indifferently.

Peering ahead, Jamil said, "That dark spot, just this side of Acre. But stay low, we aren't ashore yet."

Thirty minutes later, Jamil knew he'd guessed right.

They made it ashore without being seen. The closer they got, the more Jamil expected the black night to be shattered again by machine-gun fire and bright flares. But it didn't happen.

The spot he picked was a dark, rocky beach. Looking farther to the north up the shoreline, he saw the glow from the lights of Acre.

"Okay," he whispered. "Let's get the gear out quick. Haidar, you go up to those rocks inland at the top of the beach and post guard. Don't go looking around. If nobody's seen us yet, let's not look for trouble. We'll join you in a few minutes with the rest of the stuff."

"Ahmed," he said, turning around. "Take the boat back to the deep water and sink it to the bottom. We're infantry again."

Jamil ducked behind several large rocks and studied his map of the coast by the dim light of his hooded pocket flashlight. He saw they'd come in as close to Acre as they dared cut it, but the town might still be two miles or more to the north. Too far.

But looking closely at the map, he saw a faint ray of hope. If they hiked straight inland, they'd soon reach the coast highway. There'd be small settlements nearby, or else targets could be found on the road itself. Yes! There was an old railroad embankment to cross, but the road was only three-fourths of a mile from where they stood. It would do.

When his companions came back and kneeled around him on the high ground, he said, "It's already after four thirty, so bring all of the gear. We must hurry."

They slipped quietly through the dark, deserted country. They needed the forced march to loosen their stiff, cramped muscles and warm them up under their wet clothes. When they topped the railroad line, Jamil took a new compass bearing and led them off toward a small hill up ahead.

Crouching down to peer through the low underbrush on top of it, he broke into a broad grin as he saw the road lying in front of him. Dimly, he saw it pass to the left down a long, gradual slope to cross what looked like a small stream. It must be the one he remembered from the map. Beyond, it would go up to the lights of Acre. Off to the right, the road went down the opposite slope and disappeared around a bend. The terrain grew hilly off in that direction.

Jamil studied the position with the eyes of a skilled tactician. It would have different attributes to a mapmaker, or a construction foreman, or perhaps a tourist, but he looked at it to find the best place to kill.

"This is a good place," he said softly. "It's five fifteen, so we'll stay here and set up an ambush."

"Ambush what?" Haidar asked sarcastically. "Rocks? Trees? Nothing's here."

"I don't know yet, but I will when I see it. This is a busy road and the traffic should be starting up real soon. We'll wait for something juicy like a couple of army trucks, maybe a small convoy, a line of cars, buses, I don't know. No armored vehicles, though; we don't have enough firepower to take on something like that. But let's be patient and make it worth the trip. Right, Haidar?"

Not waiting for a reply, Jamil went on. "We'll use a two-way 'L' ambush, just like we learned at camp, so we can get anything coming from either direction. I'll stay here at the top and block. Haidar, you go down to the left. Ahmed, you go down to the right. About two hundred yards. Get well hidden in the brush—"

"How will we know what to attack?" Ahmed interrupted.

"I'll check both directions. If it's clear and the target looks good, I'll throw a rock down the road near you. As it comes even with you, start firing. Empty your rifles into the side and rear. They'll be halfway up the hill and slowing down. Remember to rake across it like a hose. Then run up after it as fast as you can. I'll move out and block. Now, the third man should get up here to help me as soon as you hear any shots. Then we'll all close in. . . . Got that?" he said, staring directly at Haidar. "Good. Get going and watch for my signal."

After Haidar disappeared down the hill, Ahmed turned toward Jamil and snarled, "I don't like him. If he ruins this I'll kill him!"

"If he ruins this, I don't think you'll have to. We'll all be dead. Get going. We haven't got much time left."

Jamil unloaded his equipment. He carefully placed his extra magazines and hand grenades where they would be within easy reach. He checked the magazine in his rifle, clicked off the safety catch, and seated a round in the chamber. Tense and nervous, he leaned forward and looked down the dark road in each direction. Nothing, he thought. No lights, no sounds, no movement. Nothing. His fingertips drummed lightly on the gun barrel, waiting for their long-sought-after moment to come.

A different time, and a different place perhaps; but he could feel that powerful white Arabian stallion beneath him. He began to gallop forward in a slow trot. The wind was in his face and behind him he could see his army spread out in the bright sun. Their scimitars were drawn and flashing like a thousand mirrors. Up ahead the enemy was drawn up before them. They huddled and talked to each other. They trembled and pointed. He could see the fear in their eyes.

He broke into a faster gallop. His line of horsemen pulled up even with his shoulders. Cheering, grinning, shouting *"Jihad! Jihad!"*, they began their thundering charge. The ground shook and clouds of billowing dust trailed back over their path. The enemy line wavered and broke as the charge bore down on them. They dropped their weapons and fled before Jamil's onslaught. He rode them down, slashing, hacking, and trampling them into the sand. None dared to stand before him. *"Jihad! Victory!"* He screamed.

Zvi Tabenkin had just picked up the last of his passengers for the early morning bus route from Acre to Haifa. He'd been on the run for over six months now and hated it.

"Give me the city—rush hour even—I tell you I wouldn't mind. But this I hate. I've always hated the long routes. Boring open road. Nothing to do. Nothing to see, just a bunch of damn palm trees and orange groves. Wind and sand. I'll tell you one thing, Dora, I'm going to see the union next week. It's that damn Shlomo, he did it to me. Crying and moaning about his bad back. 'Just a few weeks, Zvi, what's to mind?' he said. Well I mind. Twenty years I pay dues. I got the seniority. We'll see who minds."

"Oh, stop blustering, you big Bulgarian," his wife said. "Your real gripe is you got no one to talk to death. And no young ladies to look at either, you old fox!"

"Dora, it's a bore. All I carry are these damn foreigners. Greeks,

Turks, Koreans. Our own people don't even want to get on my bus no more. If they do, they sit up front by an open window so not to smell the sausage and the damn garlic. And what those Koreans eat makes you want to puke is what it does. I swear.''

"You swear too much. The fresh air does you good.''

"Ah, all they do is sleep. Acre to Haifa. Haifa to Acre. I'm just their morning nap on wheels, that's all I am.''

"Now you know they all put in long hours at the port. We need them, Jews or not. Look at the good they are doing for us. I don't see you line up down there for a job. Twelve hours a day, seven days a week. No, not you. You just exercise your big mouth.''

"I'll tell you what I'm going to do some day. If those goniffs don't give me back my old route, as soon as they are all asleep, I'll drive north to Nahariya instead of south. I'll let them all get out like it's Haifa. They'll all wander around for a half an hour before they wake up.''

"Ah, you old fool, go before you're late.''

Like most mornings, Tabenkin's bus was about half full. This was the bus most of them took for the earliest shift at Haifa. When they got off, he picked up the ones heading back home from the night shift. With peace, the port was so busy most of the work had to be contracted out to foreign firms. To lessen the inflationary pressures, they even had to bring in their own laborers. But housing was so tight they had to commute in from wherever they could find a room.

When he reached the outskirts of town, Tabenkin looked longingly up the coast highway to the north. He sighed and as usual turned the bus to the south. Leaving the last few scattered homes behind, the bus rolled out into the dark, open countryside. Accelerating to forty-five miles per hour, he resigned himself to the boring twenty-five-minute drive. It was still very dark, but the dawn would begin its first light in a little while. His return trip would be in full daylight.

Reaching the first series of low hills, he glanced in his rearview mirror. "Damn, just look at them. Asleep already!" He mumbled in disgust. "When it gets a little lighter I'll find a nice pothole. If I can't sleep, why should they!"

He came down the first hill, across the bridge, and up the long grade.

Tabenkin had wiggled and scrunched his large torso back into a more comfortable position when the quiet night was shattered by a staccato of automatic rifle fire. The bullets tore through the right side of the bus. Snapping his head to that side, Tabenkin could see the bright flashes of the gun muzzle from within the low row of bushes. The bullets worked their way along the side to the rear of the bus. The steady burst punched right through the thin body panels, sending metal and glass flying across the aisle.

The bullets ripped into seats, passengers, or the far walls without distinction. Swift and complete, the carnage left wounded, dead, or just terrified passengers scattered across the seats and floor.

Instinctively, Tabenkin stomped his foot to the floor, trying to urge the large vehicle up the long incline. In agonizing slowness it finally neared the top of the hill. At that moment a dark figure suddenly jumped out into the beams of Tabenkin's headlights. He pointed his gun at the front of the onrushing bus and began firing. Tabenkin felt the ringing impact of the bullets as they crashed into the engine and frame. His right headlight shattered and went out. As his large hands tried to turn the steering wheel away from this punishment, the front windshield was blown in.

Tabenkin saw it punctured in an instant by one, two, five, a long stream of bullets that traversed it. The individual holes laced together as the windshield became opaque, broke away, and followed the path of the bullets inward at Tabenkin and down the center aisle.

The gunman to the front leaped aside and out of his view to avoid the careening bus. From behind, the other gunman let loose another burst just as the bus cleared the top of the hill. These bullets struck the gas tank, enveloping the rear in flames. The bus rolled on over the top of the hill and down the far side, leaving a twisting trail of flaming gasoline down the black asphalt road.

Tabenkin had been slammed back in his seat and he slowly slumped off to the right side, immobile and numb from the shock of the glass that had slashed into his face and the hammer blows of the two bullets that had struck his chest and shoulder. He was conscious, but in shock. He could observe, but not comprehend. The screams of his passengers, the cold wind in his face, the orange glow of flames around him, the choking, acrid smoke; these just did not register. He sat like a remote spectator.

The bus continued to roll a short way down the hill before it ran off the road and plowed into a shallow, muddy drainage ditch. The jarring

43

halt pitched everything forward. Tabenkin crashed into the steering wheel and off against the left wall of the bus. The painful jolt brought him back to semi-alertness. Turning his head to look out the side window, he could see dim running figures illuminated by the dancing orange light. They kept shooting into the bus.

"They shouldn't do that," he moaned. "They shouldn't do that. Look at what they are doing to my bus. Oh . . . shouldn't." From instinct, his large hand groped under the front seat. Finally, it wrapped around the butt of the old British service revolver he kept hidden there. "Shouldn't do that!"

His head turned back to the front as a black shape suddenly rose up before him in the large hole in the windshield. The figure was lit in the bright orange light from the flaming gasoline. Like a creature come up from hell, Tabenkin thought. Slowly, painfully, he raised his right arm toward the figure. From inches away he pulled the trigger of the large revolver. His arm jumped up and came back down lazily. He pulled the trigger again. And again. As the scene began to fade to a washed-out orange, to gray, and finally to black, Tabenkin's head dropped forward and he lost consciousness.

Jamil had been waiting for twenty minutes when he saw the headlights come down the far hill. From the vague shape and engine noise he could tell it was a bus. This must be it, he thought. They'd impatiently allowed several cars to go by unmolested, like little fish thrown back into the sea. "You can continue in peace. We'll be back for you some other time," he whispered.

But sitting wet and cold in the damp night air, he could now see the horizon in the east was turning lighter above the hills. Dawn would be here soon. Bus—you will have to do, he thought, as he threw the rock down the road toward Haidar.

The action moved swiftly once the bus came abreast of Haidar's position. As Jamil jumped in the middle of the road, he was so intent on getting off a good burst between the blinding headlights that he'd almost let the bus run him down before he jumped aside. He felt like one of Saladin's archers trying to bring down an armored Crusader knight on his huge war-horse. The beast was mortally wounded, but he could run far before he dropped and they both crashed to the ground.

Picking himself up out of the mud, he turned to see the bus careen off the side of the road and burrow itself into the bank of the ditch with its rear end in flames. He quickly reloaded and raced down the hill as fast as he could run, firing more careful bursts now that it was immobilized. When his rifle finally clicked empty, Jamil dropped it on the road and pulled out two grenades from his pocket. He reached the front of the bus as Ahmed came up beside him. Jamil pulled out the pins on the grenades and jumped onto the front bumper with his right arm raised.

His forward momentum was stopped dead in midair as a .38 cal. bullet punched hard into the center of his chest. The colliding forces canceled out and he hung there for an eternal split second in equilibrium.

Through the large hole in the windshield, Jamil could see the bright flames leap across the rear of the bus. They illuminated the slaughterhouse of dead and dying bodies strewn along the seats and floor. Silhouetted against this scene and off to one side was a dark shape slumped in the corner behind the steering wheel. Its arm was pointed at his chest, wavering up and down. A bright red flame erupted from the end of the pointed arm. Jamil could feel the searing heat of the flash as it burned deep within him. And again. He could feel it tear into his muscle and grind through the bone of his chest. Pounding, ripping.

In complete disbelief he looked down as the power began to drain out of his body. He felt his legs go limp and rubbery. They would no longer obey him. His mind struggled in terror to regain control of his body. The scene faded out and lost focus as he toppled slowly over backward onto the ground, which he never felt.

Ahmed stood below helplessly as he watched Jamil's limp body crash to the ground at his feet. In horror he dropped down beside Jamil and grabbed his shoulders to try to raise him up. This could not be happening. If he could just get him up, he would be okay. It was all a mistake.

Looking into Jamil's limp face he screamed, "No . . . no! God. Jamil. Get up! . . . No!" as the ground around them suddenly erupted from two searing blasts of dirt, shrapnel, and flesh. The explosions of Jamil's two grenades blew Ahmed high into the air and over backward onto the hard surface of the road like a rag doll.

The blank stare and faint grin on his brother-in-law's face would be the last thing Ahmed would ever see.

Haidar raced to the top of the hill, fumbling with the magazine of his Kalashnikov and desperate to catch up with the fleeing bus. Out of breath, he pounded on down the road, continuing to fire burst after burst into the flames. Finally coming alongside the shattered hulk, he reloaded again and jammed the barrel of his rifle through a side window. Shouting and laughing he fired away on full automatic toward any dark shape he could see in the firelight—seats, baggage, bodies, or whatever.

When the rifle finally clicked empty he threw it to the ground and pulled out a hand grenade. Removing the pin, he dropped it through the window and turned away to run. Just as he took his first stride he was knocked flat by the twin explosions from the front of the bus.

Haidar had furiously scrambled to his feet and run a few more paces when the close blast of his own grenade lifted the bus off the ground and sent him sprawling across the hard asphalt road. He cracked his head and ended up in the ditch on the far side. Slowly he rose to his knees and shook his head to clear the cobwebs. Looking across the road, he saw the bus had broken in two and lay on its side in flames. He painfully stood up. His head ached. Running his hand across the back of his hair he saw blood. Burning pain now spread up his legs and back from a dozen small pieces of shrapnel.

In total terror, Haidar turned and fled down the road.

4

Corporal Avner looked out on the beach to the north while his driver watched to the south. For over an hour now they had been parked here, but all they'd seen coming ashore was the pounding surf. It was almost 5:00 A.M. Avner was anxious to be released so he could finish up the patrol. Somebody should make a final sweep up the road before dawn, he thought. He'd never heard of an Arab who could swim for an hour. If there are any left out there, they're blowing bubbles on the bottom.

As soon as the boat action was over out in the bay, they'd ordered him to leave his road patrol and bring the armored car down to the beach at Qiryat Yam. If anyone was trying to get ashore, here's where they'd head. But that was a long time ago. And no one was out on the road. That worried him.

Normally he and his crew made half a dozen runs each way between Acre and Haifa. They didn't expect to catch anyone, but they were a deterrent. Their main tasks were to watch for any new hole in the road and reinforce the small settlements quickly if they got hit. The holes could be a fresh land mine, and even the thin armor of the scout car was better than the cotton jackets the militia wore guarding these small kibbutzim. It was these settlements near the coast that took the brunt of the Fatah attacks—Qiryat Bialik, Qiryat Haiyim, Qiryat Motzkin—once they reached the bay.

He knew the guards and knew how much they needed his car if there was trouble. Having it meant they could stay inside their positions while he swept the perimeter. They appreciated it.

But Avner was frustrated just sitting there like an observation post. Someone must get out on that road before the traffic starts, he thought.

Finally, the earphones of his tanker's helmet crackled to life. "Red Sixteen, this is Base Three. We are shutting the search down. You're released to go back and continue your patrol."

The car kicked up sand as it tore across the dunes to the road. Avner told his driver to move out quickly but cautiously. He and the gunner scanned the road with searchlights. He knew they were on the edge of recklessness, but he had ten miles to cover—one very nervous mile at a time.

"You know this tin can won't make much of a minesweeper," the gunner cracked.

"Just keep your eyes on the road!" Avner shouted back. He knew this could be the most beautiful and relaxing drive during the day, a sharp contrast to the sinister and lonely combat patrol at night. It just wasn't a smart thing to do quickly. But better him than some civilians. No, not on his road. So they sped on, watching and waiting.

Finally, they got near the hilly section, which meant they were getting near Acre. They could even see its reassuring glow over the horizon to the north. Avner could feel his tension begin to relax a bit.

But he and his crew suddenly snapped to full alert when they heard the dreaded sound of long bursts of automatic rifle fire in the distance ahead. The tone was unmistakable, hated, and sickeningly all too familiar.

"That's an AK–Forty-seven. Button up and move out, quick!" he shouted down the hatch.

As the car picked up speed he heard even more vigorous gunfire. An orange glow rose up over the hills in front of them. It was followed by two muffled explosions as the glow burst into a bright fireball. Avner slammed his fist down on the side of the hatch in disgust and frustration.

Switching over to the command net he shouted angrily, "Base, Red Sixteen. We have gunfire. Coast road. Up ahead of our position. Source unknown. Looks like just south of Acre. Also explosions and flames.

We are responding to the scene. Request illumination and backup. Looks bad. Sixteen out.''

Speeding up the road, Avner watched and listened intently for any more gunfire. The chill wind flapped through his light jacket, suddenly reminding him that he was still sitting up high on the rear end of the commander's hatch, very exposed and vulnerable. He quickly dropped down into the seat below so only his head and shoulders were above the armor. He heard the gunner test the action on the coaxial machine gun below just as he remembered to cock the bolt of his own M–60 and check the ammunition feed. The orange glow was coming closer now.

They'd passed over this section of highway hundreds of times, day and night. This time, however, the sure knowledge that an armed enemy lay somewhere up ahead made each second nerve-wracking. Every curve, every dark clump of bushes, the far side of every hill, every ravine was a deadly ambush site. He waited in suspense for the flash of a powerful RPG rocket to streak out of the bushes toward the side of the car as it sped by. One of those could slice right through his thin armor plate, explode inside, and fling the car off the road like a child's plaything. It was a very, very, dark, lonely ride as they got closer to the orange glow.

Avner's driver suddenly slowed down as they neared the crest of the last hill. Peering over the top, Avner could see what looked like a large vehicle lying off to the side of the road. Bright orange flames shot up through a black cloud of billowing smoke, lighting up a dim circle around it.

Switching to his intercom, he said tensely, ''All right. Let's take it slow and easy now. I'll recon off to the left with my light and gun. Yani, you do the same on the other side. Pull up about fifty meters this side of the vehicle. Be ready!''

As they got closer, Avner could see it was a large bus, blown apart and lying on its side in the ditch. Hearing a series of faint pops, he looked up to see a string of parachute flares suddenly light up the sky and the countryside around them. He could now see a body lying in the middle of the road, but the rest of the area was deserted.

''Hey, there's someone running across those fields on my side,'' the gunner shouted. ''About two o'clock. You see him? He's heading for the trees.''

''Roger,'' Avner replied as he switched over to his external loudspeaker. "You in the field," his voice reverberated out. "Halt! Halt immediately." Avner watched the figure continue to run and stumble on.

He swung his .30 cal. M–60 lightly around on the well-oiled circular track outside the hatch. He pulled the bolt back all the way and let it snap forward to firmly seat a fresh round in the chamber while he began to figure the distance. Plenty of time, Avner thought. Distance and elevation. Add a little lead. Adjust to put him right over the sight. Track him. Lock on. Running diagonally away across the rough field. Easy now. Synchronize with him. Get his pace down. Move along with him.

Slowly pulling the trigger he squeezed off a nice short burst. The gun mount absorbed the recoil as he watched the intermittent red tracer rounds streak out over his sight. The glowing red ribbon rose up and arched smoothly back to earth, kicking up small puffs of dust in the dirt. He corrected his aim and fired off another burst. Longer this time, using the glowing tracers to walk the rounds into the moving target.

Haidar heard the car race toward him on the other side of the hill. In panic he turned and fled out into the open field toward the east. The trees, he thought. The hills. Safety. If I can only reach the trees.

But the field was freshly plowed and he kept falling down in the rough furrows. He'd scramble up again on all fours, but his head ached. He could hear himself panting as he ran, wheezing, gasping. His heart was pounding. Short of breath and in pain he stumbled on in terror. The trees. If I can only reach the trees.

The sudden burst of the aerial flares caught him alone in the middle of the field, bathed in their harsh white glare. They hurt his eyes. Can't see, he thought as he stumbled and fell. Must get up. The trees. So close now.

Exhausted, head in pain, he pounded on. But in his misery he did not hear the loudspeaker or the first chatter of machine-gun fire aimed in his direction, kicking up the dirt just fifteen feet behind.

All Haidar's concentration was on the line of trees ahead of him, just a dozen short strides away.

As the red ribbon from Avner's gun continued to rise and traverse, slowly it intersected the path of the runner. A moment after they

50

converged he saw the figure slapped off his feet in a slow tumble through the air. He did an uncontrolled cartwheel like a toy doll and crashed to the ground in a crumpled heap.

"Gotcha!" Avner shouted with a broad smile.

"Give the man a cigar," his gunner mocked. "I sit down here cramped in this shit can, and you hog all the fun!....By the way, here comes the cavalry to the rescue."

Avner looked up the road to see a string of vehicles racing down the hill toward them. "Yeah! Right on time as usual," he added sarcastically. "Head this thing out into the field where that guy's laying. I don't want to get stuck cleaning up this mess."

"You're just afraid you really didn't hit him and he might walk off on you," the driver needled. "And your medal would go right off with him."

"Shut up, you two. Let's move out."

By 6:15, the fire and rescue units had extinguished the last of the flames from the broken hulk of the bus. Army trucks, armored cars, jeeps, police cars, fire trucks and ambulances littered the shoulders of the road in both directions.

But there was little for most of them to do. Amid flashing emergency lights, small groups of grim-faced men stood around talking in low voices. Throughout the surrounding countryside, crack infantry troops swept through the woods and low underbrush hoping in vain to get a fleeing terrorist in their sights. Overhead, heavily armed helicopter gunships aided in the search. It was a sad but familiar scene that had greeted all too many cold, gray dawns in the Mideast.

An oily, acrid haze hung in the damp air as the rescue workers continued to chop and saw through the top of the bus. Others searched the shattered wreck for more charred bodies. Already, a long line of black rubber body bags lay down the shoulder of the road in neat military precision.

High-ranking officials and military officers came and went. The only purpose in their being there was to make their presence known and talk to each other. But they went through the motions of looking at the bus, looking at the two dead terrorists, and looking at the row of shrouded bodies. They also managed to find the time to visit with the

51

growing crowd of reporters being restrained by several burly MPs. So they poured their outrage into the waiting microphones to the accompaniment of floodlights and flashbulbs.

The thumping of helicopters over the scene had become so routine that little notice was given to a lone Huey that came in and landed in the middle of the open field. Swooping down to the ground, the swirling blades blew a cloud of dirt and twigs out in all directions.

Colonel Uri Ullman yanked back on the handle of the side hatch and jumped to the ground as soon as the skids touched down. Without waiting for the pilot to cut the power, he bent down and walked briskly out from under the spinning blades. Behind him, the powerful turbine began its slow decelerating whine as the pilot flipped off the switches and settled back in his seat to wait.

Ullman paused as he looked over to where vehicles were clustered on the nearby road. He slowly took in the scene with a blank expression. But if anyone had been close enough to observe, they'd have seen a hard and angry look flash across his eyes. It was the kind of look people turned away from in hopes it wasn't directed at them. He'd been at scenes such as this too often, with their red and blue flashing lights, hazy smoke, and dead civilians. He kicked the ground in disgust and set off in a straight line to where the armored car stood near the tree line.

General Gershon's call had come less than thirty minutes ago. As he listened to the brief account he wondered why bother. There was never much to learn after one of these affairs. The dead terrorists never carried any papers or personal belongings that could tell them anything. The attacks were always simple, but brutal and effective. Why go, he thought.

"I know what you're thinking, Uri, but I've got a surprise for you this time. We've got one alive. Well, at least not dead yet. . . ."

"Tell the men on the scene to put a lid on it. I don't want anyone else to know. I'll be there in a half hour. Keep the politicians and reporters away."

The field was rough and hard to walk across. Looking around, he immediately knew what had happened. He saw the staggered tracks where a man had run out here from the road. He also saw the fresh tire marks of the armored car. Where they met he saw the three young Israeli MPs casually leaning against the side of the car. A fourth figure lay on the ground in front of it, still partly illuminated by the headlamps in the half-light of the overcast dawn.

As Ullman got nearer, the young MPs became gradually more erect, but only marginally so. The eyes were looking him over, the heads more upright, and they stood a little straighter. Their tanker helmets lay on the front hood of the car and their flak jackets hung open. They had the casual self-assured manner of experienced combat troops. They knew the precise line between military courtesy and a slouch. They'd never come to attention, but they knew to straighten just enough to show a little deference. It was the universal body language of a good professional soldier. Good senior officers knew that.

As Ullman drew close, the MP with the two stripes walked out to meet him. As he began to salute and speak, Ullman cut him off with a wave of his hand. "How is he, Corporal?"

"Uh. . .not too good, sir. He took a thirty-caliber round in the side and another in the thigh. We've stopped the bleeding pretty well, but that may be because he doesn't have much left. He's lost a lot. I doubt he'll make it. He's conscious, though. We shot him up with morphine."

"Has he said anything?"

"No. He just stares up at the sky. We did get his name. It's Haidar. But he won't say anything else. We had to show him the bandages a couple of times before he'd let us touch him. And we had to hold him down to give him the morphine. I guess he thought we were trying to kill him. Not that I would have minded, but the orders over the radio were real clear on that point."

"Well, we hate to ruin your fun, but we just don't get a live one very often," Ullman replied with a short smile.

He turned and walked slowly around to the front of the car where the young Arab lay. He stared down for a few minutes until Haidar looked up. As their eyes met, Ullman pulled out a pack of cigarettes and his battered Zippo lighter. Still locked onto the Arab's eyes, he lit one and inhaled deeply. Finally, Ullman knelt down next to him.

"Haidar, I want you to listen very carefully to what I'm about to tell you," Ullman said in a soft, calm voice. "Do you understand me?"

The Arab gave a slight, mechanical nod, but his eyes were wary.

"Good, that's good. It's important that you listen very closely, because it's going to determine whether you live or die." Ullman saw the eyes flicker as he looked down.

"Haidar, it's getting late and we're all cold and tired. All the fighting's over now, it's all finished." He paused to look back at the road. "So, I'm going to give you two choices. After I ask you a couple of simple questions, you can either give me some straight answers or you can just lay there and say nothing. Those are the choices, and I really don't give a damn which you do, okay?"

Ullman paused to take another deep drag. "I want you to tell me where you came from, how many men came with you, and how many attacked the bus. . . . Now, you won't be telling me anything I don't already know. . . . We picked a few of your friends out of the sea and they've already told me the whole thing. If you tell me the same thing they did, it'll mean you're all telling the truth, and it'll go easier on all of you, see? . . .But for you, I'll let it out that they talked and you didn't. They can take the heat back home."

The Arab's eyes were sullen and defiant.

"If you make it easier for me, I'll call one of our doctors over here and ask him to do his best to save your life. You'll go to jail, of course, but I'll see to it that the sentence is a lot shorter and you'll be back home in a couple of years."

"So it's all up to you. . . . It makes no difference to me, but it'll make a big difference to you. No one else will ever know."

Ullman stopped to gauge the effect of his words, but he could see he hadn't softened the Arab's defiant stare one bit.

"Or, you can lay there and say nothing. But then you'll be of no further use to me at all. You aren't worth the cost of keeping you in jail for the rest of your life, so you might as well die right here. . . . It'll give me great pleasure to rip your bandages off one by one so we can both watch you slowly bleed to death."

Haidar's eyes flashed with hate, but his lips were sealed.

"Have it your way, but it'll be a big waste—especially for you. After you're dead, I'll spread the word it was you that talked. Might as well help the others. They'll spit on your mother's grave back home."

Ullman put the cigarette in his mouth, squinting out of one eye from the curling smoke. Then he smiled, reached down, and ripped the bandage off the Arab's thigh.

Haidar's head shot up in disbelief. Looking at his leg in terror, he

54

saw the wound open and the blood begin to flow again onto the ground. His head slowly sank back to the ground and he looked up in pathetic resignation.

As the seconds passed in silence, Ullman's eyes grew hard and cold. He reached down again and yanked the bandage off his side.

"No...stop," came the immediate response. "There...there were eighteen of us, I think. Six boats. Our two came from Ras Awwali."

"What about the others?" Ullman asked, knowing it would all flow now.

"We came in pairs...the others came from Ras al Ayn and Ras al Abyad, I think, three of us to each boat."

Ullman paused to be sure the questions would be in order.

"Where were the other boats supposed to go?"

"We were all headed for Haifa, but a lot of them, maybe three boats were caught by your Navy.... I don't know what happened to the rest. We lost sight of them. Maybe they got through, I don't know."

"All of you were heading there?"

"Yes. Some new apartment buildings...." Haidar convulsed with a choking laugh. "We...we couldn't get through. So Jamil ordered us to come here."

"How many of you attacked the bus?"

"Just us three."

Ullman stared down at the young Arab for a few moments. "Very good, Haidar. Very good." He slowly stood up, took another long drag on his cigarette and walked back to where the three MPs stood watching.

Avner asked him quietly, "Did that match what the others said?"

Ullman looked over at him with deathly cold eyes. "There were no others. He's the only one we caught." Throwing his cigarette down, he ground it out beneath the heel of his jump boots. He saw two of the MPs pass a glance at each other and stand up a little straighter.

"By the way, Corporal, were you all the way over on the road when you shot him?"

"Uh...yes, sir, just to the left of the bus," Avner replied in awe.

"That was damn good shooting. Well done." Turning to the other two, he added, "You all did well tonight. I'll make sure your CO hears that."

They smiled broadly at each other after Ullman turned and began to walk away.

Avner suddenly took a few steps after him and asked, "Sir, do you want me to put his bandages back now?"

Ullman stopped walking but did not turn around. As he stared ahead at the scene on the road he replied sharply, "No!"

Avner stood in silence as he watched him walk away across the field toward the row of black bags lying on the road.

Six days later, a bright, clear dawn was just breaking over Ras Awwali. As the sky became lighter behind the hills to the east, the morning breeze blew off the sea, chasing away the evening mist and sour smells of the village.

The first wisps of smoke rose from dozens of chimneys as the banked coals of the evening cooking fires were rekindled with fresh wood. Men and women passed each other in the narrow streets as they carried jugs of water from the communal well. Hungry dogs slunk between the buildings scavenging for breakfast in last night's garbage. Tired sentries filed back slowly from their guard posts with Kalashnikov rifles dangling casually over their shoulders. Six days and six nights now they'd waited and watched for the enemy to come.

At the far end of the long stone breakwater the last guard rises to his feet. He stretches, yawns, and shivers from the cold, damp air. Shouldering his rifle and slinging his pack over his back, he picks his way gingerly over the rocks as he heads back in. The smell of salt water, dead fish, and seaweed is very strong along the seawall.

Halfway back to land he turns his head lazily back toward the sea as he hears the screech of a flock of sea gulls fighting over their meal. But his eyes were drawn up above the birds toward the horizon. Dark specks in the sky. Birds? Moving. Fast. Toward him. Sun glinting off metal. Coming faster. In formation.

In that instant, his eyes open wide in fearful recognition. Frozen.

Walking backward, he finally turns and begins to run in terror. Screaming. Waving. Warning. Several people look out to him and smile and wave back. Too far out. They don't understand. Not that it would have mattered.

The streaking formation descends as it bears in on the coast. At supersonic speeds, they strike without warning. The pilots have already pushed their bomb releases before the planes even reach the land. Freed of the heavy loads beneath their wings, the Phantoms leap up and forward in relief. Clusters of stubby, black cylinders separate from the planes to continue forward on their own momentum. Gravity forces them down into a graceful arc that ends in the tightly packed buildings and streets below. A split second after the jets flash across the low rooftops, the quiet morning air is shattered by a crescendo of sonic booms.

Dozens of heads shoot upward in the streets below as the shock wave rocks the buildings. For a long moment, their puzzled eyes look up. Then, the looks turn to terror as they focus on the trailing wake of 750-pound bombs falling down on top of them. There is no time. No time to move, to run, or to hide, as the heavy bombs began detonating all around them.

The bombs punch easily through the low-pitched red tile roofs and on, down, through the second floors too, before exploding into the solid ground below. The heavy explosive charges rip through the small enclosed spaces. The shock wave is like a tornado trying to instantly vent its intense pressure in all directions. Upward, outward it blows, like too much air being suddenly forced into a small balloon. In microseconds it fills the space and bows out the walls, as the fierce pressure demands release. Probing, like a surgeon, the pressure finds the weakest points in the structures: those tiny flaws missed by the skilled masons of long ago.

The window glass goes, but still not fast enough. Even the window frames shoot outward, but the fury isn't spent. Roof sections are blown up and off. Walls begin to crack. The cracks expand. Joints are torn apart. Plaster, large stones, and brick tear away, leaving gaping holes in the walls. Beams strain and warp. Walls tremble and topple outward into the street. Second floors and roof beams find themselves bereft of support and fold inward, collapsing the structures upon themselves.

The impact multiplies as dozens of bombs crash through dozens of roofs, walls, or into the cobblestone streets themselves. Tons of rock, brick, wood, and the razor-sharp shards of broken roof tiles fly through the air and crash into other buildings, yards, or the streets. They smash, slice, cut, crush, and bury everything and everyone in their path.

The rubble flung upward from the first salvo of bombs begins to separate along the individual trajectory of each of its pieces. They reach their apex of flight and hang suspended for a brief moment. As they begin to fall back to earth, they are engulfed by the rising clouds of dust and smoke now billowing upward. Into this swirling melee, the second wave of jets release their bombs to begin the cycle anew.

Lehrmann sped on toward the low hills before he wheeled the flight around in a low banking turn back to the sea. Coming over Ras Awwali once again, he looked down to see that their timing and execution had been good. Precise and workmanlike, he thought. The destruction was complete. Just as he had been told to do it.

In Jerusalem two days before, the rage and frustration had finally given way to a cold determination. At his weekly Cabinet meeting the Prime Minister stared down the long table directly into the eyes of his Defense Minister.

"These . . .these bases . . .the ones they came from . . .I want them utterly destroyed! Is that clear?"

Lehrmann could see that it was.

The village had been literally blown apart, crushed, knocked flat, and buried. Around the edge a few buildings still had all four walls standing and he could see a few roofs pretty much intact. But inside this ring was where the main force of the attack had been; here, it looked like a brickyard. A few random walls stuck up amid the debris, but little else. Each of his planes had been loaded down with eight 750-pound bombs. They'd used only high explosives since the bombs would break loose all the shrapnel they'd ever need. Eighty of these bombs dropped into a few densely packed acres had an awesome effect, Lehrmann thought.

Ras Awwali had died. Or, more accurately, been put out of its misery. But those who would mourn its dead were not Lebanese.

Days later, grim-faced PLO work parties still sifted through the rubble. They no longer hoped to find any survivors, but continued to look for any valuable equipment they might salvage. Those who had survived were the few who had stumbled away or had dug themselves out shortly after the attack. Those who couldn't had died. There was no one to help the more seriously injured or those buried deep in the rubble. All

58

of the other PLO bases in the area were also bombed, so it took days for help to arrive.

The fortunate ones had been blown apart or crushed during the attack. Many more had slowly died alone in the wreckage, calling for help in vain.

The precise death toll would never be known.

On the afternoon of the fourth day, the tired workers uncovered the body of a woman that lay crushed beneath a wall. The corpse was quickly carried to the long mass grave they had dug in a nearby field. From papers she was identified as Kadri Saed and her name was added to the long list of known dead.

Four months later and five thousand miles away, her oldest brother set in motion his plan for revenge.

PART 2

WASHINGTON, D.C.
AUGUST, 1981

5

Friday, August 14

Heat, humidity, and tourists—that's Washington in August. Even Congress can usually assemble enough collective wisdom to take a vacation recess. And most of the press, lobbyists, staff, and bureaucrats are right behind them in hot pursuit. Let's face it, no one in his right mind sticks around the miserable place if he can find any excuse to leave.

Both the hot weather and the tourists were a lot more bearable in June, before the novelty wore off. But by mid-August, the patience of even the most stoic Washingtonian is frazzled. It's not that the tourists are bad people, they're more like tiresome houseguests that missed the hint.

After three months, you've had enough of being held up in sweltering midday traffic by what must be that same Country Squire station wagon from New Jersey filled with half a dozen screaming kids throwing McDonald's bags out the window onto Pennsylvania Avenue while Dad circles the White House at fifteen miles an hour yelling at his wife, who has an entire Exxon road map spread out upside down across the front windshield. And it's never his air conditioner that won't work!

In June, you'd probably shake your head and give a little knowing smile, but by August, you're besieged. It's the pits.

Things weren't much better inside the White House, either.

Actually, thought President Edward Bannon, the city was holding up a lot better than the government it housed. Six months in office and the honeymoon was over a long time ago. What a mess.

Bannon turned away from the window and walked back to his desk. He wanted to review the notes one more time before heading off to the meeting at the Executive Office Building. It was one meeting he was really looking forward to. Set all the other problems aside and dig into just one—a rare treat. And the problem was the biggest, he thought. Solving it could give him the cutting edge he needed to slice the rest back down to size.

If life was fair, Carter wouldn't have been allowed to leave all those problems behind, Bannon grumbled to himself. There ought to be a law! Just look at the inheritance he left—recession, inflation, the dollar, unemployment, and energy. That's just here at home. What about revolution in South America, race war in Africa, NATO coming apart, Cuban and Russian troops all over the place, chaos in the Muslim world, and an expansionist Kremlin.

They weren't all your fault, Jimmy, but you could have knocked a few of them down for me; then, that's what you get with government by the Gallup Poll, no policy, just fuzzy thinking.

As he leaned back in his swivel chair, Bannon could see the problems pop up in the window like targets in a shooting gallery. Each one was a big, fat turkey with a bright red number on its chest. Put your quarter down and fire away! GNP growth down to 1 percent. Bang! They're jumping up fast now. Inflation at 13 percent. Bang! Gold at $500 an ounce. Unemployment at 8 percent. Bang! Bang! Bang! The prime rate at 19 percent. Oil at $43 a barrel. Gasoline at $1.50 a gallon. Bang! Bang! Oil. Oil. Oil! The big turkey—Bang! Bang!

None are going down! Somebody should've said the gun only had blanks. The turkeys know, they just laugh and gobble away!

Oil: It's tearing the economy to shreds. The big turkey, Bannon knew. It's kept our inflation raging and drives up interest rates. Home-building and new car sales are way off, as are industrial plant expansion and consumer spending. So unemployment is up and new jobs are way down, putting the federal government in the whip-saw of lower tax receipts to pay for higher welfare. This pumps up the budget deficit so we keep on borrowing and printing more money. We are trying to export like crazy, but oil just keeps going higher and our balance of payments is worse each month. The international money markets are flooded with cheaper and cheaper dollars.

But what can we do? Despite all the rhetoric about conservation and alternate energy sources, it'll be at least a decade before these really have much effect. We completely decontrolled domestic oil this spring and our own production has come up, but now we have a shortage of pipeline and drilling equipment. And with 45 percent of our oil still imported, it's going to take years to break away from foreign suppliers. That or shut down our economy. Depressions are good ways to cut energy use.

Gobble. Gobble! After OPEC tore the dollar to shreds, they merrily switched over to the Swiss franc for exchange. Khomeini completely polarized the Muslim world with his fanatical brand of religious anti-Americanism. The Saudis and the rest of the conservative Persian Gulf states bailed out in fear and have jumped in bed with our dear friends the French and Germans.

The Mideast just keeps festering along in an ever more ominous deadlock. Egypt and Israel are at peace now that Sadat has all his land back. But in two years nothing else has moved one step closer to resolution. Here we are—the United States, Egypt, and Israel—three for bridge. Completely isolated with a whole region now turned against us. The fanatical street mobs want our blood, and the Saudis, Hussein, and the rest of the moderates are scared to death.

The balance of power is shifting out from under us daily. Beneath it all you can see the deft hand of Comintern and the Kremlin hard-liners, he thought. They'll be putting us to the test very soon now. Time's running out. And it all goes back to the big turkey in the middle. Oil!

Bannon knew he only had one bullet left. God, it had better not be a blank too. Gobble! Gobble!

Walking through the underground corridor that led to the other building, he thought, well, as bad as things are, no one ever really expected him to come up with anything dramatic when he won the election last year. That was the best thing he had going for himself. People expected him to be a tough administrator and work well with Congress, but he'd never been known as an innovative leader. They forget that during his eighteen years in the House and Senate, he never had to take responsibility for a situation this desperate.

Well, it was IOU time and he had a few surprises in store. After ten years in the House representing the west suburbs of Chicago and eight years in the Senate, he was an experienced pro who knew how to make the system work.

The Speaker had once asked him, "Ed, how do you stay out of trouble by not introducing any legislation? My district would be all over me."

"Because they aren't stupid. I've convinced them it's a lousy way to keep score. I'm a floor manager, and there are thousands of good bills that need passing. Let the others take credit, I build up the IOUs. They're there when I need them."

Now's the time to call them in, he thought.

When he walked into the room, the small group waiting for him were his closest political friends and allies over the years. Senators Jensen and Portman were old school Republicans who were still over on the Hill. Congressman Winston Fields was a southern Democrat and Chairman of the House Foreign Relations Committee. A good ole boy on the stump, he had a passion for Vivaldi and chamber music concerts. Louise Korshak went back to the beginning and his first try for the House. She became the DuPage County Republican Chairman and won his seat when he moved up to the Senate. She'd been a tough conservative on the Armed Services Committee. Bannon laughed when he thought how he'd shocked a lot of people by appointing her as his Secretary of Defense, but she was the best choice. So was Langford Andrews, his Secretary of State. Louise was a tenacious in-fighter and Lang was the sharp mind and delicate wit he needed.

"Lang, I'll never forgive you as long as I live for talking me into running for this damn job!" he told him at least once a week.

Winning even the nomination hadn't been easy. He'd been the darkest of horses. But Lang had called the race just like it did run. The other candidates fought and bled each other in a series of indecisive primaries. They won and lost; rose and fell, but Bannon waited them out. He began to take thirds and some seconds, but he held his ground and rose in the polls. Finally he won in Oregon and Ohio, giving the party pros an alternative as they gathered in Detroit for the convention.

They were all in his suite in the Sheraton huddled around the TV watching Walter Cronkite do his play-by-play as the ballots were counted through the long evening. After the third one, he was still mired in fifth place and giving serious thought to dropping out.

"Why prolong the agony. It's embarrassing." Bannon said glumly.

"Edward, open your eyes," Andrews laughed. "You've got it in the bag!"

"Lang, you're out of your mind!"

"No. Seriously. You just watch. The alchemy is about to turn your lead to gold. The old war-horses have had it. They've topped out. None of them can win, and there's too much bitterness between them. They won't support each other. The pros are starting to look around. You'll go up on the next ballot, and once you start to climb everyone'll jump on board! They know it's time to end this thing. Just watch."

Damned if he wasn't right, Bannon had to agree. It took four more ballots, but the phones rang off the hook as people made last-minute deals.

The others never knew what ran over them.

The November election wasn't anywhere near as close. NBC called it at nine fifteen that night, and the other computers soon followed.

Louise spoke up first. "You know, I was convinced we'd win, but I still don't believe it. Damn! What a trip! A Republican beating an elected sitting President. And a Democrat at that!"

"But let's have a toast to those darling Democrats Teddy and Jerry. Without the job they did tearing their party to pieces, we'd never have made it," added Jim Portman.

"Indeed," Winston Fields reflected as he poured another bourbon. "Even a Georgia farmboy should know you can't ride a three-legged mule. To Edward T. Bannon, the next President of these United States."

"Hear. Hear!" the others chimed in.

"God help the poor bastard," Bannon replied.

It was in early May when he'd called them together for the first time. Those who expected a do-nothing President were about to be in for a rude shock.

"Lang, you taught history, and you know it's always been one of my little passions. I've come to two basic conclusions about our sad state of national affairs. First, it's a mess! But more importantly, I really believe the next four years may be the last chance we have to turn the

67

country and the economy around, if it's not too late already. Pretty soon the damage will be so fundamental we won't be able to reverse it, at home or abroad.''

Bannon paused to look around the table at the stern faces. "My second conclusion is that if we don't get the ball rolling, I'm going to be the second of a long series of one-term Presidents. . . . I don't mind that so much for myself as I do for the country. It can't take that kind of instability for very long. If I'm going to fail, I'd rather it be for reaching too far than not far enough.''

"This year and next are the pivots," he continued. "A strong step now will have two years to work. If it does, we'll be heroes in the next election. If it doesn't, it won't really matter. I'll go off and write my memoirs. . . . The book'll just be a little shorter than I planned, that's all.'' He laughed as he sat back down in his chair.

"I've asked each of you here because I want you to work with me on a problem. Just one. But it's the biggest. The Mideast and what that means to us—oil. These latest attacks and reprisals just reinforce my opinion that we'll never get anywhere until we have a comprehensive peace in the region. One we force if necessary! But one that builds bridges instead of walls between us and the Arab world moderates.''

That got their attention, he thought. "That's right. For us a stable source of supply and economic alliances with the conservative Gulf states. One that'll guarantee we can isolate the radicals and put us rather than the Soviets in the position of power over there. It must be fair and equitable to Israel, but we can't keep grinding along at a snail's pace for years. They still haven't got much beyond the preliminary stages of West Bank autonomy talks and they'll keep that up without even noticing the whole region has gone up in flames around them.''

As several of the people around the table began to speak at once, he cut them off with a wave of his hand. "Not yet. I don't want your reactions now. Just think it over. I want each of you to work out a framework for a settlement in your own mind. Don't worry about how it could be implemented. At this point I just want a half a dozen formulas you think would be equitable to both sides. Let's meet next week, same time.''

As they walked away down the hall out of earshot, Senator Jensen said quietly to Secretary Andrews, "You know, Lang, it's amazing how the job sometimes makes the man.''

"Or how we never really understood the man to begin with," Andrews chuckled.

And so the meetings had proceeded forward over the next three months. They researched, debated, and probed. Gradually they moved beyond Bannon's charge to erect the skeleton of a solution. He was pleased to see their various approaches coming together. They worked in total secrecy with no fixed schedule, no agenda, no minutes, no aides, and no stand-ins allowed.

Satisfied their program was sound, in July Bannon finally began to reach out for the outside consultations that had to be made.

The pace was beginning to pick up as he convened the meeting that August 14.

"Okay, folks, it's Friday night and we've all got plans to get out of town for the weekend, so let's get started. The Secretary of State has just returned from Riyadh, so the floor's all yours, Lang."

"We are very close to an agreement with the Saudis." Lang smiled. "And I'm tired. I met for most of the last two days with King Khalid, Prince Fahd, and Sheik Yamani. We went back over the last outline many times and fleshed out some significant details."

"That's great, Lang, really great!" Bannon beamed.

"They assure us they can deliver the full support of Kuwait, Abu Dabai, Qatar, and Yemen. Plus, as we asked them to do, they've sounded out the PLO, Egypt, and Jordan, without reference to us, but they feel it won't be any problem getting them on board. Provided the program is in the general shape we've discussed."

"You know," Louise Korshak smiled, "the Saudis have really been pretty decent about bending around the sharp corners with us."

Andrews nodded in agreement as he looked down at the floor. "Yamani told me over lunch yesterday that they weren't just a bunch of rug merchants. It's too serious a business to them to haggle over. And they know what our problems are. But," he paused to look up slowly at Bannon, "he was damn blunt about one thing. I can tell you that."

"I smell a 'yes, but' coming here," Bannon cringed.

"They really want the thing to work, as much as we do," Andrews said earnestly. "I can tell they're really worried about the Soviet moves toward the oil lane and the other radical Muslim states. The 'sharks,'

Yamani called them. They want to believe you're serious, but they went down this same road with Carter, and Khalid says it's the last time they'll carry our jug to the well! It's up to us. Either quit now and don't waste their time, or else we better be ready to go through with it.''

Bannon paused to look at the ceiling in disgust. "I can't argue with them one bit, either." No, he thought, it's another of the legacies. The Camp David two-step. And Carter really led them down the path. He kept promising them he'd deliver. He and Begin would argue a lot and pray a lot, but nothing ever came of it. Just like he did with the new guy. Carter'd never drop the hammer. He couldn't, and they knew it.

"No, they're absolutely right," Congressman Fields said as he looked knowingly at Bannon. "Begin would haggle over every point and stall. . . . But to be fair, I really can't blame the Israelis too much. They never knew where we were going to stop. We always acted like it was a union labor contract and everything was up for grabs. They didn't know what was next."

"I agree, but that's only part of it," Senator Portman frowned. "In the end, it always comes down to politics. The further Carter went down in the polls, the less he had the courage to risk losing the Jewish block in his own party. When Nixon opened the door to Red China, he was in a powerful position in his own party and could hold the hawks in check. That's why I like this approach, Ed. Give 'em the whole package, signed, sealed, and delivered! They'll know it's all we'll ask of them."

Bannon looked down the table and watched the others nodding in agreement. Checking the time, he said to Andrews, "Let's move on."

"Before we all pat each other on the back," Andrews replied with a touch of concern. "Remember they have two nonnegotiable points . . . but with a little room for interpretation," he added with a smile. "First is that Jerusalem must be free of all Israeli control. Second, there must be a free and independent Palestinian state established on the West Bank. Period. Absolute! . . . but . . . there's a lot they haven't said, either."

"Well," said Louise Korshak as she doodled on a pad of notepaper, "that's what it always did come down to, didn't it?"

"Always did, and always will, so let's not kid ourselves that we'll ever get by with anything less, particularly if we want to defuse all the anti-American hatred built up in the region. But the Saudis agree that U.N. control of Jerusalem will do, provided it offers free access for all faiths. But no barriers and U.N. police."

Bannon nodded. "That would absolutely shatter the Soviets after Afghanistan. And the U.N. shouldn't object, since they've called for it since '48."

"I wouldn't think so," Andrews agreed. "Now, on the West Bank, Khalid finally agreed that so long as the state is legally independent and self-governing, we can work out the fine points. But it must have complete domestic sovereignty and full international recognition—ambassadors, a seat in the U.N., the whole bit."

"I'm more than willing for us to be the first ones to recognize them if we can get that far," Bannon conceded with a slight frown.

"Let's not be too glum," countered Andrews smugly. "I wasn't riding camels over there for two days, you know. They are more concerned at this point about the form than the substance." His eyes glittered as he went on slowly with emphasis. "They reason that any small, new nation should not be forced to squander their precious energies on building up a military force they shouldn't need against peaceful neighbors. A small constabulary, yes, but no hard weapons, no armor, no artillery, no jet fighters. They feel two things would serve this young nation better. One is to station a Jordanian brigade there to help guard the border, both ways. A modest amount of tanks and artillery, but nothing that would threaten the Israelis. Second would be a mutual defense treaty with the U.S., but it would only operate if the PLO didn't violate the border."

Bannon was obviously pleased. "The treaty idea with us won't fly, but do they think Hussein and Arafat will go along with the rest of the package?" He winced, expecting the worst.

"If the rest of the package is generally what we discussed, yes. Who's going to tell Khalid it's no dice?" Andrews raised both of his arms up in laughter. No names popped into anyone's mind, he noticed. "But they do have some major details they'll require." Returning to a more serious tone of voice, he told Bannon, "All the Israeli settlements on the West Bank and all of their bases, installations, and facilities there and in Jerusalem must be vacated. All of them, and intact," he pointed out with emphasis.

"How the hell are we going to sell that!" Bannon exploded with anger and disgust. "Damn, I can just hear the Israeli response now!"

Andrews smiled again amiably. "They gave me a few big lumps of sugar to sweeten the pot. They'll pay for all the facilities. Ten billion dollars for them. That's a lot of sweet! Besides, that way they won't just be abandoning them to the Palestinians,'' Andrews pointed out lamely. "It's a point. Anyway, the Israelis can buy an awful lot of F–Fifteens and tanks with that kind of money!''

Bannon was immensely relieved and more optimistic than he'd been for months. "We're going to have to use that carefully, though. Not just a straight offer. It's going to have to be a carrot-and-stick kind of thing.'' He rubbed his hands together as his mind raced ahead. "Yeah, we'll have to think a little on that. It's the ace of trump, no question. Any strings?'' he suddenly said, turning back to look at Andrews.

"Nothing major,'' the Secretary of State replied apologetically. "They'll give us the money when the documents are signed. The Israelis can have it when the last withdrawal is finished, and that has to be within six months. I think we could get them to release some of it, say two or three billion at the outset, so the Israelis can have some new hardware in place at the end of the withdrawal.''

"They realize that we are going to require clear statements about Israel's right to exist and the sovereignty of her borders, don't they?'' Korshak asked in a firm voice.

"That's really no problem.'' Andrews glanced up confidently. "With a free Jerusalem and Palestinian state, Khalid pointed out to me they have no reason not to do so. But it's a two-way street! The Israelis have to recognize the Palestinians too. And the Palestinians have to renounce the use of force. And,'' he went on in a slow daisy chain of conditions, "the Israelis have to stay out of Lebanon. And that means the PLO has to knock it off and get their asses north of the Litani River. It all has to hang together. That's why no one's ever been able to get the two sides to agree on a damn thing,'' Andrews said in a very tired voice as he sat down. "But that's why we're giving them both a package.''

Bannon hesitated, then asked in a careful voice, "From what they said, how much confidence do you have that they'll keep the PLO in line? The Israelis will have a whole tank corps just over the hill waiting for the first Arab who throws a cigarette butt over the fence.''

Andrews looked at him with a slight ironic expression. "Several things. First, they know that as well as we do. With the other Gulf states, they'll fund the West Bank state and the U.N.-controlled Jerusalem for ten years. They'll have 'advisors' there and they'd like for us to as well. And you have their solemn word they'll cut off the money. And that the

PLO will know that. And the Jordanians will be working for them on this. That's a lot of clout! But,'' he paused with a look of deep concern in his eyes, "they say that we must realize, and so must the Israelis, that there are some radical elements like Habash and the PFLP that neither they nor Arafat can control. That goes for Ghaddafi too; after all, that's where Habash gets his money. Khalid said to me most carefully that if, after a suitable period of settling in, Habash or Ghaddafi violate the accords, then we or the Israelis can have a free hand to eliminate them from the picture.''

Bannon looked up in astonishment and then actually smiled. "Well . . .naturally we'll all pretend we didn't hear that. Ater all, we don't do that kind of stuff anymore. But I'll make sure General Gershon and his Mossad get the message,'' he said as he broke into a broad grin.

Andrews could see that he was obviously pleased. "But remember, they also put responsibility for the Israelis squarely on your shoulders.''

"We'll just kick their asses up to their shoulder blades,'' Louise Korshak said politely with a deadpan expression.

"Louise,'' Bannon said, shaking his head. "I expected you to change the Pentagon, not the other way around.''

"Hell, we've all put too much into this and it all makes too much sense to let a few hotheads screw it all up,'' she shot back. "I'm serious! They've got to know that the full weight of this government is behind the deal, and what's at stake for them if they do anything without a damn good provocation!'' She looked across at Bannon with icy calm.

Nodding in understanding, he got up and stretched and slowly paced around the room. "What about the oil?'' he asked quietly.

"They'll keep the same volume of export and the same price of forty-three dollars per barrel until the agreements are signed, then it will drop to thirty-eight dollars. When King Khalid can pray at the Dome of the Rock in a free Jerusalem, he says it will come down to thirty-five dollars. When the last Israeli is gone from the West Bank, it goes to thirty-two dollars,'' he said, pausing. "Naturally that is to be keyed to our rate of inflation as of today.''

"Those boys sure don't miss a trick, do they?'' Winston Fields said, shaking his head in admiration. "But I guess it's as fair as we're likely to pull out of them. That's going to put Iraq in a real snit.''

"Prince Fahd gave me another jolt when I was about to leave.'' Andrews chuckled as he thought back on their car ride to the airport. "A shopping list! Hardware they want to buy from us. They want us to use it to sell the deal here at home." Pulling the paper from his briefcase, Andrews scanned the long sheet in admiration. "They really had someone do his homework on this. They even designated the contractor, the plant, location, and the name of every congressman, senator, and governor who is effected. This'll get the message to go out loud and clear: no vote, no contract; no contract, no jobs."

Andrews handed the list to Bannon, who quickly looked it over before passing it to Louise Korshak. "Here. This'll be your assignment for the week. I want you to put some of those computers you have to work. Get all of this stuff cross-indexed. And we'll get all the other secretaries to send you their domestic grants that are pending by state and district."

"Hot damn," Congresssman Fields gushed gleefully. "I do believe I see a little game of old-fashioned country hardball coming up. Sir, I volunteer to be your starting pitcher in the House. Indeed!"

"Jim Portman and I will do the same for the Senate," Jensen added. "It's a good idea to be ready with a strong deterrent. We'll appeal to their sense of national interest, but since most of our colleagues don't operate on that level, its nice to lay on some heavy lumber. I'm sure we can get all of those corporation presidents to make some phone calls along with the unions. That'll light the home fires for sure!"

"But you know," Portman replied with a thoughtful smile. "It may not be as hard as we think. Times have changed with one-fifty-a-gallon gas, Andy Young, and the Muslim fervor in the Middle East. Most of the members still talk a good pro-Israel line, but the support is becoming paper thin. In the past, there was no reason not to. The Arabs had nothing at all to offer. It was the path of least political resistance."

"Absolutely," Fields agreed as he looked over at Portman. "Remember, except for a few districts, the Jewish vote is very small. A very big and well-organized lobby, but the vote is a lot more diluted than it used to be. Where it is still sizable, you have a much larger black vote that doesn't exactly see eye to eye with them on that issue anymore. It hasn't been tested since Andy Young."

Bannon smiled as he considered the comment.

He began on a new point, surprised at the calmness of his own voice. "I want you all to believe one thing as we move forward on this deal. I wouldn't be pushing this kind of a settlement if I wasn't absolutely

74

convinced it was essential to our national interest. Or truly in the best long-term national interest of Israel, either,'' he asserted with emphasis, looking from face to face. ''What we've got to make them realize is that we're going down the tubes fast. And since they're dependent upon us, they'll come right along. If not, we won't be of any use to them at all. This is the last chance we have to keep that from happening and I'm not going to be shortsighted enough to let it slip by.''

After the room fell silent, Jensen said quietly, ''We may not have agreed with you to start with, but I think we all do now.''

''This is just flat a clash of national wills,'' Bannon concluded wearily. ''The Israelis and the Palestinians. They have honest differences, but I don't see any good guys or bad guys, just a lot of stubborn gray hats. If we assume that they both really want peace, the deal will work.'' He gestured with his right hand. ''And it is about the only one that will!''

As they all wound down and stared at Bannon, Louise Korshak asked, ''How are you going to break all of this to the Israelis?''

Bannon turned around and seemed to hesitate for a moment before he shrugged and said, ''Straight from the shoulder. There's no other way. I'm just going to lay the whole deal out in front of the Prime Minister and I guess the Foreign and Defense Ministers.'' He looked around the table at their intent faces and continued. ''I'm more than willing to explain everything I can to them. I'll even argue with them a little, but I'm not going to bargain.'' He tried to gauge their feelings and doubts but saw most of them seemed to be nodding in agreement. ''We'll have the whole package signed by the Arabs before I arrive in Israel. They can either accept or not!''

Portman drummed his fingertips on the table as he stated, ''You know, they've always rejected the idea of an imposed settlement and insisted on face-to-face talks.''

''But what has that got anyone except a de facto stall?'' Korshak snapped back impatiently.

''I realize that, Louise,'' Portman explained. ''My point is, what cards are we going to play when Ed gets the usual knee-jerk rejection from them?''

Bannon eyed them both coolly. ''No, you're right, Jim, I'm sure that'll be the initial reaction. But with the carrot of the Saudi money and the added arms we've been holding up for them, on better terms than they even asked for, it'll cause them to hesitate. They're good politicians. They should know a stacked deck when they see one, so I'm going to tell them I've got the votes to back up a complete embargo, and then invite them to check it out. I want them to know I'm serious and the games are over. But I'm going to try like hell to convince the stubborn bastards that we're on their side." He tried very hard to control his growing frustration and looked around at their faces, searching for some reassurance.

"Relax, Ed, we're all with you." Portman laughed to break the tension. "How's the schedule look? Seems to me we still have a lot of work to do."

"Lang?" Bannon replied as he turned to the Secretary. "Wouldn't you say about sixty days?"

"Let's hope no more. Problems expand to fill time. I've got some more legwork in the Arab countries, then we have to reduce it all to paper and get it signed. So, yeah, about sixty days."

Bannon sat down and pulled out his schedule book. "Today's August fourteenth. I want you to try like hell to get the loose ends tied up in thirty days. Then you've got two weeks to get out a final draft. That puts us at October first. I want the Saudis to have it to look over, after I have, of course, no later than the fifth. They've got their own little sales job. You go over there and help. I'll go over myself on the eleventh, to Riyadh first. Then a day in Amman and a day in Cairo. I'll go to Israel on the fourteenth, return here on the sixteenth, early. So I'll give the Israelis two full days." Looking up again at Andrews, he added, "Lang, you get to stick around there and use your silver tongue to wrap it up."

Jensen looked over at Bannon and said in a concerned voice, "That sounds like a very tight schedule."

Bannon nodded in agreement. "It has to be! We'll never keep a lid on this if we don't. We've got to be able to go to both sides with a complete package in hand. Once it gets out, the whole deal's going to unravel. Both sides will launch a barrage against this point or that. We'll never get it back on track." He looked back down at his calendar book again. "Besides, I'm already scheduled to make a big televised speech on the nineteenth, so we can go right up to the last moment without tipping our hand to the press. But, Lang, I'm going to insist on a simple yes or no answer from the Israelis by six P.M. our time on the eighteenth. My speech is at two P.M. the next afternoon, and we are going to have to do a lot of briefing to a lot of different people before I come out in public, whichever way it goes."

"Pardon my ignorance, but why the speech on the nineteenth?" Senator Jensen asked with a puzzled expression.

"Yorktown. Yorktown Day." Bannon paused to gauge the effect of the occasion on their faces. "Aren't there any other historians in this group? Surely you can catch why this little date would be of particular significance to what I'll be saying. What about you, Winston?"

"Certainly, Mr. President," Fields replied with mirth. "I guess they don't teach much of that subject at Yankee schools these days. That would be the two hundredth anniversary, wouldn't it? Yes, the last and most glorious battle of the War of Independence . . . and of our first peace. Nice touch, very nice. I can't think of a more suitable occasion!"

"Pure accident, but we'll all pretend a stroke of genius. Anyway, on the nineteenth at Yorktown we'll all be smiles as I announce a settlement of the modern Thirty Years War, or all frowns as I explain why we are imposing a complete embargo. Both speeches will be ready to go. Let's pray for the best."

6

Tuesday, September 8

A mile and a half northwest of the White House sits the Libyan Embassy. It is at the far end of Embassy Row, fronting on Massachusetts Avenue and backing onto Rock Creek.

From his third-floor office at the rear of the building, the Third Secretary for Trade stared out the window, lost in thought. Deep lines of concentration were etched around his eyes and mouth. He sat quite still, with his chin resting lightly on the tips of his fingers. He'd sat like this for hours and the strain and lack of sleep showed in his tired expression. From the piles of reports and paper on his desk, it was apparent he'd done little else for a long time. And couldn't care less.

He had a slight enigmatic grin on his face, but it was unconscious and had nothing at all to do with the beautiful view outside. The creek, the broad green parkway, the wooded tip of Oak Hill Cemetery, and Georgetown beyond on an early autumn morning could have been a blank white wall. In fact, Colonel Haleem Rashid detested the view on those infrequent occasions when he bothered to notice it.

To Rashid, it was a view of a hated and hateful land. Hateful by its indifference and hypocrisy. From this window, Rashid knew he could soar out for over three thousand miles to the west without ever finding one friendly or understanding face. It nurtured, armed, and encouraged his enemy. Its factories made the tanks and planes and bullets and bombs to be placed in cruel hands. It was like a perverted cornucopia that prided itself on how it could feed the starving masses of half the world. Then it mocked them by arming the very regimes that kept them that way.

He'd been here too long, he thought. That first visit he'd made to the National Archives, could it only have been a year and a half ago? It seemed much longer. But the words Jefferson had written in the great Declaration, they were noble and timeless. They were also the words of youth; of a nation burning with its ideals and seeking its own freedom. Sadly, the words were now relegated to a museum like quaint antiques. They were dangerously out of place for a nation in its old age. Fearful of change, it could only react instead of lead. It couldn't understand that the forgotten ideals of its own youth endured. Or perhaps it understood all too well, he thought bitterly. The Americans are like frightened, lonely old men, cowering deep in their armchairs before a dying fire in a dimly lit study. The doors and windows are carefully locked, but an eyebrow raises at each sound far off in the night.

Of course he knew the Russians were no better. Far more hypocritical, they'd just aged a lot faster. The liberating zealots and revolutionaries of Lenin's day had been replaced by bureaucrats and rude functionaries. But that was no consolation to Rashid.

Long ago he'd developed a deep moral and intellectual contempt for both sides. Being in this assignment only made it deeper.

He'd hated it from the day they'd told him about it.

"I'm not a spy . . .and I'm certainly not a diplomat! I'm a soldier. That's what you trained me for. That's where I'm of some use to our cause. I belong in the field with my men, not in some embassy." But his frustration fell on deaf ears.

"Haleem, you're the best man we've got for the job. That's why we want you to go," the representative of the council told him patiently. "We have all the diplomats we need. This is different. We must send someone with some real credibility who can work with the white radicals and the black nationalists. Someone they'll respect. Plus someone who knows about weapons and can work with the IRA contacts. We need a good man on the ground."

He'd lost and he knew it. He also knew he'd go where they ordered him to go. "But using the Libyan diplomatic cover—I don't like them or trust them. They spend more time watching our people than they do the Israelis. When I catch someone peeking over my shoulder, I've been known to be nasty.''

The other man squirmed nervously in his chair as their eyes locked. He would not forget the savage look in Rashid's stare. "You're just going to have to control your reflexes...to a point, at least," he conceded. "Ghaddafi's generosity doesn't fool us. But at times he's useful, and we need help. His ambitions are to dominate us and all the rest of the Arab world. He'll learn his lesson one day. But we don't want you to be the teacher! Use him, but stay away from his people.''

He put his hand on Haleem's shoulder and said with understanding, "The assignment is going to be good for you, you'll see. Learn from it. It would be a horrid waste to have your skills lost in some trivial battle. There are far greater things in store for you.''

He carried out his mission with flawless precision, but little enthusiasm. The American radical underground were silly, unkempt theoreticians, with no prospects for any success. He grew to like and respect the black nationalists. They were realists, who'd scaled down their efforts to build up their own communities, seek economic and political power, and reach out to the socialist movements in other countries. The IRA people he'd met were uniformly third rate, but why should he expect them to waste their top men on what was little more than a logistics exercise. Their people back in Belfast did know how to put what he got them to good use.

As the months wore on, he felt more and more stifled. It was almost physical. A thick, mushy cocoon wrapped around and around him ever so tightly. He couldn't move. Finally, he couldn't even breathe. It closed him in and cut off the contact he needed so desperately with his own people, his own homeland, and the things familiar to him.

He was isolated, foreign, and intensely depressed.

His last trip to Beirut was tremendously refreshing. But that was last February, and coming back was equally repugnant. His aide, Lieutenant Hafez Arazi, picked him up at Dulles.

For most of the drive into town, Rashid leaned moodily against the door and uttered little more than monosyllables. Finally he let it all roll out like an open floodgate. "I dread coming back. It's like a prison sentence. Most of all, I miss the little things. The smells, the food, a different cut of clothes. Country people in their traditional robes. Their gestures, customs, courtesies when they talk. Or laugh. Or argue. The women are so much more reserved and quiet. The street markets. Calls to prayer in the morning. Arab children running through the streets. Farmers working the dry fields with mules. Olive trees, orange groves, the dry heat, old wagons on narrow roads, and the jasmine in bloom.''

He looked out at the lights of the Capitol with barely controlled anger.

''All I have is a vacuum inside. It wears you down like a cancer!''

He didn't want to admit that what tore at him most was to be gone at a time like this. Things were beginning to move so quickly now. Victory had never been this close. He'd seen it in their eyes back home. The tide was running in torrents. It carried them forward each day. World opinion, the Muslim world in flames and galvanized like they hadn't been in a thousand years. The end of the long struggle was looming up on the horizon.

And here he was riding in a car five thousand miles away. All he could do was watch it on television or read about it in the newspapers. Attacks he didn't lead. Battles he wasn't part of. Skills not used. Rusting away. Alone. Depressed.

But that was in February. That was before his own world crashed down around him. Before the larger struggle became an intense personal hatred for the people who had destroyed his family.

Arazi had tears in his eyes when he brought in the message. He handed it across the desk but could say nothing.

Rashid scanned the teletype quickly.

WE REGRET TO . . . JAMIL RASHID AND AHMED SAED . . .
DIED HEROICALLY . . . MISSION . . . ASSAULTING THEIR
TARGET . . . ENEMY TROOPS . . . ALSO DEEPLY MOURN THE
LOSS . . . KADRI SAED . . . SISTER . . . ISRAELI BOMBERS
. . . IN LEBANON . . . OUR SYMPATHY

Reading it over time and again could not change his utter disbelief. The loss bore deeply inside him. But he could only stare down at the paper for several long minutes, paralyzed with frustration and rage.

In others the seething, blinding rage would have wasted itself in some futile act of violence, but this never really crossed his mind. Over the long hours that followed, the flaming red inferno inside died down to the hotter but less spectacular white bed of coals beneath. Returning to rationality, the mind of an experienced terrorist tactician took over again.

No, to do justice to the deed, it wouldn't be some senseless act of self-destruction. He'd have his revenge, but it'd be at the time and place of his choosing. Precise. And he'd exact the full measure. He could picture the scene clearly in his mind.

The room was packed. People leaned out over the balcony rail to catch a glimpse at the proceedings below. They fell silent when he rose.

His long black robes swished as he turned to the bench. "Your Honor," his voice rang out, "if it pleases the Court of World Opinion, the prosecution will prove beyond the slightest doubt that the defendant, America, has been engaged in a vicious conspiracy, and that they are guilty of being accessories before, during, and after the fact in the brutal murders of my father, mother, brother, and sister."

"Well, uh, Colonel Rashid," the white-haired judge sputtered as he sat forward to peer down at him, "What penalty do you seek for these crimes?"

"There can only be one, Your Honor. The prosecution demands death!"

For weeks he said nothing and did little. His work went untouched. He remained home alone or went in to the embassy and just stared out the window of his office. Eventually, he would go off by himself for hours at a time and return with stacks of books. He spent long hours pouring over them or going through thick volumes of newspapers in the embassy library.

Several times, Arazi followed him at a discrete distance when he went out to return books or go for his walks. He couldn't get close enough to tell what Rashid was up to, but he finally decided it didn't matter. He was doing something, and that was a good sign.

Twice Rashid even left town for a long weekend, telling Arazi he needed to relax and see some of the country.

On September 8 he called Arazi into his office.

"Hafez, if you're not doing anything, let's go out for a walk."

As they walked out onto Massachusetts Avenue in the mid-afternoon heat, Rashid smiled and said, "This is much better than having you follow me around. Oh, don't protest," he laughed, "I appreciate the concern. But we need to talk. And it has to be away from the friendly ears of Colonel Ghaddafi." They walked on south around Sheridan Circle.

"We've been together now for a long time, over five years," Rashid continued. "I think we respect each other, and I want you to know it is mutual. You're a fine officer and I think we make a good team. In the field, not here though. Here we are like fish out of water."

"That's the absolute truth," Arazi said in disgust. "We don't belong here."

"I'm slowly beginning to rethink that, though." He smiled, the old cryptic grin on his face. He paused to watch the traffic before he took the next irreversible step. Taking one last look at Arazi, he decided. "What I'm going to tell you must never go any further. It must stay between us as comrades. There is no longer any rank between us, Hafez. So for now, call me Haleem."

He could see the look of surprise and seriousness on Hafez's face.

"I'm not insane. In fact, I've never been more sane or coldly calculating in my life. The deaths of my brother and sister hurt me deeper than you can imagine. Hate, rage, disgust, loathing toward the Israelis who pulled the trigger, toward the Americans who gave them the guns . . . and toward myself for not being there. I went through all of that. But now I'm beyond it." His dark features were set in deep concentration as they reached DuPont Circle and turned down Connecticut Avenue.

Arazi spoke up in a sad, hoarse voice. "I knew you were troubled. That's why I followed you. I didn't want you to do anything foolish. We need you too much." His seriousness, warmed Rashid.

"I'm going to tell you of what I have concluded over the past few months. You can argue with me. Challenge the assumptions. Say I'm insane after all. Or think anything else you care to. But," he said darkly and with a quick turn of his flashing eyes, "you must swear to me now that you'll not try to interfere or stop me or notify anyone of what I'm planning, even if it goes against your orders. I could not allow that. Do you understand?"

Arazi nodded jerkily. "Yes. You know we are too close for me to do anything else." He had a sinking feeling that he'd just walked through the gates of Hell, but he couldn't think of anyone he'd rather go with.

"I know I'm asking a lot of you on pure faith, but bear with me a bit longer." As he walked he looked again at the office buildings, which housed the very people he hated most.

Rashid began to speak again, but the topic seemed strange. "I've never been very religious. I just could never believe in a God who'd desert our people as He's done, leaving them with little more than a blind faith that He'll punish evil in His own time and place . . . leaving me sitting here where I can do nothing." He paused, deep in thought. "But I was wrong. He's just too subtle for us sometimes. It's clear to me now; I was put here at this time and place for a purpose. It wasn't an accident or bad luck, there was a Supreme hand at work here."

He nodded slowly as he went on talking, mostly to himself. "No, Hafez, it was the hand of God, but not the God of old women and little children. Not the God of kindness and mercy. No, it was the hand of our Muslim God of wrath, of divine judgment, of revenge. The God of the *jihad*, the Holy War. The God who visits savage retribution on the head of the infidel. That's the God whose hand put me here, now!"

Arazi had never heard him talk this way before. Rashid had always been the model of the unemotional tactician. They walked on oblivious to their surroundings, crossing Rhode Island Avenue and continuing on to the southeast. Rashid became more relaxed as they went. His voice once again became that of calm, analytical reason. "We have a truly preposterous situation here. A classically insolvable dilemma for a thinking man. On one hand, the fervent and resolute cause of our people. On the other, the impossible situation we find ourselves in, unable to win. The Israelis won't give back our land, and we aren't strong enough to take it from them. They kill us in large numbers if we go to war, or small numbers in commando raids. Either way, we die and fail. We've only be deluding ourselves to believe it is anything else than the ultimate trap they've set for us." He exhaled slowly as he concentrated hard to keep the fast flow of his thoughts in check. It was critical to him that Hafez follow down this tortuous path without stumbling.

"All we've won is a long row of graves for our ablest young men," he continued. "We are bleeding ourselves white. We can't compete with them in open battle. We haven't got the money to buy the type of weapons it would take or the highly skilled manpower. In fact, the mere act of trying kills off our brightest men, the ones we will need to build a nation. So we resort to terror. Munich. Lod Airport. Rome. Many raids within Israel itself. But at what price?'' he asked, looking over at his companion.

Rashid swallowed hard, tasting the sour phlegm. ''A few moments of glory, but we've lost far more than they. The best of the brave. The leaders of our next generation . . . my brother. We bleed, and just give them more excuses to strike back and kill us again . . . my sister. We haven't made a dent. It's just the big trap they've set for us to fall into. We're like gnats they smash with a hammer.''

Arazi began to slowly nod his head in agreement. ''I'm beginning to understand what you are saying.'' But he looked up at Rashid with a painfully puzzled expression. ''You . . . you couldn't be suggesting that we give up? That would be unthinkable no matter how high the price.''

''Of course not,'' he shot back with a look of anger. ''And you'll soon see, that is the furthest thing from my mind. No, there can only be one winner, and it will be us. There can be no compromise with Zionism. They seek our land to the sole exclusion of all others. Religion elevated to the State itself. The Vatican with an army trying to reconstruct the Holy Roman Empire. . . . No, we'll have our land back!''

''But how then,'' Arazi asked in frustration. ''If you rule out the use of war and terrorism . . . What do you suggest, another oil boycott against the Americans? I don't see where that did very much!''

''No, you're absolutely right. It did very little, but deep inside it was a small kernel of truth. We had the right target for once, but the wrong weapon.'' Rashid smiled and surprised Arazi with a loud laugh. ''I remember when I was very young. My Uncle Abou would come visit and wrestle with me on the floor. I'd get him in a leg hold and bend and twist with all my might. He'd pound on the floor and yell and scream like he was really in pain and beg for me to stop. I thought I was hurting him until I looked up to see my mother and father trying hard to hold in their laughter as they watched us.'' His smile slowly vanished and his eyes grew narrow. ''You see, that was just like the oil boycott. We were only fooling ourselves. Another big trap, but they want very much for us to keep playing it. Their greatest fear is that we'll find out it really doesn't hurt and try something that will! That is why they scream so loud.''

Arazi stared down the street and nodded his head in complete agreement. "I see. It's like the children's story they tell about the rabbit who begs the fox not to throw him into the briar patch when he knows that it is the only place he can be safe. Yes, I suppose you're right, the boycott is an inconvenience, but certainly not much real damage to them. But how can we do real damage?"

"The pipeline! We must sever the pipeline that keeps Israel supplied. On their own, the Israelis couldn't last six months against us. Their economy could never take the strain of the vast amounts they would need to spend on their military establishment. No, the only thing that keeps them afloat year after year is the pipeline of money and supplies from the United States. This is the key—the pipeline," Rashid said emphatically. "We must do something dramatic that will weaken their resolve here in the U.S. That's why I say the boycott had the right target but the wrong weapon. We must do something that will slap them in the face and show them the price they must pay!"

"But how can we cut off this pipeline?" Arazi asked incredulously.

"We can't cut it off. We must get them to shut it off for us. But not by asking them or pleading our case. That's hopeless! It would take a hundred years to make a small dent. And we don't have a hundred years, or even twenty-five, or even five. We can't survive very much longer as a people if we don't succeed very soon. We are being assimilated. Soon we will be a mongrel people, and time is running out on us faster than anyone thinks." He shot a quick look of alarm at Arazi as he said, "Don't you see, this is the greatest trap of all. We thought that time was on our side, but it has always been our worst enemy. And the Israelis know it."

Arazi asked sharply, "It has always been against our policy to undertake a terrorist campaign here."

"I wouldn't suggest anything that crude or stupid. The Puerto Ricans blowing up a deserted Manhattan office building in the middle of the night or putting bombs in airport lockers—they only get contempt. Irritations and silly gestures . . . No, what we need is a massive shock. Something so symbolic and horrendous they'll recoil. Like the blacks burning down their own neighborhoods. Middle-class America cannot tolerate violence directed like that."

Reaching H Street, they crossed through the heavy traffic and entered Lafayette Park.

"No," Rashid continued. "It has to be something like the IRA blowing Mountbatten to smithereens. Superb. It was dramatic, vicious, symbolic overkill."

Arazi quickly countered. "But it put the British in a rage. And the ones who did it got caught."

"Yes, but as the months and years passed, the rage was replaced by doubt. People began to ask why. Was it all worth the price? Why are we still in this Ulster business anyway? It was okay as long as it didn't really affect us, but who would they get next? The security forces could react, but not prevent. And you were correct, the fatal flaw in the final episode was that they were caught. It ruins the whole effect. To do it and escape makes the security people look more helpless. You can strike anywhere, anytime. The public becomes more frustrated and the killers take on proportions larger than life."

"Getting caught does ruin all that," Arazi conceded. "It allows them to direct their attention to those who were culprits as opposed to the issue."

"Oh, but far worse, dead bodies or live prisoners bring the whole thing to reality. Like animals in cages in the zoo. They always had Sirhan Sirhan in manacles between two towering guards. Or they can dismiss you as a freak, a loner, a madman, and ignore your reasons."

"Yes," Arazi said quietly, "we must be able to escape."

Rashid smiled to himself without any outward notice as he heard the word "we." They walked on in silence past the statue of Andrew Jackson and beyond to a long row of benches along the south side of the park. Haleem sat down and said, "Let's sit here for a while."

"I must admit, Haleem, your argument is logical and impressive. But if we do something like this, we'll be breaking off on our own. They'll never support us."

"I know. It would have to be an independent operation. If it works, we'll be heroes. If it fails, they'll condemn us. But we'll be dead anyway, so it won't matter to us."

"You have a specific plan in mind, I assume?"

"We wouldn't have had this talk if I didn't. What do you think I've been working on for the past three months? Are you with me?"

"You know I am."

"Thank you. The plan requires two people. I needed you."

"But what is the target that will accomplish what you want?"

Rashid slowly raised his right arm and pointed across Pennsylvania Avenue. His face was flushed and his eyes flashed in the bright sun.

"We are going to kill the man who lives there. In a most spectacular fashion we are going to kill the man who lives in the White House—President Edward Bannon."

7

Monday, September 14

In the evening, a hotel room is boring when you are alone.

Rashid's flight to Chicago had arrived three hours ago. Rather than do something like sightseeing, he decided to just go directly up to the room and wait for the Irishman to phone. Better to be bored than to take needless risks that might attract attention, he thought. If the meeting didn't go as planned, he would need his anonymity. So he sat on the bed and waited for the phone to ring.

"Teraki speaking," Rashid answered in a soft monotone.

"Ah, Mr. Teraki, it's good to hear your voice again. It's me, Murphy. I understand you have a matter to discuss with me. I'm downstairs."

"Good. Come up to Room Eleven twenty-nine."

After Rashid hung up, he opened his briefcase and took out his .32 cal. automatic. He quickly checked the clip and the receiver mechanism before he screwed on the silencer. Lying back against the headboard of the bed, he placed the automatic under a folded copy of the *Chicago Tribune*, where it would be close to his right hand. No reason to take any chances, he thought.

He would only use this room for the meeting itself. He had booked a second room three floors down in another name and as soon as Murphy left, Rashid would make sure the hall was empty before he went to it. He could stay in the second room until it was time to go back to the airport.

The loud knock at the door pushed everything else from his mind. Beneath the outward calm, he was at a razor-sharp level of alertness like a large cat on the hunt. He listened silently through the door for any sound that didn't belong. Tense.

"It's me, Murphy. I'm alone . . . as usual," came the nervous response.

He let the fat Irishman in and leaned out into the hall to take a quick glance in both directions. Seeing no one, he closed the door and threw the bolt. Rashid turned around and looked the other man over from head to foot. His stance. Where were his hands? Was he tense? The eyes. His expression. The Arab knew that Murphy would quickly go to pieces if anything was not right. He wasn't artful enough to act another part well.

But he saw nothing. "Good to see you again, my friend. How are all of our good brothers in Belfast? Have a seat." Once the Irishman was bottomed out in the large, soft armchair, Rashid walked slowly over to the bed and took up his former position. His hand was only a few short inches from the *Trib*.

He knew the Irishman presented very little danger even if he wanted to. Murphy was quite pathetic. Short, fat, and hardly in any condition to take on a man like Rashid in a small room. Before he could raise his bulk out of the chair, the Arab would be across the room and have his throat slit very neatly and quietly with the razor in his jacket pocket. But as he looked over at Murphy in his clashing and badly wrinkled shirt and slacks, his ill-fitting raincoat, and dull, scuffed loafers, Rashid knew he was not the kind of man who would try anything. Nor was he the kind that someone else would rely upon for a hit. But caution becomes a habit.

"Well, I suppose the boys back home are doing fine. We do what we can, you know," Murphy replied with a broad smile.

Rashid watched as the Irishman pulled out his gray handkerchief and mopped his brow. "Looks like this late summer weather has got to you. There's a bottle on the desk and some ice next to it. You look like you could use a drink." Rashid said as he watched the fat man sweat.

"Oh my, yes, you're a dear fellow," Murphy said as he hurried over to the dresser. "And a fine bottle of Irish whiskey, too! No ice will

90

spoil this fine stuff, no, sir." He poured out several fingers and turned, smiling. "Won't you join me now?"

"No, no, enjoy yourself. I've gone back to observing a few tenets of my faith. I hope you'll understand."

"Well, then, you force me to drink for both of us, I guess." Murphy grinned as he belted his own drink down and poured another. "Ah, the 'milk of poets' is a good cure for the weather. I suppose it doesn't bother you all that much coming from the tropics, but I'll never get used to it."

"Did your people get that large consignment of furniture we sent them from Belgium?" Rashid reminded him just to set the right mood.

"Oh, indeed. I got word that it all arrived with no problem. But you know, the couches and chairs were so lumpy that they had to take them apart to see what was making them so uncomfortable. And would you believe," Murphy chuckled with a wink of the eye, "someone left a bunch of automatic weapons inside. Terrible quality control these days. We decided to keep them so they wouldn't fall into the wrong hands. Some very nice Swedish stuff, I'm told. With all of the fine training we've received from our other friends in Libya, we'll be putting them to very good use. Indeed. And you have our thanks."

"No thanks is necessary. You know how we fellow nationalists must work together if any of us are to succeed in throwing off our yokes of fascist oppression. A victory for one will lead to victory for all."

"You're so right. It gives us great strength. Now, what can we do for you, Mr. Teraki?"

"For once, Mr. Murphy, we are in need of your help in a matter that is very important to us."

"Just tell me what it is you'll be needing. We'll jump right to it. Yes, sir, you can be sure of that," he gushed.

"I knew we could count on your help," Rashid said with a firm smile. "There is a piece of equipment we must have for a very special job. Nothing else will do. Since you have experience in obtaining unique items such as this, we thought you might be able to get it for us." Rashid was very calm and relaxed, but his eyes never left the Irishman.

"After all that you've . . ."

As the Irishman began to speak, Rashid reached into the briefcase and pulled out a well-read U.S. Army Field Manual. It fell open to the usual page as he handed it across the bed to Murphy. "We want one of those," he said quietly.

"Holy Jesus," Murphy exploded as he took a quick glance at the picture. He looked across at the Arab in shock, then his eyes dropped back to stare at the page. "You don't want much, do you! Where are we to get one of these now?"

"Murphy," the Arab said as if talking to a very stupid child, "We wouldn't ask you to do something that was not possible. Actually, it's easier than you think. There are a number of these right here in the Chicago area. The Eighty-fifth Army Reserve Division has several. And some of the National Guard units have them. They're just gathering dust in an armory. It isn't the type of thing they watch too closely, because who'd ever steal one? They are a little hard to get out under your coat."

"Yes, but getting one of these—"

"You have never had much trouble before in taking things from armories, have you?" he asked with hard, cold eyes.

"But, Mr. Teraki, they've learned a few things about that and tightened up their security. You can only pull things like that off so often. This would be very risky." The Irishman was obviously petrified.

"We realize that, Mr. Murphy. We would not be so rude as to impose upon you simply out of past friendship or the favors we've done for you. No, we want it to be a business deal. You will have costs and risks for which you should be generously compensated. We recognize this. We are prepared to pay you fifty thousand dollars for the item. Twenty-five thousand dollars now and the other twenty-five thousand dollars on delivery. That should be enough to cover your front end expenses, or even allow you to bribe someone to get it. That is preferable to a risky break-in. Most supply sergeants can always use a little extra cash," he said, with a thin smile.

"Well . . . at least that's a point in its favor. And you're right, buying is always the best. There's never an end of those who've fallen afoul of bad whiskey and slow horses, as we say."

"See how far we've come. Now, there are two other related points that also must be attended to. In addition to the weapon itself, we need to have the base plate you see in the picture. Without it the weapon really can't be fired accurately. And we must have accuracy," he said pointedly. Also, we must have ammunition to go with it. I'd say twenty rounds would be the minimum."

"Lord," Murphy said in despair, "that makes it all the harder."

"Murphy!" Rashid snapped quickly with an undercurrent of anger. "Again, we realize you may have problems, and we'll pay you to take care of them. We'll give you an additional twenty-five thousand dollars for the base plate and twenty-five thousand dollars for the ammunition. That will be on delivery, of course. But it is a package deal. All three items, or none. That's one hundred thousand dollars for them. In cash. Your people can do a lot of good things with that kind of money." Rashid added as he leaned forward, "I hope it also shows you how serious we are."

The Irishman mopped his brow again and drained his glass, but he kept looking down at the picture in the book.

"Murphy, I know that your people don't pay you much for all the risks you take, and I know all that money I'm going to give you will go on to Belfast. That's probably not as fair as it should be," Rashid said with a knowing smile. "We want you to really do your best for us, and we know you have expenses of your own. So I'd like to change the deal a little and just say that we'll pay you seventy-five thousand dollars for the weapon and when you deliver it all, there will be an extra twenty-five thousand dollars in the bag that no one else will ever know about. Does that sound reasonable?"

"Well, that kind of extra incentive has often worked wonders to help a fellow's outlook on his job. . . . And you say it will just be between the two of us?" he mused cautiously.

"My word as a fellow soldier! We both know that your people will be happy as can be when you tell them that I offered fifty thousand dollars and you argued me up to seventy-five thousand dollars." Rashid knew he had him hooked.

"Mr. Teraki, we'll give it the best we can. How long do we have?"

"I can give you three weeks, no longer. Today's the fourteenth. That means until October eighth, but that's the latest! I'll plan on being here on the ninth."

"If we can do it at all, I guess that's enough time." He frowned.

"I know you won't fail me," Rashid said with a dark undercurrent that made the Irishman begin to sweat again. "When you have all of the items, I want you to send a telegram to the address on this paper. Just say, 'Order ready for pickup. Shaun.' I'll fly in and phone you when to arrange a delivery. It might be the ninth or sooner if we are both ready.

Rent a small U-Haul van and put all of the merchandise in the back. Roll it all up in an old carpet or something that will hide it well. Have the van all gassed up and ready to go. We'll make the exchange here at the hotel."

"Then we can both be on our way." Murphy beamed.

"Correct. Here's an envelope with the twenty-five thousand dollars we discussed. It should get you off to a good start," he said, as he passed it over. "Be assured we'll put the weapon to good use. In fact, the results will even have some direct benefits for your cause. You'll understand when it all happens. We'll be sure to point out the great role you played to your people."

"That's most kind. Maybe they'll let me out of this hell hole!"

"I'm glad you'll be able to help us out." Particularly since you'd have never left this room alive if you hadn't, Rashid thought as he smiled pleasantly. "One last thing, though. In the event you have any problems at all with this mission, I expect you to keep our security intact, regardless of the price. If things get botched, send a telegram that reads 'Order canceled per your instruction. Shaun.' You can keep the twenty-five thousand dollars for your troubles."

"Thank you. You are a fine gentleman—"

"However," the Arab said as he pinned Murphy under a harsh, cold stare. "If I come back here and there is trouble that I didn't know about, like if I walk into a trap, or if I run into problems on my way home, your people in Belfast will be notified." His black eyes bore into the Irishman. "I hear they usually deal with things such as that by shooting large-caliber bullets into the kneecaps. I assure you that it is preferable to what my people will do. Is that very clear!"

"I . . . I assure you . . . there will be no such problems at my end, Mr. Teraki!" Murphy said as he mopped his brow again.

"Good. Until next month then." Rashid smiled.

Arazi picked him up late that night at National Capitol Airport. He finally began to relax and unwind from his former state of wary alert. After years of training and operations, going into these various degrees of readiness was now a matter of habit whenever any threat of danger was possible. It had saved his life more than once.

They drove on in silence as he looked out the window. From the broad George Washington Parkway, they could see the lights of the

Lincoln, Jefferson, and Washington monuments. They were a radiant white under the bright floodlights, like tombstones in a cemetery.

"How did it go?" Arazi finally had to ask.

"About as I expected. We'll just have to wait and see. I don't trust Murphy, but he's too afraid to cross us, or to fail. A hundred thousand dollars buys a lot of loyalty!"

"I don't understand the IRA. They are such fools," Arazi said, shaking his head. "All they can do is blow up their own people and their own cities. And British security is such a joke. The Israelis would finish off the IRA in a couple of weeks."

"They are a remarkably stupid people, both of them." Rashid agreed. "The British conquered the Irish eight hundred years ago. You'd think somebody would have done something decisive in all that time. About every hundred years or so the Irish rise up in revolt and get crushed," Rashid mused with a sarcastic expression. "If you remember all of the battles they talk about like Wexford, Boyne, Aughrim, Tipperary, the Easter Rebellion—they were all defeats! But the Irish don't care, they just hold parades and get drunk. And the IRA!" He laughed. "Do you know they were organized over a hundred and fifty years ago! That's taking the long-term view!"

"It's ironic," Arazi replied sadly. "We're the best equipped, trained, organized, and dedicated liberation movement in the world. And we have the bad luck to be up against the most ruthless police state in the world."

"We bring out the best in the other side. Or the worst."

"Yes, but they do the same for us. In the end it will make the victory sweeter," Arazi said as they drove on over the bridge.

"Were you able to get the camper and the other equipment?"

"Yes, I think you'll like it. It's a new Dodge truck with one of the big camper bodies on the back. The biggest I could get around here. It was easy. The dealer couldn't have been more helpful, or stupid. I paid cash and used the phony driver's license to get the title. I have it parked out at Dulles in the long-term lot. We can leave it there until we need it. We'll get the permanent plates in a couple of days. We should put them on and then steal some new ones when we are ready to move."

"Excellent. Didn't I tell you how trusting the Americans were? Why shouldn't they be?" Rashid asked. "Did the maps arrive yet?"

"This morning. I had a good chance to look them over and I still can't believe what you can mail off for over here. Amazing! They are the best maps I've ever worked with. Beautiful. Such detail—contour lines, all buildings, roads, woods, marsh, precise elevations, everything. And all up to date. Just a couple of years old. They even show everything inside the military bases. Even the top secret ones like the Naval Weapons Station and Camp Perry. And anyone can buy them! Just send two dollars to the U.S. Geological Survey. I can't believe it. I'm sure the Russians must have a complete set.''

"Oh, the Americans probably send them all the update sheets as soon as they come off the presses! They wouldn't want anyone to have a bad set, now would they?''

"Such fools,'' Arazi laughed. "How they've managed to survive for two hundred years, I'll never know.''

"Big oceans and small neighbors. But we owe it all to them—the weapon, the camper, the maps, and even the plan, as I show you when we take our little trip down to the 'Historic Triangle.' ''

8

Friday, September 18

They drove south on I–95 shortly after noon on the beginning of a beautiful early autumn weekend. Once they got beyond the suburbs of Washington, the lush rolling hills and woodlands of eastern Virginia stretched away mile after mile, seemingly untouched by man. It was a very pleasant drive, particularly for people accustomed to the arid mountains and plains of the Mideast.

I–95 runs down the fall line, the geologic break where the upland plateau of eastern Virginia drops off to the coastal peninsulas and broad river basins of the Tidewater. More water than land, the Tidewater is dominated by Chesapeake Bay and its tributaries. The four great rivers of Virginia are born far away in the narrow ravines and creeks of the Appalachian Mountains and the Blue Ridge. Cascading down through the foothills, they broaden out and slow down after they cross the fall line—the Potomac on the north, the Rappahannock, the York, and the James. Between·them are the three peninsulas that extend to the southeast and dip their feet into the bay. From the ocean, the rivers are navigable all the way up to the fall line where they narrow. At these points grew the great cities of the region: Richmond, Fredericksburg, and Washington. On the far side of the broad Chesapeake Bay runs the thin strand of the eastern shore. At its southern end the bay flows out into the ocean creating Hampton Roads, one of the finest natural harbors in the world. Around its mouth are the large port cities of Norfolk, Portsmouth, Virginia Beach, Newport News, and Hampton.

Tidewater is as beautiful as it is historic. Its fertile riverbanks gave rise to a gentle planter economy, prosperous plantations with large manor houses that rivaled the best they'd left behind in England, and the leadership of a young and active colony and nation. Jamestown was where the first permanent colony took root and the experiment began. Williamsburg was where it matured economically, socially, and politically. Yorktown was where it reached adulthood.

About two hours south of Washington, Rashid turned east on I–64 at Richmond. Another hour brought them to Williamsburg, which lay on the spine of high ground between the James and York Rivers. Like all good tourists, plus to familiarize Arazi with the local terrain, they stopped at the Colonial Williamsburg Information Center, where they studied several of the large wall maps on display and saw the movie *Story of a Patriot*.

Its message was timeless, Rashid thought. The frustration, indecision, and slowly building anger of a people under the heel of tyranny who found themselves forced to take up arms in defense of their own freedoms could have been about colonial America or a dozen other places.

Just before dusk they drove out of town to the south and spent the night in a large campground overlooking the James River.

"After all," Rashid laughed, "it is still a camper and we might as well take advantage of it while we can."

Early the next morning they stood atop the observation deck of the National Park Service Visitor's Center at Yorktown. The panorama of the woods and fields of the battlefield spread out before them.

"Once again, we have to thank the Americans for placing this overlook here. It makes it very easy to show you the lessons to be learned. They show us precisely how we'll carry out our plan." Looking over at the younger officer, he asked, "Do you know much about the Battle of Yorktown?"

"Uh, it was in their Revolutionary War, wasn't it? I think it was the last battle."

"You already know more than most Americans," he smiled, looking out into the bright sunlight. "So it is very symbolic. It was the last battle; the one where they won their independence. As it will be for us, too! But it really wasn't much of a battle. No big charges or gallant fights on the parapets. It was little more than a short siege. The most important things happened before and after. And the only reason it was the last battle was because the British finally decided the whole thing just wasn't worth it. So they began peace talks."

"Tactically, the battle was a bore. Sixteenth-century maneuvers in the eighteenth century. This Visitor's Center here," he said, stamping his foot down on the wooden planks, "is right in the middle of Cornwallis's lines. He was the British commander. He made his stand here with his back to the river. From the high bluffs behind us, everything goes out in a series of concentric rings. He built a strong inner defense line of deep trenches and high earthworks that enclosed this field and the small village of Yorktown off to our right. Here's where he and his seventy-five hundred men were."

"It looks like a very strong position," Arazi commented as he looked around. "That's a lot of men for such a small place. I'd hate to have to assault up and over those high earthworks."

"Absolutely! An infantry assault would have been murder. Impossible. But the assault never came. It didn't have to. The Americans used their artillery to pound the British for a few days. Cornwallis made a very juicy target here. He was running out of supplies and ammunition. He couldn't see getting any more of his men killed in a hopeless situation, so he surrendered. Actually, of his seventy-five hundred men plus the sixteen thousand on the other side, there were less than two hundred fifty killed altogether. It was over before it really started."

"Not much of a battle," Arazi jeered.

"No, but you have to look at the strategy and the blunders that came before it. You know, back then, America only had about three million people. About the size of Washington today, or Israel. They didn't want independence, they were forced into it. Rather than deal with the issues, the British came to view it as a challenge to their authority. They wouldn't listen to the moderates. Positions hardened. The radicals took over."

"Sounds like an old story. Undercut the moderates and give fuel to the radicals," Arazi said as he turned his head toward Rashid. "But that's why we are where we are, right?"

"Exactly. They took it as national honor versus an illegal insurrection. That way you don't have to consider whether the grievances are valid. It's the arrogance that comes with old power." He shook his head. "It's ironic that the Americans, of all people, don't understand wars of liberation. They were the first. The model! But their battle here will also be our model. And, you know, the more I think about it, the clearer I see the parallels to the Mideast today."

"Like what?" Arazi asked in surprise.

"Well, their war had gone on for a long time. It was a stalemate. The British had a crack regular army and the best navy in the world. Just like the Israeli army and navy today," he said swinging his eyes around to look at Arazi. "The British could move up and down the coast to strike anywhere they wanted to. But the Americans would fall back and only fight on their own terms, like when they could cut the British off or surround them. It didn't matter how many battles the Americans lost, all they had to do was keep a force in the field and not quit. Finally the British gave up chasing them around and decided to just hold onto the coastal cities in the north. They relied heavily upon their navy to supply and reinforce them from abroad, just like the Israelis today. The Americans didn't have the strength to drive the British out of the fortified cities, so the war dragged on.

"Now in the south, it was a little different. Cornwallis was able to draw the Americans out into battles, and won. He conquered the Carolinas and Georgia and conquered Virginia in 1781. The British command had major bases in New York and Charleston. They told Cornwallis to find another one near the Chesapeake Bay in the middle. They figured this would help them cut the colonies in half and let them begin to bite off more states in 1782.

"So he came here to Yorktown. It was ideal. Seven miles upriver from the ocean, yet the water was so deep right offshore that his ships could moor to the trees. He could easily be reinforced or supplied from the sea. Or, if necessary, he could escape. On the other side of the river, Gloucester Point juts out to cut the channel in half. Put cannon here and over there, and you control the river."

Rashid swept his hand around in a large arc. "Look at what he had to work with on the land side. And he had four months to build his fortifications. That's the line of trenches you see in front of us. Where they met the shoreline on each side of us, he added a few small forts to make it even stronger." He grinned as he looked out at the front like an art critic admiring a master work. "But what was even more incredibly beautiful is that there are very deep creeks and marshy ravines that come in from the shore above and below here. They come inland and arc around this position like two big arms about a thousand yards to our front. In the middle there is a gap about a quarter mile across between them. But Cornwallis built five or six more forts across the gap, and that's the only way you could get here with any strength." He shook his head in wonder. "Superb. It was a superb place to defend."

Arazi looked out across the fields and nodded in agreement. "It's like a child's play set. Almost classic. Impregnable . . . . How could he lose?"

"Three big reasons—the same reasons we'll win here next month, just like Washington did! First, Washington put everything he had on the line here so he could achieve local superiority and trap Cornwallis. He marched all of his men down here with the French from New York and Rhode Island. They left in August for the long five-hundred-mile march. And the British did nothing to stop him. They all gathered at Williamsburg on September twenty-eighth. He went for a knockout punch, just like we will, with local superiority. In his case it was manpower, in ours it'll be firepower.

"The second reason was the river, Cornwallis's strongest ally, became his worst enemy when a French fleet arrived and chased away the British fleet on September fifth. Suddenly, he was trapped. No relief. No supplies. Once the American and French armies arrived, he was in deep trouble. His fate was sealed, because of the river!

"The third reason was bad intelligence and worse assumptions about the capabilities of his enemy. Here was Cornwallis's worst mistake and our key to carrying out our mission." His eyes darted over to Arazi. His excitement caused his voice to rise in strength and pitch.

"Cornwallis had been told Washington could never bring his heavy guns with him on such an arduous forced march in such a short time. After all, the British could never have done that. Plus, he expected to be relieved very soon when a new British fleet arrived to reopen the bay. He was a little short of men and figured why get them killed. He decided the best course was to abandon the outer force and pull all his men into his inner works where he could make the most of them defending against an infantry attack. They'd be invincible and could thumb their noses over the barricades at the Americans.

"It's just like the Secret Service. They rely on intelligence and close-in protection. Guard against a pistol or a knife. Watch all of the line-of-sight angles for a rifle. Three hundred yards or so. But mostly the tight inner wall."

Arazi nodded and chuckled in agreement.

"But that's the trap! Washington astounded Cornwallis when he showed up with all of his heavy cannon. Plus he borrowed some more from the French fleet. So he marched his army in through the wide-open gap, spread all around the British lines in front of us, and set up. He had fifty-two pieces of artillery with him, more than Cornwallis had. So the Americans moved to just outside rifle range and pounded him to pieces. They made a very compact target here inside these lines. Cornwallis's help never came until the battle was long over.

"And do you know what happened to the British? They were shocked and humiliated. The antiwar faction had been right. It just wasn't worth it. They had all the power, but the crazy Americans just wouldn't quit! It was the last straw. Just like it will be for us!" he shouted as he reached over to grab Arazi's shoulder.

"When the British troops marched out of Yorktown to surrender on October nineteenth," he continued softly, "their band played an old children's song, 'The World Turned Upside Down.' It'll be upside down this year, too!"

Rashid fumbled in his shirt pocket and pulled out a torn piece of paper. "There's a quotation here that I took out of a book I read about the battle. It's from a letter Washington wrote back in New York before he decided to march down here. It says, 'We are at the end of our tether, and . . .now or never our deliverance must come.' And it soon did for him, as it soon will for us. It is our time to risk it all for the big knockout punch just like he did."

They walked on across the high earthen battlements as Arazi asked, "What got you tipped off to Yorktown?"

"Well," Rashid shrugged, "there was a story in the *Post* early last spring about the preparations for the two-hundred-year anniversary that would be held here this October. I didn't give it much thought at the time, but it came back to me this summer as I decided on an act of revenge. Very few things are ever put that far ahead on a President's schedule. With all the open area here and the crowds and confusion, it just became a natural for me. We know he'll be right here on a platform in front of these battlements at a very specific time. It's a rare opportunity. He'll be pinned here. That's why it's perfect." Rashid paused to look out across the open field as he said, "It's the hand of Allah at work again."

Arazi stood next to him and concentrated on what the scene would look like. "Are you sure he'll be here?"

"How could he not be?" Rashid replied in surprise. "They have a lot of problems around the world right now. 1976 was a big success, and they'll look forward to a little flag waving." Nodding his head slowly, he said, "Oh, yes, he'll be here all right! You know it was even a fairly big event back in 1881." He turned around to his right and pointed above the trees. "That's when that big white granite monument was built. That's the Yorktown Monument. They had a whole week of ceremonies here back then. At the end, on October nineteenth, all the governors, senators, congressmen, the Supreme Court, ambassadors, and a huge crowd were here."

Arazi swallowed hard and said, "Imagine the target this'll make!"

"Precisely, all of official Washington. That's why I'm not just going to take a shot at the White House. It's probably the only time all of these people will get together at one place for a long time. And do you know who the keynote speaker was on October nineteenth, 1881? It was Chester A. Arthur, the twenty-first President. Hardly any Americans even remember the name. He only served one uneventful term in office. But there is a very strong note of irony here," Rashid paused as he glanced sideways at Arazi. "You see, Arthur had only been President for thirty days when he arrived to speak that day. The March before he'd been sworn in as the Vice-President of Garfield. Poor Garfield was shot and killed by an assassin. He died on September nineteenth. I hadn't noticed, but that's one hundred years ago today." He beamed.

"Let us hope much of this history will repeat itself," Arazi said quietly as he returned the confident look.

"We'll have a few extra bonuses as well," Rashid said lightly. "It appears that the Queen of England will also be here. So we can pay them back for starting the whole mess in the Middle East with their Balfour Declaration in 1917. They'll be here to bind up old wounds."

"Just about the time we open up a bunch of new ones," Arazi countered.

"Yes, and it'll be very nice to get back at them. They opened up Palestine to Jewish migration. Permitted them to buy our open land that belonged to all the people. Promised both sides what they wanted. Then just walked away from the mess they created. Yes, very nice!"

They turned away from the battlefield and walked down the slope to the parking lot. Arazi finally found their camper in the crowd of vehicles and they pulled out into the driveway.

"We'll drive over to Gloucester Point. I have a few more things to show you," Rashid said with a secretive look in his eye. Leaving the National Park, he turned right onto Main Street and drove into Yorktown itself.

"Here you can get a very good look at the beautiful tall white Yorktown Monument straight ahead of us on the bluff," he said.

The road curved to the right and wandered in among the well-preserved eighteenth-century town. Rashid pointed out the Nelson House, the Swan Tavern, the Customs House, the Digges House and the other old brick and wood structures that had survived the battle.

He turned right on Read Street and drove down the steep hill that led to the river and the newer part of the business district. When they reached the beach, the road turned back sharply to the left and passed in front of a series of modern stores and restaurants. A quarter mile farther it passed under the Coleman Bridge. High above them, it carried Route 17 across to the Gloucester shore.

Rashid slowed down as they passed under the bridge. "Notice these tall concrete pilings . . .the long, narrow legs of the steel bridge come down to rest on top of the concrete. But it is a very tall bridge by the time it gets out to the middle of the channel."

Arazi stuck his head out the car window and craned his neck to look up at the superstructure. "I'd say a few well-placed charges could give it quite a jolt, wouldn't you?"

"And this is the only place where vehicles can cross the river for thirty miles. People over here would be cut off, just like Cornwallis was. We're not worried about them escaping, of course, but they would have a difficult time getting over for hot pursuit. Oh, there would be a few helicopters over here, and probably some police controlling traffic over there, but the people who really know what to do would be stuck here for a few precious minutes. And that's all it will take for us to get out of there and onto some back roads. A few minutes later, we switch to a car and we're gone.''

He drove on beyond the bridge and made the first right, which took them back uphill to Route 17. When a break came in the traffic he made another left turn and drove onto the bridge.

''This is unusually high above the water.'' Arazi commented as he looked down and then back toward Yorktown.

''While we are at the top here, look down at the Gloucester shore. At the foot of the bridge off to the right is the small Coast Guard station. Those bigger buildings toward the rear are a marine biology research center. In between is a parking lot. It connects with the one on the other side of the bridge near that boat basin.''

Once off the bridge, he took a road to the right and a second one that carried them back downhill toward the river. Far beneath the bridge he pulled off into a small gravel parking lot.

''Notice what you can see from here?''

''Not much. The bridge. The high bluff all along the far shore, and the trees on top of that. You can't see any of the Visitor's Center or the battlefield from here.'' He looked harder and suddenly his face lit up. ''Of course! We can't see them and so they'll think they're safe! All we can see is that beautiful white monument standing above the trees. It's an aiming stake!''

Rashid smiled. ''Again, complements of the U.S. Government. And if you plot this point and the monument on those lovely U.S. Geological Survey maps they sent us, you'll see that the field in front of the Visitor's Center is five degrees to the left and seventy-one hundred feet out from here. That's one-point-three-four miles. Just right.''

Arazi stared out across the river for several minutes. ''It's all tailored for us! So beautiful. So totally unexpected.'' His gaze gradually clouded over with a look of concern as he turned toward the other. ''But even still, to be really accurate at that distance it's important to have an observer at the other end who can adjust and correct our fire. Should I be over there?'' he asked.

''No, you'll be needed here. Besides, we'll have three observers over there. They'll give us enough to work with.''

Hafez frowned. "I don't understand."

"We'll have CBS, NBC, and ABC!" he roared. "What could be better?"

At 10:00 A.M. on Monday, Rashid drove into the side yard of Dante's Garage, in Columbia, Viginia. He'd chosen it carefully. Located in a run-down section of the small town, it didn't look too prosperous, but it was big enough to do the type of work he wanted. Getting slowly out of the car, he sidestepped several piles of rusting parts. Behind the old metal building he noticed the carcasses of dozens of chopped-up automobiles, a few trucks, and a smashed-in schoolbus. Across its ripped side ran the letters LIBERTY BAPTIST CHU.

Columbia wasn't the type of place where people asked a lot of questions about the type of work they were paid to do. It was downriver and downwind from Richmond; the "chemical capital of the South." It smelled like Gary and looked like Birmingham, but on a small, trashy scale. The jobs paid well, considering the other choices, and only longhairs or the nosey EPA seemed to pay much attention to the foul air and water. You minded your own business.

Rashid walked through the body shop's door and glanced around at the three or four cars being worked on amid the dirt, grease, and clutter. Fenders, doors, hoods, and welding equipment were lying against the two outer walls. He walked over to the small unpainted corner office and stuck his head inside.

"Mr. Dante? I'm Samir . . . I called you about some work I need to have done?"

The large grimy man in the blue coveralls frowned for a second and then broke into a broad smile. "Oh, sure! Ya'll come in. Have a seat. Just let me move a few of these catalogs here." He leaned over and threw several big stacks onto the table in the corner.

"Thank you. As I told you, I'm with Virginia Gas Pipeline. I was told you were the best in the area for some special work we need done."

"Well, we do try. But we're awfully busy right now. What's it you need?"

"We have a new Dodge camper we need to have modified. You see, we want it to hold our equipment so it can go out to the field with us, rather than bring the work back to the shop. We are getting behind schedule. And time is worth a lot of money in our business." He smiled earnestly.

"To all of us, Mr. Samir," Dante said as his eyes lit up, "all of us."

"You see, the camper gives us the type of mobility we need. But we can't have the suspension bounce when we are at work. It throws off our calibrations. We want a metal floor put in above the regular one, with hydraulic jacks that go at each corner. Here's some drawings that show what I mean," he said as he handed over the sheets. "You can see the jacks go down to the ground. If we extend them four inches further, it lifts the false floor up, so we have a solid, level platform to work on."

"That's right clever, you know," Dante said, truly impressed.

"The floor is three-quarter-inch steel plate," the Arab continued. "We want it reinforced with three-inch steel bars. The jacks retract up inside the body. And away we go." He looked over at Dante and asked, "Can it be done?"

"Can't see why not."

"We also want a five-foot-square sun roof put in. Hinged in the middle so it opens out to each side. Then about six inches of styrofoam insulation on all the walls and under the floor. The equipment can be noisy and we don't want to disturb anyone," he explained. "Cover over the whole inside with some plywood paneling so it looks nice. Now, you see these brackets here on the floor? That's where we mount our machinery, so they must be welded on very strong. Down each side we want some wooden cabinets built in and finished flat on top so we can use them as places to sleep. We'll stow some of our gear inside."

"That's a whole lot of work you got there," Dante smiled as he shook his head. "It ain't going to be cheap, you know."

"How much?" Rashid asked, as if it mattered.

"That's tough to say. Maybe three or four thousand dollars, and material, of course," he added as he looked up to get the Arab's reaction.

"No problem. I already have the jacks and the brackets. I assume you can get all the other material here locally." He looked directly at the other man and asked, "How long will it take?"

"Gosh, we got a lot a work already backed up here now. I'd say six, maybe eight weeks, at least."

"I'll be frank with you, Mr. Dante. We can't wait half that time. Today's the twenty-first of September. I'll double your high estimate. We'll pay you eight thousand dollars if you have the whole thing complete by the twelfth of October. Plus I'll give you a special bonus in cash of two thousand dollars if it meets all of my high expectations for quality. But it must be done by the twelfth. I'll knock off a thousand dollars from the eight thousand for every day you go over. Here's four thousand dollars as a deposit. Can you get it done?"

"You can count on it, Mr. Samir," Dante beamed. "Just leave the keys."

"Fine, I'll see you at noon on October twelfth."

As Rashid walked out the door to where Arazi waited in the rental car, he heard Dante's voice boom across the garage.

"Ralph . . .push that damn Ford of yours out the back door and get your ass in here, boy. We got us some real work to do!"

A week later, on the twenty-eighth, the first faint tinkle of a distant warning bell went off. But it was enough. Rashid knew they'd waited as long as they possibly could.

It was a very mildly worded cable, but Beirut wanted to know why he had withdrawn the thirty thousand dollars. Hadn't he already made all the payments to the IRA? Or was something wrong with the records? No time to waste now. They'd have to take out the rest. And that would really set off the bells.

He motioned to Arazi and they walked outside.

"The time's come. We must be taking off. You go get the car. I'll go back in and leave word we have to go to New York for a few days. Meet me outside the bank in an hour."

They looked at each other and smiled.

"I had hoped we'd have a little longer," Arazi replied.

"We'll just take a little vacation and wait to hear from Mr. Murphy. I figure we have a week to kill. Maybe two."

108

PART 3

WASHINGTON, D.C.
OCTOBER 7-13, 1981

9

Wednesday, October 7

October always comes as an immense relief to Washington. With the tourist season finally over, the residents have the place pretty much to themselves. That's something worth the wait. Worth savoring.

The first tantalizingly cool fall weather had arrived. Dogwood leaves were turning a crimson red—the first sign that another spectacular autumn was only a few weeks away. It is busy weather. Dry, clear, and sunny, but with the last tinges of Indian summer. It's a marvelous time to get outdoors where you can begin to smell and taste the leaves drying out.

October. The summer reruns were over. School had been in session long enough for thousands of mothers to return to sanity. And, most important, the Redskins were back on the field.

"Mr. Halperin, you have a call on your private line. It's for Capitol Cleaners again, about the green drapes," his secretary's puzzled voice came over the intercom. "You sure you want to take it?"

"No problem, Julie, it's good PR. Let me handle them."

Halperin picked up the phone and asked in a pleasant voice, "Hi, can I help you?"

"I'm not sure. I just dropped off a set of green drapes. I forgot to ask, can I pick them up tomorrow, around two forty-five?" The mildly accented voice inquired.

"I'm really sorry," Halperin said apologetically. "You have the wrong number. You must be calling Capitol Cleaners, right?"

"Why yes . . . This isn't it?" The voice asked tentatively.

"No," he smiled. "This is the Israeli Embassy. No problem, it happens all the time. We're four-three-six-five, they're four-three-six-six."

"Please excuse me," came the embarrassed voice. "I'll dial again."

Halperin slowly replaced the receiver and leaned back in his chair.

"I wonder what the Egyptians want this time," he said softly, with a quizzical look on his face. Well, this was just the excuse he'd been looking for to get out of the office, anyway. The daily intelligence summary could wait.

It was a nice little system he and Mouse had set up several years before. They used it infrequently, but it was a good way to arrange a quick meeting. God only knew how many bugs were on the phone, or whose, but this allowed them to go to a prearranged spot without attracting too much attention, he thought. Every security service has the same problem. Most of them figure out ways to work around it.

There really was a Capitol Cleaners. And they really did have a number only one digit away. And Halperin really did get calls for them by mistake. That was the beauty of the system. It was also what gave him the idea in the first place. But Capitol Cleaners doesn't do drapes.

His secretary always put these straight through, and he always said the same thing to the caller. It must drive his uninvited audience crazy, he thought. Sometimes he went out when it was a real wrong number and just walked around. Usually he stayed in the office, but there was no pattern.

The key was the drapes, and the last two digits of any number such as money, an address, or time. The number told him in how many minutes to be there. Simple yet effective. It was now ten thirty, he noticed. So add forty-five minutes and they'd meet at eleven fifteen.

Currently the prearranged meeting place was the French Impressionist hall of the National Gallery of Art. Needless to say, that was

112

Mouse's idea, not Halperin's. "Of all things, only great art endures," he invoked.

They took turns picking the place and changed it every few months, depending on how frequently they met. It had become a little game between the two of them. One-upmanship. Pick a place the other guy couldn't stand.

"You know, David," he'd said at some diplomatic reception Halperin couldn't remember. "We need a new spot once more. Since we are both supposed to be assistant cultural attachés, I think we should look for somewhere that will offer you something on a higher plane." Mouse rubbed his chin and pretended to concentrate very hard. "Yes . . . I believe I have just the right place." His eyes lit up in mirth as he told him. "But it is also a very practical choice. It's a snap to spot a tail there."

Halperin's choices leaned in a different direction. He'd picked the intramural fields at nearby Georgetown University. There was always some type of sport going on and people milling around. Or the tennis courts at Bannecker Recreation Center. The ninth tee on the Potomac Park Golf Course was one he'd been particularly proud of.

Mouse had sent them off to the east portico of the Kennedy Center, the Hirshon Museum, the Folger Shakespeare Library, or the National Gallery.

Halperin had schemed for months to try to figure a way to meet in the upper deck of RFK Stadium during a Redskins game, but the timing just wouldn't work out. "I'd like to see him top that," he thought.

Reaching over to the intercom, he said, "Julie, I'm going out for a couple of appointments. I won't be back till after lunch."

As he left the building he began the careful, painstaking process of shaking any possible tails. He drove quickly down Massachusetts Avenue and looped around Scott Circle before turning north on Sixteenth Street. Two blocks later he swung east on P Street, checking the rearview mirror with each change.

He turned south on Fourteenth Street and drove straight for about a half mile through the business area. He spotted a car pulling out of a parking space just ahead and swung into the vacant spot. It looked like the only one for blocks around. Dropping some coins in the parking meter, he dashed ahead to the front door of Garfinkel's Department store. Even if he was followed, he knew this would split the tail. The driver would have to frantically search for a space while his partner continued on foot.

Halperin marched smartly through the busy aisles, turning as quickly as possible to get out of sight from the front door he'd just come through. Moments later he wound his way to the F Street door on the far side and went back outside. He walked out through the traffic and turned the corner to head south onto Fifteenth, crossed Pennsylvania Avenue, and passed into Pershing Square. On the other side of the park, he walked into the north entrance of the Department of Customs Building.

From its dark shadows he looked back to take note of anyone heading in the same direction, particularly anyone in a hurry. But nothing seemed out of place. He turned around and walked quickly through the long first-floor hall to the south exit.

On the other side of Constitution Avenue he entered the Smithsonian Museum of History and Technology, looking back once more. Tacking east, he repeated the same steps at the Museum of Natural History. Finally, he reached the National Sculpture Garden, which lies between Natural History and the National Gallery. He took a seat on one of the side benches that faced the door he just came out of, and opened up the *Post*. This would tell the tale, he hoped.

After killing ten minutes, it was almost eleven fifteen. Well, if there was anyone still out there, they were masters, he thought. So he folded the paper under his arm and walked slowly over to the door.

"David, it is good to see you again."

"Hi, Mouse. What's up?" Halperin replied, looking around casually.

"Not to worry, we're alone. I checked your approach, and you're clean, too." He took a deep breath and continued. "Now that we're at peace, we get together too seldom, too seldom." He smiled warmly at the much larger and athletic-looking Israeli. "You know, you look like you're putting on weight. Fat middle-aged operatives don't wear well," he warned. "About five pounds, I'd say—a little in the gut and a little more rear echelon." He had a most sarcastic and expressive tisk-tisk.

"None of my Arab girl friends have complained."

"They have notoriously poor taste . . . but let's get on with our art tour, shall we. We have all these lovely Impressionist paintings to enjoy. It's not the Louvre," he shrugged sadly, "but one must make do."

"Mouse," Halperin said, shaking his head, "it's not the Louvre

114

because this isn't Paris. You aren't in Paris because the Foreign Minister's nephew probably got Paris. You probably spilled a martini in his wife's lap, and you ended up in Washington."

"It would have been white wine! But that would have been superior to that terrible American beer you drink," he stated imperiously.

"I guzzle or slurp. I admit it, I'm addicted. It is a carryover from my college days here. I'm hooked." Halperin beamed contentedly.

As they walked on slowly through the gallery, Halperin added with a furtive glance and soft whisper, "By the way, you'd better enjoy the art while you can. Our top agent in Cairo told me that you're on the list to be posted to either Burundi or Guyana next."

That one cracked him up. Halperin looked at the dirty stares they were starting to get from the guards as they walked on snickering.

He still couldn't figure out how or why they'd become such good friends over the years. They had no common interests whatsoever, except a good joke. Halperin was rough and fairly crude, while the much shorter and slender Egyptian was the epitome of a smooth, urbane continental. "Mouse" was a nickname he'd picked up in graduate school at the University of Chicago when a professor couldn't quite handle Mustapha. He didn't even try Amin Khalidi.

Mouse was from a prominent Cairo family. Halperin, on the other hand, was from a long line of Eastern European peasants, the remnants of which—those that had survived— settled in Israel in 1946.

While Mouse studied economics and political science at the knees of the great minds at Chicago, Halperin attended Nebraska to learn agricultural science on a government scholarship. His taste for Budweiser was an acquired one from football weekends rooting for the Big Red in Lincoln. He was thoroughly Americanized and had asked for this posting.

After college, Halperin returned to Israel in 1971 and went into the Air Force. He'd seen heavy action in the 1973 War on the Syrian front. Six days and three planes later it was all a blur. Too many tanks and too many SAM missiles. The burnt-out hulks of the Syrian tanks dotted the Golan, right up to the southeast rim. They'd almost broken through. It would have been open tank country from there on, but they never quite made it. All that was left was the world's biggest junkyard of countless Russian T–54 hulks. Flying over it at night, it looked like hundreds of campfires across the high plateau. But there weren't any Boy Scouts down there. In the first few days it took some incredible heroics by army units outnumbered ten and even twenty to one to merely slow the armor advance long enough for help to come before the Syrians made it to the rim. Reserves were thrown in nonstop as soon as they arrived. But they held. Later, it was the Israeli's turn. As the Syrians tried to flee, the whole Golan turned into a shooting gallery. But after all their losses, the revenge was only bittersweet.

"Let's sit here before all of these beautiful works," Mouse broke in. "Look at them . . . Monet, Degas, Lautrec, Gauguin, Seurat, and my personal favorite, Pissarro." He sighed deeply as his eyes moved down the wall. "Well, I suppose we are going to have to mix a little business in with my pleasure."

"I certainly hope so."

"There is this fellow we've been keeping an eye on fairly casually for some time now. A dear Arab brother who is employed at the Libyan Embassy here in town. He's been here for a year or two posing as an economic specialist. He goes under the name of Hassan, but of course that's only a cover."

"Someone at the Libyan Embassy under cover?" Halperin replied in a mocking tone of surprise.

"Yes, that does come as a rude shock to all of us," he continued acidly. "But there are too many probable suspects around the world to keep a close watch on most of them. Unfortunately, some just slip through the cracks. Like this one. We've just found out his real name is Rashid, Haleem Rashid. He's a Palestinian, not Libyan. Actually a high-ranking operative, a colonel," he said with a tone of concern.

Halperin nodded wearily. "We've been aware they had several men here, and have done a little routine surveillance, but we had to be careful. The Americans are more sensitive about that stuff these days. We never turned up anything that would give it a high priority. They keep in touch with some of the radical groups here and with some naive congressmen, but nothing of any direct threat to us." Scanning his eyes to both doorways, he assured the Egyptian, "Of course we turn over what we get to the FBI or to you people if it looks interesting."

The Egyptian's face twisted in a look of slight pain. "It's always been a waste of time to turn it over to the FBI. We do it, too," he admitted, "but they just klutz it up, as you would say."

Halperin slowly turned his head to look over his shoulder with a completely blank stare, "I don't care how good your Yiddish is, my sister's still not available."

"... To her eternal regret, I would point out. Now, seriously, the rest of this conversation must remain in strictest confidence between our two governments, and so on and so forth. In other words, you can pass onto your chief that it's an official contact, not just our usual social amenities."

"Okay, I'll wake up and start to pay attention, and you can report back that we'll as usual treat this as an official confidence, et cetera."

"We may have a real problem here," Mouse went on as he too checked to be sure they were still not being observed. "It seems our Colonel Rashid disappeared. Probably a week ago."

"Vacation?" Halperin vounteered lightly.

"No. This came from a source of ours in Tripoli. Apparently the wires have been burning up between here and there, and Beirut. They don't know where he is. Neither the Libyans nor the PLO. They are really in quite a snit," he emphasized. "He hasn't been recalled or reassigned, of that we're positive. And our people are fairly sure that the other side doesn't know where he is. He seems to have just vanished."

Halperin sat silent for a moment. His eyes narrowed as he turned and said. "I think I'd rather know where he is. But he could be off somewhere on a special assignment, or just out in the field, couldn't he?"

"No, I haven't gotten to the most curious part. It seems that there is a substantial sum of money missing from some of their bank accounts here. Several hundred thousand dollars. That's what set off all the alarms in Tripoli."

"I suppose it's too much to hope that the good life here got the better of him and he just cashed in the chips and ran?" Halperin asked hopefully.

"We doubt it, for two reasons. First," he ticked off on his finger, "we're talking about one of their senior officers, not some codes clerk. He's a skilled and dedicated commando. A fanatic. But not a defector. Besides, where would he go? He really doesn't have any critical intelligence data that would be of use to anyone except you or us, so no one else would have any reason to take him in off the street. And his friends will be after him soon enough. So where could he hide?"

"That's a point."

"Second, it seems that his aide is also missing. Two highly skilled commando officers . . ." he raised one eyebrow in scorn, "not likely."

"Have you begun running the usual checks—customs, passports, other cities, airports, all that?"

"Some, but it's going to take a long time. We can assume they would use phony passports, and they could have gone from and to an infinite combination of places. Just checking all the international airports here is hard enough, much less Mexico and Canada, but we're looking. We've also asked our contacts with the PLO and Libya to let us know what they find out. After all, they have as much reason as we do to track him down. What they do can tell us a lot. But they've been at it for three or four days and haven't come up with any more than we."

"Okay, we'll start with our sources. Each of us can go a lot of places where the other can't. Maybe we'll kick over a rock and get lucky."

"We feel it is worth the effort. Just in the last few days we've found out quite a bit about him that has us very alarmed. That's why I was told to call on you. He isn't well known, but he was one of their leading tacticians and strategists. Back-room stuff, out of sight in recent years. Before that he was active in the field, but it's the last few years that are the most disturbing. Apparently he had a hand in the assassination of our diplomat in Cyprus as well as many commando raids against your country. I suspect we've only scratched the surface."

"When you locate him, I know some people who'd like to meet with him," Halperin said with a quiet determination.

"I'm afraid you'll have to wait your turn," Mouse snapped, "and it may be a long wait." He composed himself as he looked over at the Israeli. "I must ask you a most important question. You may assume it comes from the highest levels of my government. I can appreciate it if you are unable to answer right now, and we don't want an answer if you are unsure whether or not it is entirely correct, but when you give an answer it must be correct, because it is important. We also need to know the answer fairly soon."

"Okay, I'll try, what is it?"

"We know Rashid is dangerous. We know he has done substantial harm to your people. Let us assume for a moment that he has in fact disappeared, voluntarily or involuntarily. If the latter, we could well understand and be in sympathy with your government if they learned of

118

his record, tracked him down, and decided to terminate him with 'extreme prejudice,' as they say. Let me quickly add that we would consider this to be none of our affair if that were the case. We would shed few tears for our dearly departed Muslim brother. But—"

"If he disappeared voluntarily . . ." Halperin nodded ominously.

"Precisely. So, you understand, it's vital to all our interests for us to attempt to eliminate all of the other possibilities as quickly as possible. Let us hope that we discover someone else took him out of the picture. It is unlikely that we'll be able to prove he's gone voluntarily, except by a very slow process of elimination. And that bothers us."

"Is it possible the Americans could have him, or have taken him out?" Halperin asked in a thoroughly puzzled voice. "No, I guess that's a stupid question."

"That thought crossed our minds for a few seconds too, but we don't see how they would even be aware of him. And if they were, what reason would they have to move against him? Even they must know they'd botch it! They'd never risk infuriating the Libyans, no matter how thin Rashid's credentials are. No, the Libyan natural gas and crude oil is far too important to them, even if we or you had asked them to do it," he said with a quiet logic.

"So, what you're saying," Halperin concluded, "is that leaves you or us . . . and you think it wasn't you."

"And, I assume if it was your people, David, you would be aware of it since it would have been within your area of operations."

"I should, but I'm not. But I'll check with Jerusalem and see if there's something they haven't been telling me."

"One other thing. You are a lot closer to the Americans than we are. Just to make sure, why don't you check with them—very carefully, of course. It makes no sense to get them involved if they're not in it already. Who knows," Mouse smiled. "Maybe he went down the wrong street in Harlem and he's in the intensive care ward at Bellevue? Who knows?"

"I have a good contact at the FBI. I'll see what he might know. They could surprise us, but I doubt it."

"Good. That will allow us to check off one more out. But for a moment, let's consider some of the other alternatives. What if he and his aide have disappeared voluntarily. Two skilled terrorist officers, perhaps still here in the U.S., or, in any event, dangerous wherever they are.

They have enough money to do quite a bit. What if they are on some very secret mission, or what if they have some grudge of their own. Maybe they're cooking up something with the IRA or some of the other terrorists around here. What if they've gone to ground?'' Mouse went on ever more alarmingly as his eyes grew more and more dark and harsh.

''You think they might have gone in business for themselves?''

''Who knows, it's possible. But that or some top secret mission are the best of the lot if you want my opinion.''

''Good Lord,'' Halperin moaned as he leaned back and stared at the ceiling. ''One of our greatest fears over the years has been that they might move the scene of action over here, but it is against all their policy. They keep hands off as long as there is any hope they can turn the United States around.''

''But that's a very slender thread. Some day it will snap! And remember, we have no evidence whatsoever that he has left the U.S. That doesn't mean a whole lot, but it's possible.''

''And what a possibility.'' Halperin said sickeningly. ''This place is so wide open. They'd have a field day. Another thought just struck me. If they were on some secret assignment, it would be no surprise that very few people would know what they were up to, but just enough would to keep those alarm bells you mentioned from going off. They'd never have allowed any attention to be drawn to these guys if it was that secret.''

''You are beginning to see that there are not too many good choices left that make any sense. The odds are that they are either dead or up to something we aren't going to like. We have to narrow the range of alternates very quickly.''

''It'll take me a little time to check this out. Let's meet again, tomorrow. Say . . . three fifteen. But let's change the place. It's my turn, so how about the south door of the Air and Space Museum? It's got good visibility.''

''David, you're hopeless! How can you opt for all that crass junk and glitter over the serenity of the masters? Tomorrow, then.''

Returning to his office, Halperin went directly to the communications room and began to pencil out a message.

REQUEST ALL AVAILABLE DATE ON RASHID, HALEEM, COLONEL, PLO: AKA HASSAN. CURRENTLY ASSIGNED TO LIBYAN EMBASSY

HERE. BELIEVED MISSING. BELIEVE PLO/LIBYAN SEARCH NOW
IN PROGRESS TO LOCATE RASHID. SOURCE: EGYPTIAN INTELLIGENCE
HERE. CONCERNED AND COOPERATING. WANT JOINT
EFFORT. WANT TO AFFIRM THAT WE WERE NOT INVOLVED WITH
RASHID'S DISAPPEARANCE. WERE WE? IF NOT, CONSIDER A
CONDITION AMBER, REPEAT, AMBER. EGYPTIANS ADVISE MONEY
AND AIDE ALSO MISSING. AM CHECKING LOCAL SOURCES. NEED
DATA BY NOON TOMORROW. H.

"Dani, send this off priority to Mossad HQ in Jerusalem. Eyes only for General Gershon. Let me know as soon as there is any reply."

It was nine fifteen that evening before Halperin was finally able to call an old friend at the FBI.

"Hello, Daniels speaking," the reply came after the tenth ring.

"Frank, old buddy, this is David," he said, trying his warmest voice.

"Oh, shit . . . I finally sit down to relax and watch the damn baseball playoffs, and you have to pop up and ruin my evening."

"I need a favor."

"You've really got nerve," Daniels exploded angrily. "Do you have any idea how much hell I caught about the last little favor I did for you?"

"Haven't I always tried to even up the score? Don't I always give you anything I think might be of use to you? Come on now, let's be fair," Halperin said soothingly, "besides, we denied that we ever got anything from you guys, didn't we? This time I really don't need anything. Actually, I want to pass some stuff on to you."

"That's bullshit! You guys never give us a damn thing unless you got a whole bunch you want in return."

"Now, now, let's not be testy," he responded quietly, hoping Daniels' well-deserved irritation had run its course. "I really do have something to pass on. We have recently picked up on a very high-level PLO operative—one with a very nasty record—who has apparantly set up house over here. His name is Rashid, aka Hassan. He's now with the Libyan Embassy here in D.C."

"I think I've heard the name Hassan. But so what, half the Arabs at any of the embassies have records of action against your people. We aren't taking in laundry, David. If they aren't doing anything against Uncle Sam, then they're no business of ours. And you guys keep your damn hands off, or it's your ass we'll be after."

"Frank, cut the crap. I'm not talking about parking tickets. This guy is a full colonel, PLO, and one of his main assignments over here is to work with your radical groups and the IRA. Arms, money, and terrorist planning. Do you want me to rattle off the number of your laws that violates? This is a bad dude!"

Daniels was silent for a few moments and Halperin just let him hang there.

"Okay, okay David, what else have you got? I'll look into it."

"That's the problem. He's missing, or at least we haven't been able to find him for the past few days. We assume he's off on an assignment. That's what would bother us and you the most; but maybe he's had an accident, maybe he's in a hospital somewhere, or maybe he got in real trouble and is a John Doe in some morgue?"

"We'll put out the trace on him. Thanks a lot," Daniels concluded.

"Whoa. Easy now. I said I need a favor, remember?"

"There was silence at the other end of the line. Finally, Daniels said, "What?"

"Well, we are a little concerned about this guy, too, you know. If he isn't up to mischief here, then he may be after us somewhere else. We need to know which."

"Okay . . . So?"'Daniels said nonchalantly.

"So, I need to know what you come up with. I'm sure you'll need to check with the CIA, and we'd like to know what they find out, too. Maybe they have him?"

"You're pressing!" came the annoyed warning.

"You wouldn't even be calling them if I hadn't phoned," Halperin pointed out quietly. "Also, maybe your contacts with the IRA, or the FALN, or the blacks will know something. We only want to know so we can rule out that he's after us, okay? We aren't going to go after him. We could have done that a long time ago if we wanted to."

"If you try to go in business over here, I'll have your tail end on a plane to Tel Aviv so fast it'll give you nosebleed."

"All we want is to trade a little information."

"All right, but this must stay as a 'nameless source.' If you tag me with this, you'll be in a whole lot of trouble."

"No problem, you can go back to your ballgame."

"After you, Howard Cosell is a dream," Daniels snapped.

"Don't be anti-Semitic now," Halperin joked.

"The two of you don't make it easy."

10

Thursday, October 8

It was a nice place to catch a few rays.

Halperin sat on the cool cement apron of the south portico of the Air and Space Museum with his back leaning up against the pristine granite of the building face. It was three fifteen, but the sun was still high above the trees on the far side of the street.

While he was relaxed and enjoying the scene, he kept alert and continually checked the view up and down Independence Avenue and across to Sixth Street directly ahead of him. But that was the deal, the one who called the place was the first one there and kept watch as the other approached. If you were there first, you got a good vantage point where as many approaches as possible could be observed, he thought. If you were there second, you made sure your route allowed you to be seen a long way off. This makes it much easier to spot a tail.

But Halperin wasn't too concerned; the Egyptian was good.

It was a good place to meet, too. Good vistas and plenty of people moving around, yet not real close. Safe, but with privacy. All along the north side of the street were hot dog, soft drink, and ice cream wagons, which guaranteed a continuous swirl of people passing by on the sidewalk just below him.

Halperin got a clear view of Mouse while he was still two blocks away down Sixth. He watched closely as he approached and passed between the NASA Headquarters buildings on each side of the street.

Their eyes locked when Mouse waited to cross Independence. They were alone.

"Hi, Mouse," Halperin greeted him as he came up the wide stairs. "Have a seat. I bought you a hot dog."

The Egyptian's eyes closed as he looked down at the tightly rolled waxed paper. "How can you eat those things," he cringed in disgust and sat down next to the Israeli. "They are terrible—cold, dry, and God only knows what's really in them."

"You're not trying very hard to blend in, you know."

"Some standards just won't blend," he looked over with an aristocratic smile. "Were you able to find out anything about our friend?"

"Yes and no, as you might expect. First off, we were not involved in his disappearance. They assured me of that. You can relay it on as official. Also, I called a friend over at the FBI and he ran it through his NIC network. So far everything is negative, but it is going to take several days at least to get a complete report. There's a lot of bases to touch."

Mouse nodded as he listened. "Anything more direct—could they have gotten to him?"

"No. He said they didn't touch him. He checked with the CIA this morning, and they're clean, too."

"Do you think we can believe them?"

"Well, I believe the guy who told me, but that's not saying he got a straight story. I guess we have about as much as we're likely to get. We'll just have to keep after it. If he finds out anything, I think he'll let me know with some hint. But I don't want to set them off. They already have about as much curiosity as we can stand."

"I agree. It looks like we are still on square one. We know a few haystacks where the needle isn't."

"It isn't going to get much easier either." Turning to look at Mouse, Halperin added, "Oh—my people want to express their thanks for the tip. They really mean it."

"Thanks. It's our little way of reciprocating for the information about the plot to kill Sadat in Bonn. Let's hope we can continue to share when it has momentous consequences for the other side."

"I exchanged a few messages with Jerusalem," Halperin turned serious as he went on. "They are finally leaning in the same direction you are. Rashid's up to something. They want us to assume he's still in the United States until we can prove the negative. Other people are looking for him elsewhere and we have our whole network on alert. I sure do hope he turns up somewhere else!"

"This is one of those assignments that gives you a very sick feeling in the pit of your stomach as each minute passes." Mouse said, speaking each word slowly. His face was drawn and tired and tense. "Our contacts in Mexico, Canada, and Cuba have found nothing. We're also checking out all the Libyan embassies we can, but so far that has also turned up nothing. By tomorrow I expect to hear from our people in Moscow and some of the Eastern European countries. But since our PLO and Libyan sources are still upset, I really doubt that he's gone to any of those places. It wouldn't make any sense."

"It doesn't make any sense that he'd be here either, but that's becoming more and more possible as we eliminate the other choices."

"That's what makes me sick." Mouse said in frustration.

"Our people did come up with a few more bits of information and I reached a low-level contact we have inside the Libyan Embassy here. The word around the embassy was that something really hit him last spring. He was hurt bad. Kind of dropped out of sight for a while. The rumor was he had a brother and sister who were killed in an attack against our people. The timing coincides with the commando raid on the bus and the reprisal bombings we launched against the PLO bases. He spoke to no one and looked very bad for a while. I'm not sure what it means, but it gives a little insight into the guy."

"Family ties are strong among many Arabs. I suppose revenge could be a very strong motive." Mouse shrugged and said, "It's nice to know he has some virtues, anyway."

"He's probably nice to his dog, too! But I tend to agree with you on one point at least, that he didn't take the money and run off to Acapulco. No, it's more likely he's on a blood hunt."

"But where? After who?"

"Hell, I don't know. But let's try to reason it out a little. Let's assume he's here, anyway that's all you and I have to worry about. In fact we'll have to make a lot of assumptions just to find a place to start. Continuing on with what you said yesterday, suppose he did go to

126

ground—worst case, okay? Suppose his aide is with him, and they have a big fistful of cash to use.''

''All right, consider me assuming. Now what does that tell me?''

''I'll get there . . . We turned up a small piece of his murky background. It seems Rashid had been closely allied with the Al Saiqa faction of the PLO. Very radical. Bad people. You remember about two years ago . . .''

''Mohsen, Zuheir Mohsen, the head of Al Saiqa. Your people shot him to death on the Riviera, wasn't it in Cannes?''

''Well,'' Halperin smiled as he looked over at Mouse, ''let's say that someone decided to cut his vacation short. Maybe he undertipped a waiter, you know how surly French waiters can get.''

''Six shots in the head?'' Mouse raised an eyebrow scornfully.

''Anyway, Rashid apparently planned and even carried out a number of black jobs for Mohsen. Far beyond the hit on your man in Cyprus. We think he might have been one of their top planners and there is some evidence he carried out some hits on other Palestinian leaders, like civilian moderates on the West Bank. The guy is ruthless and completely dedicated.''

''But the worst is that he is a planner. If he has decided to do something over here we can assume he has the talent not to pick something stupid or simple. It would be big. A major target, or he wouldn't waste his time.''

''I agree,'' Halperin said as his eyes glinted in the sun. ''I can think of three types of targets that he might be able to take on. First would be an attack on something of interest to Israel, or a major Jewish symbol in the United States, like our embassy or a large concentration of Jewish population. Second, he could be off on some high-level project with the IRA or some American radical group to hit some industrial or military target here in the U.S. Or, third, he could be off to hit some American target on his own, regardless of the PLO policy.''

''That covers a lot of ground.'' Mouse nodded solemnly.

''We are already in the process of greatly increasing the security at all of our embassies and consulates here, and we are passing the word to all of our community leaders in New York, Chicago, and a few other places. So that's covered. Second, I think we should tip the FBI a little more heavily that we think Rashid is up to something with the IRA and the other terrorist groups here. If that's what he's really up to, it won't hurt our searching. Anyway, who knows, it might turn up something. And they have a whole lot more people to do that legwork than we do. You buy that?'' the Israeli asked.

Mouse twisted up his face in a look of indifference. ''I guess . . . but let's not let them know too much. Start with the angle that he's thinking of bombing one of your places. That will help the security and lead them to the IRA and the rest. It also gives us a more plausible reason to be snooping around and to keep going back to them for information.''

''That's good. They're going to be tough to deal with unless we do.''

''But,'' Mouse asked coldly, ''what if he's after an American target? With their lousy security and that guy's record, he could be out to blow up Congress, hijack the President's plane, or steal an H-bomb!'' He threw up his hands in desperation. ''Do you tell the FBI something like that?''

Their looks were in total agreement.

''Even if we had proof, it would backfire on us,'' Halperin replied. ''They wouldn't believe us but they'd still shut up tighter than a clam. And they'd never find him. I'm sure he's too clever to have broken any laws they could pin on him, so even if by blind luck they caught him, all they'd do is deport him. And he'd be on the loose again. No,'' Halperin said with finality, ''we each have some scores to settle with him and he's in bad need of killing! It will be a lot easier to get him if all we are trying to do is locate him as opposed to convict him. That's what my government wants anyway, and this time I tend to agree with them.''

''So does mine. They feel we are much more prepared to deal with the workings of a skilled terrorist than the Americans are. But that sick feeling of mine tells me that we don't have a whole lot of time.''

''You know, one point puzzles me a little.'' Halperin looked up thoughtfully. ''He's been gone now for over a week. Set off the alarm bells. If he were going to do something here in Washington he'd probably have stuck around here to the last minute and acted normal. But he wouldn't have raised any suspicions.''

''One thing you're overlooking—the money. That's what triggered the alarms. And he would have known it would. So we can assume the very last thing he'd do before he went to ground was take the the money. He wouldn't touch it until he absolutely needed it. So he needed the money a week ago. A lot of it. We can assume he had to buy something or pay someone to do something. But the delay would suggest there were still things that had to be done once the payment was made."

Halperin's eyes sharpened as his mind raced to get in step. "Yes. And two hundred thousand dollars. That's an interesting number. Not really a whole lot for something illegal. For a really hairy mission you could hardly hire one good pro for that. And if he's used it to buy something, it's too little for anything really exotic like a missile or an H-bomb. Yet we can assume that all he'll want is a fraction of that to cover his needs, so he might have bought something moderate. Certainly not a rifle or a case of grenades."

Mouse pursed his lips together. "I agree. He's not just taking a shot at someone. . . . Damn," he snapped angrily. "It has taken us so long to get so many issues settled between us, and then these hotheads have to keep throwing gasoline on the dying fire. It took fifty years and a lot of people to mess up the Middle East. How can they expect it all to be settled overnight? And then we get preposterous situations like this! Two completely rational adults sitting on the steps of a space-age Disneyland talking to each other about the relative possibilities of a man blowing up Washington with an atomic bomb, or something." Mouse's face was livid with rage. "If I went down and asked that hot dog man what he thought about it he'd call the police and tell them there was a crazy nut over on the steps of Air and Space. And he'd be right!"

"This business has made all of us a little crazy." Halperin said sadly. "It's all gone on too long . . . too damn long. A lot of people say that, but those of us who've seen it, who live with it, know it worst of all. We're going to try like hell to stop this guy Rashid, but if we do, it won't make one damn bit of difference. He's very dangerous, but totally irrelevant."

As they looked at one another, a knowing bond was sealed.

"You are correct," Mouse sighed. "I assume you are going to work with me on this little project?"

"Yes, but my people are sending a guy over to take charge from our end who can work in the field."

"Why? I think we'd make a great team."

"Oh, I'll still be in on it," Halperin said, "but let's say that in the great department store of Israeli Intelligence I'm the clerk in charge of women's lingerie, down in the bargain basement."

"You disappoint me, David!"

"I'm just a retread jet pilot. Codes and cocktail parties. Nothing heavy. I'm not the guy to go after Rashid. They know it, and I agree. But the man they're sending over is. He's a counterterror specialist. I've heard of him vaguely. Real hard core. If anyone is a match for Rashid, it's this guy. You may not like him, but he's effective. Cheer up, though, old pussycat Dave will still be along to offer you lunch." Halperin smiled.

"All right, but when does he arrive?" Mouse asked in resignation.

"Tonight. On the ten fifteen flight into Dulles. We'll go out to pick him up. I'll swing by your place at nine, okay?"

"Fine. What's his name, by the way?" Mouse asked.

"Ullman, Colonel Uri Ullman."

They arrived at the floodlit terminal a half hour early and sat down to wait for the flight to arrive. But Dulles isn't like most airports, it has a fairly intelligent layout. Contrary to JFK, O'Hare, San Francisco, or almost anywhere else, O. J. Simpson hasn't got anywhere to run at Dulles. It isn't laid out like an octopus. There is no linear main terminal with a half dozen radial arms stretching out in all directions waiting for the plane to snuggle up and disgorge its passengers down connected ramps directly into a lounge. Not Dulles.

It's a little more sensible. The terminal is a big rectangle. Along the far wall are a series of passenger lounges. When the plane is ready, the lounge doors close and it drives off on tall legs to go out and meet the plane parked on some distant tarmac. It's like a giant bus. Very logical, and a lot less running.

So they waited, drinking vending machine coffee in the busy hallway. Finally the PA system announced an arrival at the international gate, so they headed down to the far end of the terminal.

The lounge doors hissed back and 188 passengers scurried to queue up at Customs. Most were middle-aged or elderly American Jews returning on a charter tour of Israel, so the checks were cursory at best. A gray-haired, four-foot-ten-inch grandmother from Skokie with two shopping bags is hardly the profile of a heavy drug mule.

When the line had just about finished, a lone figure finally got up from his seat and joined the end. He carried one small carry-on suitcase and a canvas flight bag.

130

Mouse rested his chin on his knuckles as he sat and carefully examined Ullman. He stood silently in line, his face utterly devoid of any expression, slowly smoking a cigarette in long, deep drags. By Egyptian standards he was a very large man. Well built, no fat, and he moved with ease and sureness. He was about six feet tall and around two hundred pounds. The cigarette looked small in his large, square hands.

Mouse couldn't tell his age. He could be thirty-five or fifty, but that was probably due to his short, pure gray hair and weathered face. He was well tanned and had deep lines around the eyes and mouth. Vaguely handsome, but rugged. No, he was younger than he looked at first glance.

But what was most striking to Mouse was his clothes. They didn't look good on him. They didn't quite fit, looked a little uncomfortable, a little out of place. He didn't look like he cared much about it either. Army. He had army stamped all over him. The kind of man who belonged in a uniform and only wore his limited array of out-of-date civilian clothes when he had no choice. A no-nonsense army colonel out of uniform, that's exactly what he looked like, Mouse concluded.

The Egyptian watched as Ullman turned and slowly scanned the room. Like radar searching out a target it knew was there. The body never moved, but the eyes were alert and active. They finally came to rest on David and him, but without the slightest reaction. Like looking at a couple of bugs under a microscope.

As their eyes met, even from a distance of a hundred feet or more, Mouse felt the uncomfortable urge to squirm. They held steady on him for a few seconds and bore through to his backbone. Finally the line moved once more and Ullman turned away toward the Customs clerk.

Mouse leaned partway over to David and whispered, ''You were right, I don't think I'm going to like him!''

11

Friday, October 9

The next evening it was Rashid who arrived at an airport, but it was O'Hare, in Chicago. Leaving the plane, he casually walked along with the other passengers until they reached the main terminal. While they bunched up to take the escalator down to the baggage area, he slipped away into the large, milling crowd nearby. He was traveling light and the small canvas flight bag he carried was all he'd need. Except, of course, for the briefcase.

Retrieving it was not something you did rashly, he thought. He approached the wall of lockers casually, slowly, obliquely, and ready to walk away if his close observation found anything out of place. But more than that, it was the feel of the place that mattered most to him. The best solution, since he had plenty of time, was to simply sit down with a magazine right in front of the lockers and begin to read. Smiling to himself, that's exactly what he did.

Thirty-five minutes later he glanced at his watch. Standing up, he took a last look around the room and walked over to the locker. He opened the door and pulled out the case without the slightest hesitation. Walking back through the terminal he thought, if you feel out of place, you are.

Seeing the long line of cabs outside, he walked up to one in the middle and hopped in behind the startled driver. "I know, I know, it's against the rules." He smiled and handed her a twenty-dollar bill. "I'm superstitious . . . the O'Hare Inn, please." And I never take the first cab, he thought.

He had her drop him off on the street so he could enter the lobby through a side door after taking a stroll around the lot. He checked in as quickly as he could and went up to the room to make the phone call to Murphy.

"Well, now," the Irishman answered. "I've been expecting your call any day."

"Is everything ready for me?" Rashid asked bruskly.

"Just as your requested. You'll notice I even made it with a few days to spare. And, to be quite frank, I'd like to make the delivery just as soon as possible. You might say it's red hot around here."

"Fine, come right over to the hotel. I'm at the O'Hare Inn this time. Park in the north lot. I'll expect you to call me from the front desk in half an hour, no longer. Have everything in the van as I told you." He hung up without waiting for a reply.

Rashid opened the briefcase and carefully checked the mechanism of the automatic. As he screwed on the silencer he knew it was a wise decision to leave the hardware over at the airport rather than take the chance of two extra trips through airport security. Once was risk enough, and Rashid was far too experienced to press his luck one bit further than he absolutely had to. "Never take an unnecessary risk," they'd told him. "Only do that at the execution stage of a mission when there is a big payoff, and even then only when you can't avoid it. But never take the risks while you're only planning or preparing for the action. Walk away. Start over again. That's what separates a dead amateur from a live professional."

It wasn't the kind of thing Rashid would forget.

He put the gun in his small shoulder holster, grabbed the two bags, and left the room.

Thirty minutes later when the telephone rang, Rashid wasn't there to answer it. He was standing in the shadows behind the large dumpster outside on the edge of the parking lot. From this vantage point he could get a clear view of the lot and the access road beyond. Since he had changed hotels, if it was a setup he'd know it soon enough. Murphy wouldn't try to take him on alone. There'd be a small army of police, FBI, or other IRA people backing him up. Rashid would simply disappear along the rear side of the long commercial strip. But he wouldn't forget, he'd be back to even the score with Murphy.

Finally he saw the orange U-Haul van make the turn and pull into the quiet lot. A few other cars went by on the road but nothing looked out of place. Murphy got out and lumbered across the lot to the lobby doors of the hotel.

Once Murphy was out of sight, the Arab waited a few minutes more to be sure there were no trailers. He left his hiding place and crept along the rear side of the lot to a point where he could approach the van from a blind corner. Standing next to it for a few moments, he listened hard for any sound from within. Satisfied, he crept over to the rear window and suddenly lit up the interior with his flashlight. It was empty except for the long dark roll of carpet lying on the floor. Maybe Murphy was smart enough not to try anything after all, he thought.

Rashid turned off the light and walked quickly over to the side door of the motel lobby. Through the window he watched Murphy arguing with the desk clerk. He paced up and down a bit and went over to the house phone once more. There was no one else in the lobby except two women and a young couple. Finally Rashid opened the door and walked over to where Murphy stood.

"Oh . . . there you are," the Irishman said as he was about to return to the desk. "I was . . . I just tried to . . ."

"I know," Rashid cut him off before he could explain. "Let's go."

Outside the motel, the Arab again scanned the lot and the road, but nothing had changed.

"The van's back over here," Murphy said nervously.

"I know," Rashid replied coldly, "Key?" he asked as he put out his hand. The Irishman fumbled through his pockets and handed them over as fast as he could. "Good. While I examine the merchandise, you go over behind that big dumpster. You'll find two bags back there. Bring them to the van."

Once Rashid had the door open he stepped up inside and unrolled the blanket far enough to get a good look. Under the beam of his flashlight he quickly counted the shells and the main pieces of the weapon.

134

When Murphy stuck his head in the door, Rashid smiled faintly and told him pleasantly, "Good. Very good, you did well. It looks like everything is in excellent condition."

"I told you we'd do our best, didn't I?" he stuttered anxiously. "And I tell you, you have no idea how hard it—"

"And I don't want to, either," Rashid's sharp voice cut him off. "You did a good job. That's what you were paid handsomely to do, but we appreciate it." He looked down and took the bag from Murphy's hand. Reaching inside, he pulled out a large manila envelope and handed it over.

"Here's the balance of the money I owe you. . . . It's all there," he added with a smile as he watched the sweating Irishman squeeze and feel through the thick paper.

"I'm sure it is. Yes, sure indeed."

"I do want to know one thing though. What's been the reaction to the theft? Anything unusual yet?" Rashid asked as he stared into Murphy's face.

"Oh, there's been a lot of reaction, all right. Me and some of my boys were called in and questioned twice, but that all blew over when they found that nigger sergeant's body. Now they blame it on some black terrorist gang. I guess I'm getting ahead of myself," he said in apology. "We paid this one supply clerk to get the stuff for us. He was white, see . . . but there was this nigger who worked under him. He'd be the only one who might figure out that the first guy was involved. We was going to kill the white guy at first, but then I had this flash of brilliance, you might say," he beamed. "What we did was to kill the nigger and dump his body near where the Muslim mosque was on the south side. . . ." Murphy's smile suddenly vanished in panic. "Oh, Lord, I hope that didn't bother you about the mosque part, I . . ."

"No, there's no connection at all, go on," he said reassuringly.

Murphy pulled out his handkerchief and wiped his brow. "Good. I never thought . . . Anyway, see, this way the white guy knows he'd go down for murder if he opens his yap, it sends the coppers in the wrong direction, and doesn't point a finger at us like it might somehow if we'd have killed the white guy. Of course he'll have a little accident in a few months, just to make sure."

"Not bad, not bad at all. You surprise me, Murphy," Rashid said with an undercurrent of real feeling. "No, you did well." He paused to let his expression get more serious. "I just hope you have remembered what I told you last time about what will happen if I have any problems on my way back."

Murphy flinched as if he'd been slapped across the face. "No... No need to worry, no, sir!" He tried to avoid the Arab's flashing black eyes, which reached out at him from the darkness. "There will be no trouble from my end, I can assure you of that."

"I certainly hope so, for your sake," Rashid said softly. "Goodbye then. You stand right here until this van is out of sight down the road. Then you can call a cab for yourself. I think you can afford one now."

Rashid got behind the wheel and drove out of the lot onto Mannheim Road. The Kennedy Expressway wasn't too far away. Once out into the sparse traffic, he checked his rearview mirror and the gauges on the dashboard. Everything looked fine.

As he sat back and relaxed he thought about the long drive ahead. Nine hundred miles. He'd go straight on through. Early tomorrow afternoon he'd be there. It would be a long night.

As the miles began to roll by, his sense of exhilaration rose. It was October ninth. The pace quickened, he could feel it. He was on edge, excited. Only nine days to go. So far no problems. No alarms. No signs of surveillance. No interference.

The past few months had passed with excruciating slowness. It was painful and frustrating. The mission consumed him so that everything else seemed too trivial to be bothered with. He lived for the plan and his revenge, and knew that it was a lot more personal than he'd dare to tell Arazi. But that was no matter; it was enough that he could have this one act of intense pleasure.

The plan. He'd gone over it countless times. Every detail rechecked. Maps restudied until the creases had to be taped to keep them from falling apart. Books reread. And a continuous game of "what if," whereby he tried as hard as he could to think of anything that could go wrong, no matter how bizarre. What would he do if . . .

It was an intellectual exercise that helped him to fill the void, but it crowded everything else out and became an obsession. Deep in the recesses of his mind he knew, but he did not want to admit even to himself, especially to himself, that something had snapped. If he had thought about it, he'd have known by the simple fact that all of his plans

136

and concerns ended with the act. He gave Arazi a full sketch of what they would do to get away, but that aspect really did not matter to him. All of his thoughts went into what went before. All.

Returning to the battlefield a week ago had helped. Walking the ground where it would happen. This was tangible. He lay on the very spot where the reviewing stand would soon be built. He closed his eyes and could feel it through the blades of grass. The shock waves from the rain of shells exploding all around him. He could sense the black earth and green grass erupting upward. Thousands of eyes filled with terror as they look up to see the small black objects falling from the sky, arcing downward, plunging, in rapid succession. The wooden platform shattering into splinters of flying wood. Everywhere, he could see the air filled with flying dirt, shrapnel, grass, wood, and bodies. Shouts, screams, explosions tearing through the air. The huge crowd turning as one to stampede away in panic. Trampling those in their way. Escape. Anywhere! As the rain of death fell down among them.

He opened his eyes and the sky was blue. The ground was still. The field was empty and quiet. But he knew he was alive, if only for a few moments. It helped.

It gave him strength as he drove down the Kennedy Expressway. Nine hundred miles away, but a quantum leap closer than he'd been yesterday, or even an hour ago, he thought. They'd passed the point of no return. He'd taken the money and now he had the weapon.

Motive, opportunity, and now the means, he thought. Just like on the American police shows. The means.

No turning back now. He knew he'd already be wanted very badly by people in Beirut. He could just picture the council in a frantic debate.

"What is Rashid up to?" they'd ask. "What could he be doing?" "Did anyone authorize him to do something?"

Silence. Puzzled faces. Worry. Rage.

The point of no return.

But he knew there was nothing they could do. They'd never be able to find him. Wouldn't even know where to start. And they could never report him to the Americans, because they didn't know what he was up to. What if he was on some normal mission, but the cable had been lost? And even if he was doing something crazy, do they admit they have an agent in Washington? Much less one they'd lost control of? Rashid

137

laughed. That argument would have them going in circles for days. Questions, but not one answer!

It was like a random motion machine. Slowly a pattern would emerge. Slowly time, space, and the seemingly innocent motion would come together. At the right time and the right place.

Murphy had stood without taking a single step as he watched the van go around the line of buildings. At that second he turned and bolted in a waddling gait toward the door of the motel. Out of breath, he lunged for the pay phone and quickly dialed the number of the McDonald's a few blocks away.

"Tim . . . the bastard's gone. Get over here, and turn the machine's on. I don't want to lose him."

Murphy dashed out the front door and waited impatiently.

"We'll see who's so smart now!" he snorted.

12

Monday, October 12

It was just after 1:00 A.M. and Rashid was right. A lot of questions were being asked, but in a basement room of the Israeli Embassy, not Beirut.

"What the hell are they up to?" Ullman said as he rubbed his fist into the palm of his hand. "We've been over and over the same ground now for days. And we're not one step closer to them."

"That's not entirely correct," Mouse replied evenly as he filled his coffee cup again. "All of the foreign sources have drawn a complete blank and we haven't had one piece of solid news about them for over a week. I think we can begin to infer a few things about that, since we have little other choice."

"Like what," Ullman asked as he eyed him coldly.

"Well, we've each had significant intelligence resources thrown into this. Some well-placed operatives that we only use in emergencies. Plus cover on all the likely spots they'd have gone to. The PLO, the Libyans, and the rest. So far we've come up with nothing. Nothing at all," he said, very casual and relaxed. "I hate to admit it, but I'm becoming convinced it's because there's nothing to find. They're here in the United States, and none of their contacts know what they are up to. They have gone underground and are hiding from everyone."

"I think you're right, Mouse," Halperin agreed. "It's the only thing that makes any sense."

"All right, let's assume they are still here," Ullman challenged irritably. "So what. We still don't have the slightest idea what their target is."

"And we aren't just going to, either," Mouse said as he stared back at him. "We are just going to have to work hard and use a little logic."

"What do you think we've been doing?"

"Looking for more clues. And I'm telling you we already have all the clues we are going to get. Somewhere in them is the answer. For instance," he said as he leaned back and rested his chin on his knuckles, "the money. Here he is in a foreign country. He's struck out on his own. He has a well-developed plan. But I can't believe he went into this with all the equipment he would need. That's why he took the money. He has to buy something or someone. A service or a thing. The only other possibility is that he is financing some other group. But two hundred thousand dollars just isn't enough to do that."

"You mean like the Japanese attack on the airport in Rome?"

"That kind of thing is a possibility, but it could only be a group that would do something for pure ideals, not money. You could ask your friend at the FBI if there is some new super-crazy group on the loose. But my bet is that he needed to buy something, not use someone else. If it was this big to him, he isn't the type to put it in the hands of someone else," the Egyptian said calmly but persuasively. "And if he wanted to buy something, the odds are he'd go to someone he'd already worked with and trusted."

"The best word we have on that," Halperin added, "is the IRA or the black nationalists here."

Ullman shook his head skeptically. "That's just not their style. The PLO almost never goes outside for anything they have to depend on."

"Oh, I agree, back home. But he's cut off over here. Plus he knew he couldn't get anything from his own people since this isn't sanctioned."

"I think you're right, Mouse," Halperin stepped in as referee. "I think the best course is for me to check back with the FBI and see what they turned up. They have the only contact with those groups. We'll just have to hope they've found something."

140

"Agreed," Mouse said as he stretched and yawned. "Gentlemen, I'm tired. I'm going to go home and go to bed. I suggest you two might do the same. I think we're going to need to be at our best."

"You're right. Let's get together in the morning. Hopefully I'll have something from the Americans by then," Halperin said as they all stood up and straightened the chaotic stacks of paper on the table.

After the Egyptian's footsteps had faded away down the hall, Halperin sat back down and watched Ullman for a few moments, debating in his own mind whether or not to say something.

Without looking up, Ullman said, "All right, Halperin, what's bothering you? Since you don't seem to be able to say it, let me try. You think I should be more polite to our Egyptian 'ally,' to your 'friend.' You think perhaps I've been a little rude to our 'guest,' " he said sarcastically. "Well, you're right, I have been! And I have no intention of changing, either."

Ullman leaned forward on his hands, drawing closer to Halperin and continued. "I don't like having an Arab involved in this. It wasn't my idea and you can be sure it was over my objection. It goes against my grain."

"I don't think he likes working with you very much either," Halperin replied. "But he's a professional and has a good mind for intelligence. I've worked with him before, and the little guy doesn't make mistakes. He can be trusted. He's done many things for us he didn't have to do."

"I'm sure you're absolutely right, Halperin. But you're losing sight of the key point. He's an Arab. I don't mind using them for anything we can, but I'll never trust them, regardless of their pedigrees!" Ullman said sharply.

"His being an Arab gives us access to a lot of information we are going to need very badly, and maybe it gives him an ability to get inside Rashid's head that we'll never have."

"Your background is airplanes and now a foreign embassy. Mine's been dealing with terrorists—Arab terrorists—for too many years. When the chips are down, do you really think he's going to look out for our interests!" Ullman asked. "Do you think he'd chop down another Arab as fast as you or I would?"

Halperin had no answer.

"And I'll tell you right now," Ullman said as his eyes flashed, "if he ever crosses me, he'll be Minnie Mouse . . . and I don't have a sense of humor . . . at all!"

"That comes as a real surprise," Halperin replied flatly. "Look, we've got to get along—all three of us. So let's change the subject." He looked over in the corner where two large bags lay. "Is that what was brought in with the diplomatic pouch yesterday? I heard the mail clerk grumbling. He isn't used to schlepping heavy packages from Dulles. What's in them anyway?"

"A little equipment I had Mossad HQ send over. You can never tell what we might come up against. This place isn't exactly well equipped. Go have a look."

Halperin kneeled down and opened the top bag. "Jeez, what are you expecting, World War III?"

Ullman ran his hand through his hair. "Maybe I'm just tired. Maybe you're not as stupid as I think you are. There's two collapsible Uzi machine guns and two thousand rounds of ammunition in the top bag. And a sniper rifle, a scope, a couple of Belgium nine-millimeter automatics with silencers, some grenades . . . and some sodium pentathol."

Halperin was in shock as he looked down at the open bags. "This isn't the Golan," he shot back as he turned his head to stare at Ullman. "This is Washington, D.C., the capital of our best ally. You can't run around shooting up the place!"

Ullman's face grew livid and the muscles in his neck stood out. "Listen, you ass!" He shouted. "If you think this is some kind of Hadassah tea party, some kind of joke, you should have been with me last spring on the road outside Acre after they butchered that bus. Rashid's little brother was probably part of that group that set out from Lebanon. Trying to follow in his older brother's footsteps," he spat out angrily. "You know we think there were twenty people on that bus, give or take a few, but it's only a guess." He waved his hand in frustration. "All unarmed civilians. Most of them weren't even Jews. They didn't care. There were five bodies we never did identify. And a lot of pieces we just put with bodies so that the total added up. Two arms. Two legs. But they were all shot up, blown to pieces, burned to charred lumps. You know," he said as his voice cracked, "a couple of times when the rescue people were trying to clear out the bus, they had to kick at one of the lumps to see if it was a body or a seat cushion. Everything was black and burned."

Halperin stood up and slowly walked back to his seat. "But. . . ." he began.

Ullman cut him off with a fierce stare. "There are no buts. That's what these bastards do. Like at Nahariya a few years ago. Women, children, old people, even other Palestinians if they don't quite agree with them. It makes no difference. It makes no difference to Rashid either. Look at his record. I came here to kill him, anyway I can!" He leaned forward, very close to Halperin. "I want very badly to kill him! You could never understand how much. . . . And I couldn't care less if you ever do." He paused to look at him with complete contempt. "But make no mistake, when the time comes, I'm a cold professional. You don't have to worry about me shooting up the Washington Monument. It's only Rashid I'll be shooting up. And neither he nor the Americans will ever know who hit him. But it's very satisfying work, so don't you comment on things you don't understand." He glared. "And don't ever get in my way!"

Halperin shivered and shrank back from one of the most savage looks he had ever seen.

Ullman paused while he rubbed both hands down his face. The tension was broken. "I'm sorry, you didn't quite deserve that," he said quietly. "I shouldn't expect you to understand what it is that we're up against. You and the Egyptian have been here too long. You've become civilized. But it isn't a civilized war. They are animals. They are out to do no less than to liquidate our people without distinction."

Halperin said in frustration. "I know that every bit as well as you."

"But you don't! You think you do, but you don't. I can't expect you to. You haven't seen the atrocities up close. You haven't looked into their eyes. They will never stop. Never! We only have two choices. We can give in and surrender or we can kill them before they kill us. One by one if we must."

His voice was calm but intensely serious as he tried very hard to explain the depths of his feelings to Halperin. "We must demonstrate over and over to them that the only people in the world that are more determined than they are are us. Just as vicious and just as serious. More so if we have to be. That's the only way a counterterrorist program can work. I want them to know that we actually want them to keep coming. To send the best they've got. So we can kill them, without mercy, wherever we can."

Ullman paused to light another cigarette. He inhaled deeply as Halperin watched, mesmerized.

Ullman went on as he looked over at Halperin again. "Eventually, they must learn deep in their bones that we will kill them, and the people who sent them. No sanctuary. As sure as the sun will rise. . . . Some day, one terrorist will pause, stop, decide it just isn't worth it, turn back, put down his gun, and just go home. On that day we will have won. And it will happen," he said as he grew agitated. "It must happen. It is the only solution that we can ever allow . . . we have nowhere else to go. So it is the only thing we can do."

Halperin could think of nothing to say in rebuttal.

"It has fallen to our generation, and maybe the next," Ullman said as he looked down vacantly at the table. "We must hold what others have won at a staggering price. We safeguard the last hope of a thousand generations of our people. The millions who died in the gas chambers, saying to each other 'next year in Jerusalem.' I'm a few years older than you. I grew up in Israel before the war. I can still remember what the survivors looked like as they limped or were carried off the boats. They aren't just pictures in Yod Vashem to me. My family was German."

The pause was deafening. "They paid for our land, for our home. Ours. The one place where we won't be kicked around. The one place where Jews are not a subhuman minority for someone to have fun with. That's why safeguarding Israel, regardless of whatever other claims anyone else might have, is the most sacred responsibility any Jew has had in two thousand years. That's what it is all about. That's why I'm here. That's why I'm going to kill this Arab Rashid that I've never even met. It's a historical imperative. Can you understand that?" he asked quietly.

Halperin had a puzzled look on his face, so Ullman sat forward in his chair with his fingers knit together. "Let me explain. As a people we've come full circle. The Biblical kingdom of Israel lasted less than three hundred years, and that was almost three thousand years ago. We have been scattered to the four winds ever since. Oh, there was a brief rebirth of a second kingdom about two thousand years ago, but it lasted for only sixty years and could not hope to survive as an independent nation against the might of Rome. So we have been scattered across every continent and nation in the world ever since." His eyes gleamed and he took a deep breath. "No other people could have survived under such circumstances. But our religion, our culture and heritage have been our salvation. It binds us together no matter where we are. But it has also been our curse. It has always served to set us apart by our tormentors.

"We are unique in that our religion and our heritage are all rooted in this small land we now call Israel. Without it we are nothing as a people. I'll be the first to admit that our actual title to the land is a joke. Our area has been conquered by the Canaanites, the Babylonians, Egyptians, Greeks, Persians, Parthians, Romans, Christians, Muslims, Byzantines, Turks, Ottomans, and even the British. And most of them ruled it longer than we did. Even the Arabs ruled it for six hundred years or so.

"For the last two thousand years we have been truly without a home. Unwanted outcasts. In the Middle Ages even the British, the French, and the Spanish expelled us from their lands.

"We came to Israel as strangers, but we had no choice. It was the only place we could go, and at least we had some dim tie to it. But it wouldn't have mattered if it was in the middle of Africa or the South Pole, we'd have taken it!" he exclaimed.

"And God knows we got no bargain. We came here from every corner of the world, dirt poor. We settled it, built cities, and made the deserts bloom out of a wasteland. What we have today we built and we must defend, because we are safe nowhere else! That's why the State is so important to us. It is the only place in the world where we are not a minority.

"But we didn't get it because we waited and deserved it. Oh, no. Do you know why we got Israel?"

Halperin shrugged his shoulders. "It was a long struggle to convince the world, I guess," he replied lamely.

"No. It was a long struggle, I'll grant you that. The Zionist movement started over a hundred years ago. But they were irrelevant, except that they began the slow migration of Jews back to Israel. In 1922 we were only eleven percent of the population of Palestine. Even in 1946 we were only thirty-two percent. Hardly more than a large minority. My parents were some of those early settlers. They told me about the bloody riots by the Arabs in 1929, 1936, and 1939. But that meant nothing to the

British, or the rest of the world for that matter. If they did, why wasn't a Jewish state set up there and then? Our case had been before them for years, and it hadn't changed. No, that wasn't the reason. Do you know what it was?''

Ullman paused as his eyes burned through the narrow space between them. ''It was the death camps. Nothing else made any difference. The horror of the Holocaust shocked them into action. They were embarrassed that a civilized nation like Germany could do something like that. And what were they to do with the survivors? Send them back? Take them in themselves? Far worse, because that would serve as a reminder of something they wanted very badly to forget. After all, the same level of barbarism lurked under the surface of every nation in Europe. Just look at their histories. . . . No, we had them in a corner. They could not turn down our request, particularly when it cost them nothing. They had a long history of giving away things that belong to someone else so they could settle a pressing present-day problem. All they needed was the slimmest of pretenses.

''So it solved their problem, and ours, but never forget that we owe it all to the six million who died so that it could happen. The only way their deaths have any meaning at all is if we hold what they paid for! It is a sacred trust.

''It's like at Masada.'' Ullman laughed to himself. ''Have you noticed how fashionable it has become for foreign commentators to accuse us of having a 'Masada complex'? If they only realized what a compliment that was, at least to me. I really wish all of our people had a Masada complex. There were nine hundred and sixty of our people trapped on top, hopelessly surrounded by the Romans. Eleazer Ben-Yaer, our leader, stood before them and said, 'a death of glory is preferable to a life of infamy.' And so all nine hundred and sixty men, women, and children took, their lives—rather than surrender. They had nowhere else to go. And neither do we!''

Ullman was silent for several long minutes as they looked at each other. Finally he said, ''Can you understand that?''

Halperin slowly nodded in agreement as the realization of the truth in Ullman's words scored deeply into him.

Ullman sat quietly and finished his cigarette. He then rose and dropped it to the floor. Crushing it out under the heel of his boot, he took

146

one last slow look at Halperin, nodded back in understanding, and walked out of the room.

Halperin sat there alone, drained of all but an embarrassed understanding which he hated himself for, like a chastened student.

That same evening, another meeting was well underway in Beirut.

"Is there no word about Rashid yet?" Arafat pleaded with his hands as he looked around the table at his silent entourage. "Surely someone must know what he is doing!"

'No, Yassir,'' the operations man replied. ''The embassy has found out nothing. He and Arazi have just vanished! But it was his signature on the withdrawal slip and the bank manager identified his picture. He was alone, very pleasant, and under no stress that the manager could see. He counted the money, put it in a briefcase, shook hands, and sauntered out of the bank. There is just no explanation for it.''

Arafat looked around slowly at the vacant faces. "Well, someone had better have an explanation . . . and soon! You all know what has been going on in Riyadh. You know how sensitive the talks with the Americans are. You know I'll be signing the papers tomorrow." He took off his sunglasses and stared at each of them angrily. "Someone had better find out what Rashid's up to, and quick! He frightens me like few other men do."

"Should we notify the Americans?" A nervous voice asked.

"No! No! You idiot. That would be the worst thing we can do! You want to tell them that our discipline is so lax that we seem to have lost a colonel and would they please help us to find him before he hurts himself!" His derisive voice sliced through the room and left them squirming.

"Find him!" he screamed. "Go through his room, his office, his papers, every message he ever sent, every letter. Everything. All his contacts. I want every stone kicked over. There must be a clue. Find him!"

Daniels was sound asleep when the bedside phone began to ring. And ring. Finally his wife rolled over and jabbed him in the ribs with a sharp elbow.

"Frank . . . Frank! Answer the goddamn thing, will you!" She rolled back and angrily pulled the pillow over her head. "Bastards!" she muttered.

He groped for the phone and knocked the receiver off the table onto the floor. Leaning over, he grabbed for it as it bounced noisily across the hardwood floor. Finally grasping the cord, he reeled it in and raised the phone to his ear.

"Yeah. Whozit?" he rasped.

"Wake up, Frank. This is David," came the bubbly reply.

Daniels's eyes shot open. He reached over and brought the alarm clock close to his face. "What the hell!" He grimaced. "What are you calling me at this hour for?"

"Take it easy. I had to get hold of you before you left for work. I got standing orders from you never to call there, remember?"

"What do you want?" Daniels groaned in resignation.

"That matter we discussed a week ago has really heated up. We are very concerned that the guy is out doing something. I need to know anything you've found out. Any little piece might fit something we have. Can we meet later this morning?"

"We haven't found the guy. I told you that before."

"Anything you've found, anything unusual about the groups we talked about. Anything . . . okay?"

Daniels slowly got his brain going into second gear. "Look . . . I can't get away until late morning. I've got a meeting. I'll meet you at eleven o'clock. But not in town. Out at Tyson's Corner. The big mall. In front of Walden Books. I'll dig through the files and see if we have anything, but I'm not too optimistic."

"See you then, you're a peach. I'll put you back on my Chanukah card list. Now that you're wide awake, why don't you roll over and nibble on your wife's ear?"

"She'd hit me with a table lamp."

It was noon before Halperin finally opened the door and walked into the basement conference room. As he looked over at Mouse and Ullman, it was painfully obvious he'd broken in on a long silence.

"Where the hell have you been?" Ullman asked irritably. "We've been sitting here for almost two hours."

"I was meeting with my friend from the FBI. Sorry, couldn't be

148

helped. He doesn't like to talk on the phone, so I had to meet him out of town."

"Well . . . did he at least come up with anything?" Mouse asked.

"It's hard to say. Some slim leads, perhaps, but I'm not sure. Neither is he. Since I didn't want to tip our hand, I only threw out a very big net. We'll just have to sort through it all and see if any of it makes sense."

"Well, let's get started," Ullman said wearily.

"There are four groups they feel might be up to something or at least have some usefulness for a guy like Rashid. They are all active, all somewhat dangerous, all have their own rabid cause, and all have some tie to foreign sources of money or arms. Probably Mideast, but some also work with the Chinese, Cubans, or even North Vietnam."

The other two nodded in frustration.

"The first is a radical Black Muslim splinter group in Harlem. Very crazy. The FBI hasn't been able to penetrate them, but the talk on the street is that they have money and are planning something big. The problem is that they are really paranoid and have never dealt much with outsiders. So who knows?"

"Let's mark them down anyway," Ullman said. "Next?"

"Second is the Puerto Rican nationalist group, the FALN, also in New York. Mostly bombers. They like 'symbols of capitalist oppression' like Manhattan office buildings." Halperin shrugged quizzically. "Anyway, they definitely get outside money, but most of their ties are to Cuba for training, money, and weapons. Yet there are ties to Libya as well. The word is they mght do a little contract work if the price is right."

Ullman shrugged his shoulders. "They are organized and do have a track record at least. That makes them a little more likely."

"Third, we have the IRA. They have well-established ties to Libya and the PLO, as we all know. The other two groups hate the American government and just might take on a target over here for Rashid, but not the IRA. They are only here for supply and finance. I doubt they'd do anything that might backfire on them and result in losing their American support. They don't want to get moved up on the list of the FBI's priority. And they don't have their better people over here either. Poor quality, and under orders to keep a low profile. The best shot for us is probably Chicago; that's where their most active supply base is right now. It moves around fairly often. The FBI says several armories got hit there in the last few years. One only a few weeks ago.''

"From what you've said so far, we can look at this two ways,'' Mouse reflected. "If he were looking for a group to carry out a violent mission for him, that would be one thing, and probably lead us to the FALN or someone like them. On the other hand, if he intended to do the job himself but needed some equipment, that would be a different matter and he'd probably lean toward the IRA, since that is their forte. The question is, which is he up to?''

"Good point,'' Ullman conceded. "We'll have to pick out the top choice on each list unless something comes up to narrow the choice. You said there were four groups?'' he asked looking over to Halperin again.

"Maybe. But it's a real loony. In California...''

Mouse broke in, "It just wouldn't be American without one.''

"True,'' Halperin continued. "It's a group of splinters and castoffs from the SLA, Manson family, and some others. They've done some bank jobs and have arms. Maybe some international ties, but the FBI doesn't think that anyone abroad would take them seriously. They may have met with some of the Japanese radicals, and maybe that could lead back to the Libyans... who knows? They are crazy enough to try anything. Their idols are the Red Brigade and the Bader-Meinhof Gang. But these people are pure crazy and high most of the time. They tried to blow up a nuclear power plant last year. I can't believe a guy like Rashid would be stupid enough to rely on people like that.''

"Unless he had a totally crazy mission in mind,'' Ullman pointed out.

They sat quietly for a few moments rethinking the information. "That's a splendid set of choices we have before us, isn't it?'' Mouse said, shaking his head in disgust.

"I have some names and addresses to go with a few of the leaders of these groups. What do you want to do?'' Halperin asked.

"Well,'' Ullman said in a slow, measured tone. "The best of the worst in my book are the FALN and the IRA.'' He paused to look at the others, who seemed to agree. "We'll work it this way. Halperin, you stay here. We need a base and a communications center worse than we'd need a third man out in the field. Your job will be to keep in touch with the FBI and our intelligence posts back home. Frankly I think you'll come up with something here a lot faster than we will out there. Okay?"" he asked, looking up.

"I can't really argue with that. I'd rather go out with you, but what you say is the smart play." Halperin tilted his head as he looked at Mouse.

"He's right," Mouse agreed. "So I assume you and I go out to check these leads?"

"Correct." Ullman replied. "You are dark complected and can probably get by better posing as a Libyan than I can. That might at least open some door with the FALN or that black group. I can probably take the lead with the IRA, but we'll work them together. If we're not careful, we'll get slit throats if we make any mistakes! It's going to take some finesse. We have to figure out a few ruses to come at them from an angle, feel them out to see if they've been meeting with Rashid. Assume we're following up for him and see what we can draw out of them."

"And stay out of corners if they don't know what we're talking about," Mouse warned. "But it's a good approach."

"We'll go to New York first. It's closest and we can assume Rashid wouldn't make this any harder than he had to." Ullman went on. "Let's start with the Puerto Ricans. While we're there we'll check out the black group to save time, but I don't think they're much of a prospect. Then we'll go on to Chicago. Let's reassess after that. If we have anything else we'll go on. California's the last resort!"

Mouse and Halperin nodded in agreement.

PART
4

JERUSALEM
OCTOBER 14–18, 1981

13

Wednesday, October 14

"Mr. President, with all respect, these proposals of yours are impossible. We have rejected them before. We reject them now, and we'll always reject them," the Prime Minister declared angrily. "You propose to leave us defenseless—and with a Palestinian state on our narrowest border! Now, as to the idea that we vacate Jerusalem; well, that is absurd! This sets back the peace process ten years, sir."

"You haven't heard all the details yet, Mr. Prime Minister," Bannon said as he began to realize this was going to be a very long day. "I suggest you make no evaluation until you have." His voice was calm but with a noticeable undercurrent of irritation. "I wouldn't come here to rehash old ideas."

"But you could have no understanding of the ancient or modern history of this complex region if you seriously believe we could accept this."

"And you, Mr. Prime Minister, could have no understanding of the much larger state of current affairs in the world around you, if you think we can delay much longer without a settlement of the issues!" Bannon responded as he looked sharply at the Defense and Foreign Ministers, who were seated across the table on each of his flanks.

The Foreign Minister spoke up in a clear, calm voice. "It is the position of this government that the issues you speak of have already been solved, or are in the process of having that happen."

Bannon waved his hand. "With the Egyptians, perhaps. But the rest are simply held at bay by force of arms. That is a stalemate, not a solution! There has been no progress on any other issue, and you know full well there won't be any. Besides, the proposals I've put forth are ones Israel has already accepted."

"What?" the Defense Minister yelled.

"The November 1948 U.N. resolution to partition Palestine. You agreed to it, the World Zionist Congress approved it, and Ben-Gurion cited it as justification to establish the State of Israel the next May. It called for an independent Jewish state, but also an independent Palestinian state and an internationalized Jerusalem. It is the only solution that will ever make sense," Bannon said calmly.

The Prime Minister laughed. "Mr. President, and just what happened to the Palestinian state? We did not violate it. We set up our nation and they were free to set up theirs. We stuck to the U.N. boundaries and did not interfere. It was they who did it. They attacked us," he said, stabbing the point of his finger into the table. "They rejected the partition, not us. We defended ourselves, but we still did not invade their land. Even after the '48 War was over, they still could have set up their nation, but Hussein invaded the West Bank and incorporated it into Jordan. We did not kill the Palestinian state, he did!"

"And the Arab League condemned him for it," Bannon pointed out. "A lot of water has gone over the dam since '48."

"And three more wars!" the Defense Minister argued. "They attacked us in '56. Finally in '67 we pushed them back to borders we could defend. But only after they proved we needed them!"

The Foreign Minister added, "It was the Arab League that rejected the Partition of '48, not us. That's one reason why we reject U.N. Resolution 242. They could have had it for nineteen years, but the opportunity has passed. Why should we give up what they were unable to take from us? We paid for it in blood!"

"I don't deny that," Bannon replied, lowering his voice. "But this is the 1980's. Back then your nation was young, and the Arab states only a few years older. It was a neighborhood streetfight. We were all-powerful and there to back you up if need be. The region was in the

156

turmoil of a power vacuum. The Turkish Empire fell apart and the British tried to iron things out for a while. We're still trying to get things back in balance, but thirty years of interim solutions won't work. We need a permanent one," he said as he spread his hands out on the table.

"Not at our expense," the Prime Minister stated emphatically. "Turning the other cheek may be part of your religious heritage, but it isn't part of ours. You ask too much."

"It won't be." Bannon said. "Look at the balance of power in the region. You are superior to all your neighbors put together. You cannot be touched so long as you have two things."

"And what are they?" the Defense Minister asked in a patronizing tone.

"Your mobile armored columns and your total control of the air. That is your true defense! And we intend to add to them significantly. Boundaries are a joke. There haven't been defensible borders in this region for four thousand years, but with your air and armor forces you are invincible in a general war. You know that as well as I do, that's why the Egyptians have given up. And now, the combination of your elimination of the Sinai front plus your tremendous power makes any attack by Syria suicide!"

The others looked back at him in silence.

"But look at the larger scene," Bannon continued. "You have no defense against the terrorists. And more alarming still, with the Arab nationalist uprisings all across the Middle East, the moderate and conservative Arab governments are terrified that if they do not bring about a settlement in this matter, they'll be overthrown. We'll be kicked out of the region and the radicals will be in control. They are pleading with you to join with them in a solution that might just save all of us!"

"Why should we believe what the Saudis say?" the Prime Minister asked quietly.

"Just look around!" Bannon replied in exasperation. "Look at what has been going on since Iran and Afghanistan. . . ." He looked at each of them, then directly into the eyes of the Prime Minister. "Where will you be in five years? If you accept, or if you just drift on as you have been going . . . If it comes to it, I suppose you could win another war fairly easily, but how many more after that? We have very little capability to help you, and neither does Sadat. How long do you think he will last? The balance of power has shifted out beneath all of us, whether we

157

like it or not. Just look around you. I suppose it is the supreme irony that just at the time Israel has its greatest tactical strength, it faces its greatest strategic weakness!''

After a strained pause, the Foreign Minister asked, ''What guarantees do we have that these pieces of paper will mean anything?''

''The same guarantees you've always had,'' Bannon replied. ''None. But let's look at this logically. It is you that will have the Palestinians surrounded, not the other way around. The Saudis want this to work very much and will have complete control over them by the purse strings. They know you can retake the West Bank and Jerusalem any time you want. Also, it will neutralize the Lebanese front for you and reduce the threat of terrorist attacks. Finally, it rebuilds the credibility of the United States in the region, and ultimately, that's where your security lies.''

The Prime Minister had a polite but strained smile as he replied, ''Your points are well made, Sir. But in the final analysis they are only a handful of promises from our sworn enemies. This nation long ago adopted the policy that we can rely on no one but ourselves to defend our people.''

Bannon was trying very hard to gauge their true feelings and doubts. His expression softened noticeably as he said, ''That is a very admirable position for any nation to take, so long as it is feasible. Today you have the strength and the courage to make it work. I am asking you to act out of that strength and take a chance that really entails little risk. Tactically your defense sits in the turrets of your tanks and in the cockpits of your jet fighters. But strategically, I am offering you the only kind of security that has any permanence at all—to be at peace with all your neighbors!''

The strain was beginning to show on the face of the Prime Minister. ''Would that it could be so, Mr. President. Would that it could be so. . . . But I bear the responsibility daily of weighing the potential for that peace you suggest may happen against the potential annihilation of my people. I can only deal with things I know.''

Bannon looked thoughtful and slowly nodded. ''Then I'll talk about some things that you do know. Believe me when I say that I realize the risks that I'm asking you to take. You would not be responsible leaders of your people if you threw away your security.'' His hands were steady as he turned to look at each of them. ''We are prepared to offer you

158

substantial new military capabilities that will more than offset the dangers you fear. Initially we'll deliver thirty new F–Fifteen Eagles within sixty days of your complete acceptance of the proposals. Plus fifteen more per year for the next four years. That's ninety of the very best planes in the air. We desperately need them ourselves, but we'll give them to you."

"Give?" The Defense Minister asked incredulously.

Bannon smiled wearily. "Yes, there will be no charge to you. They will be paid for by the Saudis. In secret, of course, but you may consider them to be an added bonus." He enjoyed watching their uneasiness. "You asked me what assurances there were that the pieces of paper meant anything—well, you have your answer. I said the Saudis were serious. What stronger token of faith could they offer than to hand you a gun pointed at their own heads! The United States will also provide you with forty new tanks per year, the latest model M–Sixty for the next five years. But these you'll have to pay for, on some very generous terms."

He paused to study their reaction to his words, but they were deep in their own thoughts, trying frantically to detect the trap, the flaw, the con.

"You know as well as I do," Bannon bore in, "that ninety F–Fifteens and two hundred new tanks give you all the security you'll need for a long time. The proposals gracefully avoid the issue of the Golan, the only border area where you have a valid concern. But with a peaceful Egypt, Jordan, and Lebanon around you, the overkill is already sufficient. What possible threat can Syria, with her antiquated MIG–Twenty-ones and T–Fifty-four tanks, or the West Bank with irregular infantry and no real hardware be?" He paused and forced himself to relax.

"In total the Saudis are giving you ten billion dollars. That will pay for the F–Fifteens, the settlements and installations on the West Bank and in Jerusalem, or whatever you like. Your economy can use it, so I'd give a little thought as to how it could be best used."

"This all sounds very attractive, Mr. President," the Prime Minister said as he coughed to clear his throat and think of a reply. "But . . . this must go to the Cabinet, and frankly . . . I'm not at all optimistic that there will be much support for it. The West Bank and Jerusalem . . . that is an impossible task. They aren't for sale at any price."

Bannon nodded solemnly. His face was drawn and tired. He went on very slowly, emphasizing each word. "You are a sovereign nation. It's your choice to accept or reject. All I can do is lay the proposals before

159

you and try to explain them. It is the whole ball of wax, all that we expect of you. Signed, sealed, and delivered. I will put no pressure on you here or through the American Jewish community at home, or through your supporters in Congress. It's your decision. But I want to make clear that it is the position of my government that the package is a fair one. It is solid and workable for both sides, and it is in the highest national interest of both of our countries that you accept it. You are the ones who must decide. I'll go no further in trying to convince you that I'm right.''

''That's a very constructive attitude, I must say.'' The Foreign Minister smiled in relief, thinking they were off a very delicate hook.

''I'm not finished!'' Bannon snapped as his eyes narrowed. ''It is your decision, but that decision carries certain consequences with it. First, today is the fourteenth of October. I want you to take a few days to think it over and review it with your cabinet. But we must have a definite yes or no answer by the eighteenth at six P.M., our time. No answer will be considered a rejection. My Secretary of State will stay here to be available. Perhaps we can make some minor adjustments, if he considers them minor, but the package at six P.M. on the eighteenth is final. Accept or reject.'' His gaze was hard and unwavering.

''That's preposterous!'' the Defense Minister stammered. ''That's not negotiating, it is . . . a fait accompli!''

''You are absoultely right,'' Bannon stared back with barely controlled anger. ''This is our new policy—to settle the issue, not argue about it. If you accept, all remaining details will be concluded in thirty days. All withdrawals will be finished in six months. That is when you receive the ten billion dollars.''

''And if we make the 'free choice,' as you called it, and do not accept,'' the Prime Minister asked as he leaned forward to stare right back.

''Then we wash our hands of the whole matter,'' Bannon stated firmly. ''I have a major speech scheduled for the nineteenth. I'll describe the terms offered, and what your answer is. If you reject, all the Saudi and U.S. aid disappears forever. You will be going your way while the policy of my government goes another. We will invoke the terms of the 1952 Military Aid Agreement we have with you that prohibits the use of our equipment for other than defensive purposes. Your continued attacks on Lebanon violate that. So we'll place a complete military and economic aid embargo on you as we did on the Turks. I'll do this by executive order, and I have the votes to back it up in Congress. We'll also seriously downgrade the status of your bonds, limiting their sale in the United States to that of other foreign securities."

"That's blackmail!" The Defense Minister screamed.

"Not at all!" Bannon replied calmly with a faint smile. "As I said, it is a free choice, with consequences on each side. You have your interests and we have ours. We can no longer afford to jeopardize ours if you are not at least willing to share the risk a little. If you choose to go your own way despite the clear direction of our policy, then do so, but don't expect us to nurture you in that effort. There is a price."

"Mr. President, do you seriously think you can enforce this?" the Prime Minister asked skeptically.

"Gentlemen . . . do you seriously think I'd be sitting here if I couldn't?" He looked around as their confidence began to visibly evaporate. "You know my background. Oh, I'm sure you can make a fight of it, but I'll win. You can accept the deal now while there are some major advantages for you, or you can fight us and end up with nothing. Think it out, have your people in Washington check behind me. It's a stacked deck, but the deal is a good one."

"We will not be treated like this, like some third-rate banana republic that you can sail into and order around," the Defense Minister lashed out.

"Quite the contrary. These days we can't order anyone around even if we want to. It's the Achilles heel of big power politics. Actually, I'm trying to treat you very much like a first-rate power by demonstrating that there are concerns that go beyond your narrow situation and by demonstrating that if Israel and the U.S. are to have an enduring, co-equal relationship, there are problems on each side that the other must recognize and respond to. We are in trouble and we are asking for your help. If you are a true partner you'll give it even though it will hurt. If you are only in it for yourselves, you won't and we'll redefine the relationship."

The room was silent for several long minutes as they stared at each other. "You have really got the Arabs to sign all of this?" the Foreign Minister questioned.

"Yes." Bannon bent down to pull a thick folder out of his briefcase. He handed it across the table. "It wasn't easy . . . so look them over carefully. It has complete reciprocal recognition, full treaties, and the rest of the details we discussed.''

The Prime Minister stared down at the neat package, his eyes unblinking. Finally he looked up at Bannon. He had the look of a very old man. ''But at such a very high price . . . very high,'' he said as his voice trailed off into silence.

14

Friday, October 16

"Hi. Is this Mr. Murphy?" asked the softest female voice he'd heard in a long, long time.

"Well, I guess it could be, dependin' on who's doing the calling."

"Great! I'm really glad I was finally able to get you. I'm kind of a free-lance public relations consultant, if you know what I mean. A very nice gentleman from a Mideast export company asked me to give you a call. He said he just did some business with you and you'd know just what I meant. It seems he was very, very pleased with how it all came out," she said coyly.

"Oh! Yes, I guess I do, now that you mention it, darlin'."

"I knew you would," she gushed. "Because he was so very appreciative of your fine efforts, I'd hate to think I had the wrong Murphy. You see, he's very busy and he sometimes hires me to do special assignments like this for him. He wanted to be sure you were thanked properly, and I'm . . . in business to make sure people are given only the warmest regards."

"Well, now! That was very thoughtful of him, wasn't it?"

"Oh, yes, very thoughtful," she laughed huskily. "He said I should phone you right away and see if there wasn't some time when we might be able to get together so I could express his warmest regards . . . personally," she emphasized.

"Personally? Well, we all know what a very dear and generous man he is, indeed!" Murphy said, playing right along.

"Yes . . . and he didn't think he'd be able to thank you the way he thought you really should be . . . personally. Maybe you could come over to my place, say this evening? I've kept the evening free just for you."

Murphy was trying very hard to keep himself under control. "You know, I think that might be a grand idea," he stammered.

"Great! How about nine o'clock? I'm in a cozy little apartment in New Town. Twenty-three eighteen North Clark, Two–B. The door is right next to the Disco Lounge. I can count on your being there, now, can't I?"

"Oh, darlin' . . . with bells on. After all, you know how these foreign people get when you don't accept their hospitality. It's like an insult! Kind of lose face, you see. And I wouldn't dream of insulting the man!"

"See you at nine then," came the singsong reply.

Murphy wiped the saliva off the mouthpiece as he hung up. "Well, I'll be damned!" He snorted to himself. "The man's a bastard, but there's no denying he's got class. That he does."

"Who was that on the phone, Thomas?" his wife called out from the kitchen.

"Oh, just some business, darlin', just business. I have to go out tonight. It's another shipment of goods I have to attend to at the airport. Always some problem, you know. I'll probably be out very late." He called down the hall. "In fact, the way these planes and customs people operate, I may not be back until morning, so don't be worried."

"You do too much night work, Thomas. I sure hope they appreciate all the work you do."

"Oh, don't worry about that," he chuckled. "I'll be getting my rewards soon enough, I'm not worried at all."

Murphy finally found a parking space for his battered 1973 Chevrolet on a dim side street just off Clark. It was a few minutes after nine, so he quickly locked the doors and scampered off toward the better-lit street nearby. His eyes nervously scanned each dark doorway and shadow as he hurried along. It wasn't the kind of place where you took casual late-night strolls.

New Town wasn't new. It was an old neighborhood of three- and four-story walk-ups, bars, head shops, and discos. It had a brief fling with fashionability in the mid-seventies. Like Rush Street in the fifties and Old Town in the sixties, it had its day. But fads don't last long, and the smart money knows it. Ride it up, but don't ride it down. Just when things are really beginning to roll strong, look around to see where the new action is starting up. Take your money and run, there's always a gynecologist from the suburbs looking for a hot investment in a thriving club.

It was now well past its prime. By night it still had some of the old noisy glitter if you didn't look too closely. Its economy was now dependent upon hookers, drugs, and gay bars.

Murphy walked quickly up Clark until he finally found 2318. It was a narrow doorway in a four-story walk-up. The whole first floor was taken up by a lounge, and the band was just beginning to blast forth as he went through the door into the dimly lit vestibule. Inside, he scanned the bank of dented mailboxes, but most had no names, only numbers. To his chagrin, he noticed that the other exit from the vestibule was a steep staircase that went up to the second floor. He slowly took a firm grip on the handrail and began to labor up the long incline. Twice he stopped to catch his breath. There were very few things that would ever get him to attempt such a feat, but this just happened to be one of them, he thought. And she'd better be good!

When he finally reached the second-floor landing, he stood for a few moments to rest and mop his brow on the sleeve of his coat. Looking himself over, he tucked the tails of his shirt in around his large gut and hitched up his slacks. Feeling slightly more presentable, he stood up straight and walked over to apartment 2–B to give the door a firm, playful knock.

As much as he detested the strenuous exertion, he'd have walked to the top of the Sears Tower for the attractive, shapely brunette who answered the door.

"You must be Mr. Murphy. I'm Lilah. Come on in," she smiled. While he was having a quick look around the room, she was having a quick look at him and having a hard time keeping a straight face. The

165

rumpled, chunky Irishman with the whitish-gray shirt and narrow black tie was worse than she'd expected.

"Well, now," he said, turning around to get a better look at her. "It's a real pleasure to meet you, darlin', and why don't you just call me Tom."

"Great, Tom, let me take your coat. Say, why don't you go into the kitchen and pour us a couple of drinks. There's a bottle in there on the counter."

As Murphy walked on through the small apartment he noticed it was sparsely furnished. Just an old couch, a couple of cheap overstuffed chairs, and some end tables. No books, pictures, odds and ends, or other personal belongings. As he made the drinks, he saw that the kitchen also had only the barest array of appliances and utensils. The counters and stove didn't look like they'd seen a meal cooked in a long time. Must be the girl's business office, he thought with a snicker.

Walking back into the living room, he could see three doors along the far wall. One opened into a bedroom, as he could clearly see from the light of a small bedside lamp. The second opened into a small bath. The third door was closed, but must be a second bedroom or closet, he thought.

"I see you even got me some fine Irish whiskey," Murphy said in his most pleasant voice. "Just like our dear friend to remember all of my weaknesses." He plopped down on the couch next to her and handed over one of the glasses. "Here you go. A little toast is in order, I think. To our dear Mr. Teraki."

"To Mr. Teraki," she replied. "You know, Tom, he was really pleased with the work you did, from the way he talked to me. What's your secret—what did you do to make him that happy? I'd sure like to have him that happy with what I do for him—wow."

"Oh, it really wasn't all that much. Let's just say I was able to lay my hands on something he wanted," he said cautiously.

"It sure must have been something he wanted pretty bad." She decided to drop it there, rather than press her luck any further. "Tom, I'm going to slip into something more comfortable. Why don't you go into the bedroom and do the same. So I can express Mr. Teraki's thanks the way he told me to," she winked.

"You hurry on up, darlin', I'll be in there waiting." He gulped down the rest of the drink and walked lightly into the bedroom. Whistling along with the loud music coming up from the disco lounge on the floor below, he kicked off his shoes and threw his rumpled slacks onto a chair. Pulling off his damp shirt, he sat back on the bed in his red-and-white-striped boxer shorts and white socks. "All ready, darlin'," he sang out as he turned off the light.

After a few expectant moments, he heard a door open. Sitting with his hands folded in his lap, he craned his neck to see around the doorway.

He suddenly looked up to the dark figure of a very large man coming through the doorway toward him. The shape was back-lit by the lights from the living room and Murphy couldn't make out any features. To the rear he now could see a second man stop just inside the doorway.

"What the hell is this," he bluffed nervously as he stood up. "If this is some kind of a setup, I'll wring that bitch's neck. You don't know who you're—"

His angry voice was cut off in midsentence by a short, powerful punch to the solar plexus. He never even saw the gloved hand coming. Murphy crumpled to the floor like a large fat balloon with the air let out, gasping and clawing for breath.

"Get up, Murphy," Ullman said in a quiet, bored voice. He watched Murphy lay on the floor wheezing. "Get up, I said . . . now!" The voice was more ominous. Getting no response, he gave the Irishman a sharp kick on the shin.

"Oh, Lord, stop," Murphy called out. "I'll . . . I'll get up, wait." Slowly he dragged himself up the side of a chair and leaned on it, holding his stomach.

"Get in the kitchen. I said move!" Ullman said harshly.

"All right, all right," he said as he limped across the room. "God, I feel sick." Once into the living room, he turned on his sore leg and made a break for the front door. He hadn't gone three steps before the big man caught up and slammed one of his boots into Murphy's back. He flew forward and smashed into the hard wood door, coming to rest in a heap on the floor.

Ullman walked over and pulled Murphy's head up roughly by the hair. "That was a very stupid thing to try to do!" Looking down into Murphy's dazed but terrified eyes, Ullman gave him a short, chopping right cross that flattened his nose.

Ullman released his grip on the hair and Murphy's head bounced unconsciously off the wood floor. He stood up and reached for the girl's glass on the end table. After taking a slow swallow, he threw the rest in the Irishman's face.

The cold sting of the whiskey brought him around, but he just lay there moaning.

"Murphy," Ullman called. Getting no response, he jabbed him in the ribs with the toe of his boot. "Murphy!"

"Yeah, yeah," came the hoarse, nasal reply.

Ullman bent down and grabbed him by the chin. Twisting it around to where he could look directly into Murphy's eyes, he said, "You dumb shit. You're too stupid and too slow to even try that crap with me. The next time you don't do exactly what I tell you, I'm going to have to start getting rough with you. Now get up!"

"Okay." He cowered. "Don't hit me." He slowly rose to his feet, wobbling and leaning against the wall.

"Now get into the kitchen and sit down in that chair."

Ullman turned to the girl who was standing in the bathroom with her coat on. "Nice job, Lilah. Go on down to the car and wait for us there. We won't be very long. But before you go, wipe off everything you touched, and take that glass with you."

He followed closely behind Murphy and prodded him in a straight line to the chair. He slumped down on it heavily.

"Put both of your hands out flat on the table, palms down so I can see them." Ullman took up a position on the far side and leaned over menacingly.

"Who are you guys, huh?" Murphy asked. "You can't do this to me, you know. There's laws in this country. You FBI bastards can't just come in here like this and roast a guy around." He was getting a little of his old bravado back. "I'll have my lawyer on you first thing in the morning, then we'll see who's hurting."

Ullman slowly began to walk around the small kitchen. "Shut up and keep your eyes riveted on that far wall, Murphy." He walked around behind him and watched the sweat run down the middle of the fat man's back. "We aren't the FBI, but you're going to wish we were before too long! No, Murphy, this is the big leagues now. You've been messing around with something way out of your class this time. If you don't start talking real polite, and only when I tell you to, you'll need a lot more than a lawyer in the morning."

Mouse stood in the doorway watching Ullman work. He was terrified, even if the Irishman might not be.

Ullman began slowly and calmly. "It's very simple, Murphy. We want to know about the Arab, Teraki you called him. Describe him to me, everything you can remember about him."

For the first time, Murphy detected a slight accent and a wave of nauseating fear passed through him. "I was just clowning around with the girl. She made the big come-on, so I played along. I don't know anybody named Teraki, I was just putting the bitch on. You see, I was—" Suddenly his head exploded in excruciating pain as Ullman's two cupped hands slammed into his ears.

Murphy screamed and crashed forward onto the table in agony.

Ullman let him stay for a few moments as he looked over toward the Egyptian with the look of an arrogant professor demonstrating to a hopelessly backward student. Turning away, he walked back to the far side of the table.

"Okay, Murphy, let's get back with the program. Sit back and put your hands on the table." As he complied, Ullman could see his face was livid and lined with pain. "That's better, Murphy. Head throb a little? Could be a lot worse, but that was just your first warning." He leaned over so their faces were very close to one another. "Let's get this straight. This is no joke at all! I do this for a living. If you don't start telling me exactly what I want on cue, I'll slowly tear you into little pieces. Your pals in Belfast are complete amateurs compared to me. The only prayer you have at all of not dying very painfully right here tonight is if you tell me everything you know. So stop the bullshit! You hear me."

Ullman slowly lit a cigarette and inhaled deeply. He watched Murphy's eyes and could see the pain and terror behind them. "Every time you give me some shit," he said, "I'm going to give you more pain than you can imagine."

"All right . . . all right," the fat man said, frightened now.

"Good. Now tell me about the Arab."

"He's dark . . . late thirties, maybe. Black hair, short, parted. He's about six feet tall, I guess, but he looks big, well built, maybe two hundred pounds. He speaks pretty good English, but with an accent. . . . I don't know, what the hell do you want me to say?"

Ullman looked over at Mouse, who handed him an envelope. He took out a grainy eight-by-ten glossy. "This isn't the best picture, but it's good enough. Is this Teraki?" Ullman held it in front of Murphy's face.

The Irishman closed his eyes and nodded. "Yeah, that's him."

"What were your past dealings with him?"

"Mostly one way. He gave us money and got us weapons . . . kind of coordinated with us over here for the Libyans and the PLO."

"When was the last time you saw him, exactly."

The Irishman became very nervous.

"Murphy!" Ullman said sharply.

"A week ago . . . a week ago . . ." he stammered.

"Where?"

"Here. Here in Chicago, out near the airport."

"What day was that, and what time?"

"Uh, Friday, last Friday, the evening, about ten o'clock."

Ullman was silent for a few moments. "What was it that you got for him?"

Murphy sat silent again, too scared to answer. Before he could react at all, the big man's gloved hand flashed out from behind his back. Murphy saw the glint of steel, but was too stunned to move as the powerful arm drove a ballpeen hammer down onto the back of his open hand. Murphy felt the bones crack. He stared down with his eyes gaping. As the pain shot up his arm, he screamed, "Oh, my God. You . . ."

Ullman stood there shaking his head. "Murphy, how many more demonstrations do you need? Now stop screwing around. And God is the very last place you'll ever get any help from. Scream all you want, no one in this neighborhood will even bat an eyelash."

As Murphy's eyes were drawn upward, Ullman tapped the hammer lightly against the palm of his hand, then laid it onto the table. Leaning back on the cabinet, he saw that Murphy's eyes never left the tool. "Looks like this is going to be a longer evening than I thought," Ullman said.

"Are you crazy?" Murphy screamed.

"I guess I am!" Ullman replied with a laugh. His face suddenly turned savage as he leaned forward again. "Now put your other hand down on the table. If it isn't there when I want it, I'll use the hammer on your fat head!"

The trembling hand slowly came up and was laid on the table as if it were a bed of coals. "Okay. Okay. I'll tell you anything you want to know, just leave me alone. Okay?"

"That's better. Now we'll pretend you didn't hear me the first time. And if I don't get the truth, I'll turn your hand into a bag of Jello . . . then I'll start working my way up."

Murphy swallowed hard to keep the bile from rising in his throat.

"Now what did Teraki want?"

"He needed some equipment."

"How do you contact him?"

"We don't, he contacts us . . . except once. I had to send him a telegram to a P.O. Box in Washington. Normally he'd just phone and I'd meet him at some hotel out near O'Hare, a different one each time. He's a very careful type. Doesn't trust us."

"I can't understand why not. What was in the telegram, what did you tell him?"

Ullman saw the Irishman was really terrified now. There was something he was hiding. But it wouldn't stay hidden for long, he thought. His fist lashed straight out and smashed into Murphy's already battered face. The sound was like a week-old Halloween pumpkin being flung onto cement.

Mouse watched Murphy's head snap back. His body rocked back and then collapsed forward as it crumpled onto the table. "If you kill him, we'll never find out anything!" Mouse raged.

"Oh, shut up, he's a long way from getting killed. Get me a glass of water." When Mouse finally handed it to him, he threw it in Murphy's face.

Murphy's eyes fluttered open as he lay with the side of his face in a pool of water and blood.

"Wake up, sweetheart, the dance has hardly started," Ullman said as he pulled the slumped form back to a sitting position. "Now talk. What was in the message?"

"That . . . that he could pick up his order . . ." Murphy shook his head to clear away the fog. "Look, if I really tell you some things you don't know, if I really cooperate, will you let me go?"

"That depends on whether it's something we really want to know, and on whether or not it's the truth." Ullman sat down on the other side of the table. "Get started, before I lose my patience again."

"It's the truth, I swear it is to Mother Mary. Look, I know the guy isn't from Washington."

Ullman didn't bat an eyelash as he asked, "How?"

"Well, I hate the bastard. I didn't trust him any more than he didn't trust me. I wanted a little protection, just in case . . ." Murphy's eyes became filled with hate. "He was always threatening me, treating me like some dirt, like I was too stupid, you know. So I decided to learn a little more about that heathen bastard. Always so damn superior he was. Indeed!"

Murphy's eyes had a faraway look, so Ullman let him go on without breaking the spell. He knew the Irishman had reached the point where it would all just flow out without any further prodding.

"When he met me at the airport hotel this last time and took the van, I had one of my boys put a small, high-frequency radio transmitter onto the muffler. Way up underneath where he'd never find it. We went after him, me and one of my boys," he laughed painfully. "All the way back east, we did. Well, we just followed him straight on back to Virginia! Drove all the night through . . . and us right behind him, about three miles back, we was." He started to smile but winced in pain. He turned up to Ullman and asked, "I'm in pain, man. Can I at least have a drink?"

Ullman nodded to Mouse and said, "Go on."

While Mouse poured out several fingers of whiskey into the glass, the Irishman continued. "He went all the way to Washington, like we thought he'd do, but then he went around on the expressway and drove past into Virginia." When Mouse handed him the glass, Murphy nodded thankfully and drank it half down in the first gulp. He closed his eyes as the searing flame of the uncut whiskey burned a path down his raw throat. He coughed and savored the lift it gave him for a few seconds.

"He . . . he went on down the Interstate and east to Williamsburg. When he got off there, we pulled up a little closer so we could get him in sight. He stopped there. That was where he was going . . . the Colonial Arms Motel."

"What did you do after that?" Ullman asked quietly.

"Nothing. We got a room in another hotel across the street where we could watch. That was Saturday afternoon. He never came out until Monday. We just sat there and waited. Monday morning, he and another guy left and drove off in the van. We followed them again. They went up to a town named Columbia, about an hour away. He picked up a big red and white camper van from a garage.'' Murphy looked up at Ullman again and shrugged. ''That's all. He's a real bastard, that one. I didn't want to take no more chances of getting caught, so we drove back home. I just got back here Tuesday afternoon.''

Ullman sat quiet for a few minutes as he tried to figure out the pattern.

''What do you think he's up to?'' the Israeli asked.

''I don't have the slightest idea,'' Murphy replied.

''What was in the van? What did you get for him?''

Murphy had the panicked look in his eyes again, so Ullman sat forward once more and looked down at the hammer.

''No . . . wait,'' he stammered. ''Look, you're Jews, aren't you? Israelis. That's what this mess is all about, isn't it?'' Murphy looked quickly from one of them to the other. ''Holy Jesus. I never done nothing to you people. I had to cooperate with the bastard, don't you see? We need their help to fight the British, just like you did. That's all we want, to throw the damn British out. But sometimes we get forced to help these Arab bastards out. . . . You know how it is. They're a lot of heathens, but it's none of our business. We just had to help him. Don't you see, for God's sake?''

A very hard look crossed Ullman's face. ''Murphy,'' he said through his clenched teeth, ''what did you get him!''

''Oh, Lord . . . We stole something for him from an Armory. He paid us a hundred thousand to get it for him. . . . I couldn't refuse. You gotta understand that,'' he pleaded.

Ullman picked up the hammer.

''Okay. Okay. It . . . It was a mortar, a really big one, one of those Four-Deuces they call it, a four-point-two-inch mortar. I don't have the slightest idea what he wants with the damn thing, I swear.'' His eyes darted between them again. ''We stole some other stuff too, but we kept all that for ourselves. All he wanted was the mortar, and two dozen rounds of ammunition to go with it.'' His eyes were pleading now.

''Good Lord!'' Mouse groaned out loud as he leaned against the doorway.

Ullman laid the hammer back down on the table. For once, it was the calm inquisitor who was stunned into unbelieving silence. A shiver ran up his spine as the consequences of what he'd just heard sunk in.

Gradually, his eyes came back in sharp focus as he felt the hatred toward the fat Irishman rise up in his throat. Bringing his emotions just under the fine line of control, he smiled faintly and asked, "All right, Murphy. Is there anything else you remember, anything he might have said about what he was going to do with it? Anything!"

"No, just that he had something big planned, and we'd like it. It would have some benefits for us, too. That's all. He never said what he was up to, and I knew not to ask."

"Nothing else?" Ullman leaned forward to closely watch his eyes.

"No . . . that's all, I swear it," he replied, staring straight back. "That's all I know," he pleaded.

Ullman looked at him for a moment longer. "You did fine, Murphy, fine."

The Irishman slumped down in his chair, numb from the ordeal. He looked up slowly as he saw the Israeli pull an automatic out from under his arm. In the brief second it took for the barrel to line up on the gap between his eyebrows, he barely had time for one agonizing groan. His eyes were frozen on the small black hole of the silencer six inches in front of his face.

Murphy never heard the soft phut!phut!phut! as his view suddenly went crimson red with a brief flash of searing pain.

The heavy 9 mm. bullets blew the top half of Murphy's head off, splattering the kitchen cabinets and sink with blood, bone, hair, and brains. The violent impacts rocked him backward, tipping the chair over. His limp carcass crashed to the floor, pulling the table over on top of him.

Mouse could not move. He could only stand in the doorway gaping at the sight. Finally he whipped around to Ullman and shouted in anger, "You . . . You had no reason to kill him like that!"

"I had every reason to kill him like that . . . or much worse if I had the luxury of time," he spat back with contempt. "Just what the hell did you think I was going to do, let him go?" He slid the automatic back inside the coat. "You're as stupid as Halperin. What the hell do you think this is all about? I should take you over there and stick your face in it so you won't forget, because there's going to be a lot more people die worse than that if we don't find Rashid before he uses that little toy Murphy got for him. Just remember that!" He glared savagely.

Ullman turned away and said, "Get the glasses and the bottle and shut up. Wipe off everything we touched."

After he made his final check, Ullman went back into the kitchen and pulled out a bold black magic marker. He wrote across the cabinet doors. DEATH TO ALL INFORMANTS and IRELAND LIVES.

As he locked the front door of the apartment, he said, mostly to himself, "There, that should have them at each other's throats for a while."

After they dropped the girl off, Ullman drove straight out of town toward the airport. They both sat in silence, trying to figure out what their next move should be.

After twenty minutes, Mouse was the first to speak. "If we can assume Murphy told us the truth, and I think he did as best he knew it, we've finally got our first lead on Rashid," he said, turning to face Ullman. "If he really was in Williamsburg only four days ago, then we'd better get down there before the trail gets any colder. He has his weapon now, so whatever he's planning, we don't have much time left."

"You're right," Ullman conceded as he thought on. "We'll catch the first plane back to Washington and check in with Halperin. We've got to get this on the wire back to headquarters."

"Why don't you do that?" Mouse said. "It doesn't take both of us. Meanwhile, I'll go straight on down and start checking around. Every hour might be important. Maybe our networks can tell us what it all means."

"Okay," Ullman said halfheartedly. "Just don't try to get too close to Rashid. Some phone calls and distant snooping, that's all. I'll be there in a few hours, so don't tip our hand!"

"Don't worry," Mouse replied. "I have a healthy respect for my life."

15

Saturday, October 17

It was almost noon when Ullman rushed through the front door of the embassy. Late flights and slow cabs, he swore to himself.

"Is Halperin here?" he asked the startled receptionist.

"No, sir, he just left for lunch and I believe he said he had a meeting to go to after that, but he'll be back."

"See if you can track him down, it's important. Tell him Ullman is back and to come down to the conference room as soon as he can get there." He strode away impatiently without waiting for a reply.

Once inside the conference room, he threw his bag in the corner and picked up the phone.

"Give me the communications center." The time dragged as he stood there. "This is Ullman, Colonel Ullman. I want this teletype down here in the basement put on line to Jerusalem immediately. Get me through to Mossad headquarters, Priority Red. Ask them to get General Gershon on the line, eyes only. And I want the line scrambled and secure at both ends. Call me back as soon as you have them."

He sat down at the table and lit up the first of a long series of cigarettes. The time passed slowly as he watched the silent machine sit there against the wall.

Twenty minutes later, the lights came on as it chattered out a few test letters. The phone rang and the communications officer said, "We've got them on the line for you, sir, but they're still looking for the general."

"Fine, I'll take it from here. You get off the line."

He pulled a chair over to the console and began to type.

ULLMAN HERE. IS GENERAL GERSHON PRESENT? U.

He sat quietly and waited for the reply.

NEGATIVE. WHAT IS YOUR MESSAGE?
GET GERSHON! U.

Smart-ass clerk, Ullman thought.

STANDBY.

It was thirty minutes before the machine sprang back to life.

GERSHON HERE. WHAT THE HELL IS SO IMPORTANT, URI? G.

That sounds like the old boy, Ullman thought.

REAL PROBLEMS! TRACKED RASHID TO CHICAGO HE HAS
MET WITH THE IRA. PURCHASED A US 4.2 INCH MORTAR AND
SHELLS. NOW BELIEVED IN WILLIAMSBURG, VIRGINIA. WAS
THERE EARLIER IN WEEK. OBJECTIVE UNKNOWN. ANY
THOUGHTS? OBVIOUS CONDITION AMBER, REPEAT AMBER. ASSUME
IMMINENT. EGYPTIAN THERE, I WILL FOLLOW. ADVISE. U.

He punched transmit again and lit another cigarette.

Minutes passed as he waited. Finally the machine clattered,

STANDBY. WILL RESPOND. G.

"Damn," he swore.

It was late evening in Jerusalem. Gershon stood stiffly as he reread the message. The conclusion was obvious.

He picked up a phone and dialed the Defense Minister's private number.

"This is Gershon. I hate to bother you this late, but can you come over to Mossad headquarters right away? It's important. It has to do with that American problem we were discussing this afternoon. . . . Good, I think you'll find it's worth the trip. I'll be in the signals room."

He turned to the clerks in the room and said, "When the Defense Minister gets here, I want all of you out, got that!"

It took twenty-five minutes for him to get there. He threw his coat over a vacant chair and turned to the general. "All right . . . I'm here, now what's up?"

"This just came in from Ullman," he replied with a barely concealed smile. "If you remember, he's in the United States, trying to track down a very nasty PLO colonel who is missing. 'Amber' is our internal code for a probable local terrorist action at the location of the sender." He handed over the message and watched the Minister's face as he read the message.

Gershon continued on, "You realize what this means. . . . I remember that in the transcript of the meeting with Bannon, it said he was going to be giving a speech in Yorktown. I've been there. It's just down the road from Williamsburg. It's no coincidence . . . the dates and places just don't match together like that by accident. Not with a guy like Rashid. Not with a weapon like that. He's after Bannon."

The Defense Minister read the message again in silence. He looked up at Gershon with a look of complete bewilderment. "But why? The treaties we've been going over give them everything they want. It's insane! Arafat has already signed them. Why would this Rashid go after Bannon?"

Gershon shrugged. "Who cares? When were the treaties signed?"

"By Arafat? Just a few days ago."

"So, in all likelihood, the PLO knew nothing about the deal until just a few days ago! Bannon's little secret may cost him his life."

"The Secretary of State said that it was all worked out between the United States and the Saudis, and the other parties were only brought into it when Bannon got over here, or not much before, anyway."

"That could be the key," Gershon said as his expression lit up. "This Rashid has been missing for several weeks. Let's suppose he's off on a top secret job, as this would be, and now Arafat can't get hold of him to call him off. Or maybe Halperin was right and the guy is off on his own with some personal score to settle. But it doesn't matter to us, does it?" He broke into a broad grin. "And it's so damned ironic, isn't it!"

The Defense Minister's eyes grew hard and cold as he nodded. "You have a point there. If Rashid makes a play for Bannon, for whatever reason, it will really undercut the Arab position. Their credibility would be in shreds. Yes," he mused with a thin smile. "And I don't see that it would matter much to us whether he succeeded or not. Bannon's no big friend of ours, and a martyr would just inflame the Americans that much more."

Gershon leaned back in the chair and roared with laughter. "And that dumb bastard Rashid doesn't even know!"

The Minister sat down quietly and reread the message. He looked across at the general and said, "Let's take this very slow. We must be sure we aren't making any mistakes. We must be completely out of the picture. Let's get Ullman back on the line."

Ullman sat on the edge of the table watching his feet dangle in circles, bored and impatient. His head shot up as he heard the machine start to type out the long-awaited response.

ARE YOU ALONE? G.

YES. U.

AM HERE WITH DEF. MIN. DO AMERICANS KNOW ABOUT RASHID'S MISSION, LOCATION, OR MORTAR? G.

NO. ONLY THAT HE IS MISSING. U.

CAN HE BE TRACED AGAIN THROUGH CHICAGO? G.

NO. TERMINATED. U.

There was another long pause before the machine clattered.

STANDBY. G.

Ullman sat back in the chair and waited, wondering what they could be debating for so long.

WE DO NOT WANT YOU TO INTERFERE WITH RASHID ANY FURTHER.
G.

Ullman read the paper in disbelief and began to slowly type:

PLEASE SAY AGAIN??? U.
WE DO NOT WANT YOU TO PURSUE OR INTERFERE WITH RASHID
ANY FURTHER. REPEAT, ALLOW HIM TO PROCEED AS HE IS DOING.
BUT WE DO NOT WANT OUR INVOLVEMENT UP TO THIS POINT TO
BECOME KNOWN. WE HAVE OUR REASONS. G.

As he stared down at the message, he slowly began to smile. He understood what they were doing, but not why. Not that that made any difference, he thought. He'd find out, or they'd tell him when they wanted to.

All nice and neat, he thought, except for one small complication.

ROGER! WILL COMPLY. WHAT ABOUT THE EGYPTIAN? HE IS
ALREADY IN HOT PURSUIT. U.

There was another long pause after he put the ball back in their court.

IMPERATIVE THAT NO ONE INTERFERE WITH RASHID AT THIS
TIME, OR AT LEAST FOR THREE DAYS. ALSO IMPERATIVE THAT
OUR INVOLVEMENT UP TO NOW BE KEPT STRICTEST SECRET.
SUGGEST YOU USE YOUR BEST JUDGMENT AS TO HOW THAT CAN BE
ACCOMPLISHED. BUT NO ONE CAN BE ALLOWED TO INTERFERE WITH
RASHID! G.

"Well, I'll be damned," he mumbled to the machine, knowing full well what the order meant. "That sly old fox!"

WHAT ABOUT HALPERIN? U.
KEEP HIM IN THE DARK IF YOU DON'T THINK HE CAN BE

RELIED UPON. WE'LL ORDER HIM BACK HERE FOR REASSIGN-
MENT IN A FEW DAYS. BUT COVER ALL YOUR TRACKS! WE'LL
REST UPON YOUR JUDGMENT. G.

Ullman thought about it for a minute as he lit another cigarette. He couldn't think of anything he couldn't handle by himself.

ROGER. WILL COMPLY. U.
AFTER YOU HAVE, RETURN HERE IMMEDIATELY AND CLEAR
THE AREA. WE DON'T WANT YOU ANYWHERE NEAR THERE ON
THE 19TH. G. OUT.

"You realize what we've just done." The Defense Minister turned nervously toward Gershon.

"We haven't done a thing . . . not a thing. We had some people check on the whereabouts of a suspicious Libyan attaché, but they found nothing. We tipped the Americans off to be looking for him, but we aren't the FBI. How could we have any idea what he was up to?" Gershon stated very matter-of-factly. "Now just because that crazy Arab happens to do the only thing right now that could save the State of Israel . . . well, that just couldn't be helped, could it?"

"This scares the hell out of me, though."

"Why? There are only three people who know about this, and it'll be our job to see that it goes no further. I'll have every piece of paper on Rashid destroyed tonight. Ullman's my best man, and I trust him completely. If anything else starts to unravel later, like Halperin; well, we'll just have to snip off a few loose ends if we have to. But now isn't the time! Everything has to look normal right up to the afternoon of the nineteenth." Gershon's eyes narrowed to two dark slits. "You do see my point, don't you?"

The Defense Minister's face grew pale as he turned away. "Yes, I know you're right. But it still scares the hell out of me. If it leaks, they'll hang us."

"But if it works, the three of us will have the silent satisfaction that we did more for the future of our people than a whole armored corps could do. We just have to go about our business like nothing happened . . . and not lose our nerve!" he said pointedly.

"Let's hope you're right," the Defense Minister said, looking vacantly in the direction of the teletype machine. "Let's hope you're right."

Ullman had just locked the conference room door and was turning to walk down the hall when he saw Halperin come out of the elevator.

"You should have phoned and told me you were coming back here," Halperin called out, "I could have met you at the airport."

"No problem. We had a hard time getting a flight, and there was just no time. It was better you stay here." Ullman said with a faint smile as he stuffed the folded teletype sheet into his coat pocket.

Halperin looked around and asked, "Where's Mouse?"

"He's, uh, he's out at the airport. Yes," Ullman said, looking at his wristwatch. "Damn , I didn't notice how late it was. I'm heading back out there right now to meet him. We've decided to take a try at Los Angeles."

Halperin frowned in surprise. "No luck at all in Chicago?"

"No, a complete waste of time. Just like New York."

"Huh! That's really surprising. I would have put money on Chicago. . . . Nothing? If it was a waste of time, I hate to think of what L.A.'s going to be."

"You never can tell. Oh, I just spoke with General Gershon to bring him up to date on our progress. He agreed that we should go on out to L.A., but he thinks they may have picked up some leads on Rashid finally. Nothing definite yet, but they think he's in Damascus."

"Damascus! That doesn't make any sense."

"It may not fit your theory, but that's where they think he is. Anyway the focus of the search has shifted. You can kind of relax here. Take the weekend off, he said. We can call you at home if anything turns up, but I really doubt it will. I'm probably going to fly straight home from L.A., so it may be a while before we meet again."

"I don't understand any of this. How could it change this quick?"

"You don't have to understand, that's just the way it is!" Ullman snapped. He suddenly smiled again and wiped his hand across his forehead. "I'm sorry. Look, I've been a little short on sleep the past few days. As I said, the guy's probably slipped out and is back in Damascus. That's what Gershon said, and I'm hardly going to question him. His judgment isn't usually too far off."

"Yeah, Okay. I'm just surprised, that's all."

182

"That's the way it goes sometimes."

"Should I at least check with the FBI again?" Halperin asked.

"No, definitely not. Gershon doesn't want them out on any wild goose chases. Let's save our credibility with them for a time we may need it. We've pushed this thing far enough on too little. If they call you, tell them we are beginning to think there was nothing there. Suggest they drop it." Ullman put his arm around Halperin's shoulder as he steered him back toward the elevator. "By the way, Gershon said he liked the work you did on this even though nothing was there. He likes follow-through and attention to detail. There may be a nice surprise for you at the end of this, so don't blow it with the man now. Do exactly what he says, Okay?"

Halperin was completely puzzled by both the tone and the words that Ullman said. "Yeah . . . Uh, Okay, if you say so."

"Good, I do! Get some sleep. I've got a plane to catch."

16

Sunday, October 18

President Bannon stood before the dresser mirror in the State bedroom on the second floor of the Lightfoot House fighting with the last uncooperative pearl stud on his dress shirt. It was almost 6:00 P.M.

"Damn these things, Sid! Can you get this one?" He said, turning in desperation to Senator Jensen.

"Would you relax, Ed! It's just six now. You know the Israelis are going to keep haggling and going over the details right up to the last minute. They've had five Cabinet Meetings in the past three days. If Lang knew anything, he'd let us know."

"Dress shirts and long waits were two things I never could stand." He raised his chin while Jensen worked the stud into place. "I'd have never taken this job if I knew how much of each I'd be forced to put up with."

"There . . . got the little bugger. Now sit down and finish your drink! You know, I always thought it was the pressure of decisions that got to Presidents, aged them so soon, but it isn't. It's the waiting. I can see that being around you." Jensen paused as he took a sip of his own Scotch. "It's like being a fireman between fires. You know deep in your bones that something is going wrong right now. You know it! So you

184

keep looking at the alarm, waiting for the damn thing to go off and confirm your worst suspicions. And when it does, it's already too late."

"I suppose you're right. But at least the firemen know what to do when the alarm goes off. The thing that is most maddening around here is that every expert we have has a different way he thinks we should fight the fire. Every way except common sense. But with a big emphasis on hindsight."

They sat quietly and drank. Bannon looked up and said, "Another thing I noticed around the White House was how none of my predecessors ever kept any old pictures of themselves around, like at their inaugurations. As I looked in the mirror last month, I realized why.

"Maybe you should have the water checked—it could be the well has tapped into a reverse Fountain of Youth." Jensen's laugh petered out into an embarrassed silence.

Bannon went on as if he hadn't noticed. "You remember how Carter looked when he took office—Lord, he must have aged ten years, at least, in just four. I think every President dies in office. Sometimes they just have to wait a few years to bury us, that's all." He took another big swallow of the drink. "Damn! Where is he?"

Bannon got up and began to walk around the room. Reaching the front window, he paused to savor the view. It was nearly sunset and he thought that the sight was one of the prettiest he'd ever seen. The long, fading rays of the sun exploded through the red and yellow leaves of the trees outside, creating a spectacular autumn scene.

Turning back toward Jensen, he said, "I love this time of year here in Williamsburg. I always think it is tops, until I get down here in April when all the flowering trees are in bloom. The dogwoods, azaleas, and all the rest."

"Maybe when all of this is over, we can get appointed professors at William and Mary. Think HEW can swing that for us?"

"May take a couple of grants, but it isn't a bad idea," Bannon mused. As he looked back out the window, he shook his head and swore again, "Damn! Come on, Andrews. We've done nothing but wait for four days now. And those Israelis haven't given one hint as to which way the tree is going to fall."

Jensen shrugged. "At least they haven't turned us down yet."

"I hope to God they don't. My heart really isn't in that second speech." Bannon said with a pained look in his eye as he returned to the

185

chair. Sitting down, he paused to look wistfully around the room and say, "Six or seven years ago, I came here with Jerry Ford for his debate with Carter . . . you know, his famous Polish joke. He stayed here at the Lightfoot House and had some of us over for drinks. I've always loved it. True class! Authentic. Not some gussied-up imitation." He looked down and rubbed the arms of the chair with the palms of his hands. "Real eighteenth century. Helps to put things in perspective. Gives you real mental roots," he said with a satisfied smile.

"That's the magic of the town, I guess . . . makes things relative."

There was a knock at the door.

"Come in," Bannon said expectantly. As the door opened and Secretary Korshak walked in, Bannon said, "Oh, damn. Sorry, Louise, that really wasn't meant for you. Glad you finally made it."

"What a great welcome. I take it you still haven't heard anything."

"Very perceptive," replied Senator Jensen.

"Are all the computers ready to roll at your shrill command?" Bannon asked with a smile.

"Sure are. I have an army of colonels back there sitting by the phones ready for the sound of my whip . . . black patent leather, of course, to go with the boots they all assume I wear."

"I'll leave your management style up to you," Bannon said deadpan.

"Anyway," she went on, "the briefings are all set for the morning with the Congress and the diplomatic corps, press, and various political leaders, either here or by phone depending on where they are."

"Great, Louise, I appreciate it," Bannon said sincerely. "But from the looks of town, I imagine almost everyone is here. What's the weather report for tomorrow, anyway?"

"Perfect. Crystal-clear skies, high about seventy degrees," Korshak replied. They expect over two hundred fifty thousand people to be at Yorktown for the ceremonies, by the way."

"Well, one way or the other, it'll be a hell of a show," Jensen said. "Just imagine all the federal expense reports that will flow in on this trip next week."

Bannon shook his head. "When I see Governor Lane of Virginia tomorrow, I'm going to tell him that this whole thing was just cooked up as Yankee foreign aide to help out his depressed economy."

As they all laughed, Jensen asked, "When are you going to get with the other heads of state who are here?"

"I'll corner them at dinner tonight and ask them to ride over to the battlefield with me tomorrow. Fifteen minutes is all they'll need." Looking at his watch again, he said, "Almost showtime. Let's head on to the lodge. I want to work the crowd a little and do a little last-minute politicking."

They followed him out the bedroom door and down the steep open staircase to the first floor. "Larry!" Bannon called out to his aide, "let's go."

"Yes, sir. Your car is waiting out front."

"That's ridiculous. It's only a couple of hundred yards, we'll walk."

"Mr. President, the Secret Service gets real heartburn when I let you do that," his aide pleaded.

"A compromise," Bannon said, raising his hands. "We'll go out the back. Nobody expects to see the President coming out from between the garbage cans, right?"

"As you wish, sir," his aide sighed. "I'll be right with you."

"No, you stay right here by the phone. When Andrews's call comes in I don't want just the maid here to answer it! Then I expect you to beat feet and find me, wherever I am."

They walked out into the ornate boxwood flower garden so beautifully arranged behind the white picket fence. The sun had already sunk below the lodge off to their right. The strong, pungent aroma of the boxwood hedges was even more powerful in the still evening air.

"Louise," Bannon asked with a smile. "Do you think LaGrange would be mad if I decided to put my presidential library here instead?"

"Since all it will have is your collection of *Playboy*'s from 1968, I doubt they'll stay mad very long," she cracked.

They walked on across South England Street and turned up the crescent driveway of the lodge. Hearing footsteps quickly running up from behind, the half dozen Secret Service agents alertly spun around with their hands in their coat pockets.

"Mr. President," Larry panted as he caught up. "I've got it, sir! The Secretary just called and I wrote it all down. Here," he said as he handed Bannon the small slip of paper.

The sunset was no less beautiful as seen from a boat out in the middle of the York River thirty miles to the northeast. Most of the wide orange ball was just settling behind the dense line of trees along the far shore farther upriver. It cast the Yorktown side in deep shadows, while the Gloucester Point side was still bathed in a soft yellow light. Along its shore could clearly be seen the deep green pines, crimson maples, bright gold poplars, and russet oaks. They stood out in relief high above the narrow ribbon of white sand along the water.

It was spectacular, but even more spectacular to people accustomed to arid rolling hills, cedars, orange trees, and palms.

"What kind of fish did you say we were supposed to be looking for, anyway?" Arazi asked as he threw his line back in the water.

"The man said bluefish, or something like that," Rashid replied as he kept the boat on its meandering course upriver. "Just keep your line out. If anyone asks, say it's a slow night and ask them what bait they're using."

"This must not be a very popular time to fish," Arazi said as he peered up and down the river. "We're about the only boat out here."

"There's been a few around . . . but you're right. So let's not look any more conspicuous than we already do. It'll be dark soon, and I don't want to get to the bridge too quickly."

They'd finally come down to Tidewater that afternoon. For most of the past week it had been an aimless trek through the Blue Ridge country. In this season, one more camper wasn't noticed in all the crush of tourists. They changed campgrounds every night. Geting off on their own in some of the huge National Forests enabled them to find a nice secluded place to drill the intricate plotting, assembly, loading, and aiming. Day after day they practiced until it became automatic. Only one more detail required attending to.

The day before they left the mountains, Rashid went to an automotive supply store. The clerk was surprised but pleased when he bought all thirty-one cans of midnight blue touch-up spray paint in stock plus a dozen rolls of three-inch masking tape.

Alone in the woods all that afternoon, they carefully repainted the red trim on the truck and the camper to deep blue. They also gave a generous coat to the white top and added some new trim panels to the sides.

As Rashid looked over the finished job he said, "Well, Hafez, it isn't body-shop perfect, but it'll do. The main thing is it doesn't look like the truck we drove up here in. Yes, for a day or two, it will do.''

As they made the long drive to Gloucester from the valley Arazi said, ''So far things are going right along with your plan. I can't believe it!''

''That bothers me. I'd be a little less nervous if we'd had some trouble. No operation ever goes perfectly, so the longer we make it with no trouble, the more it sets me on edge. And this is such a slow-developing plan that I'm just waiting for someone to get a whiff of us somewhere. This's the time when we really have to be careful. We're on the last leg, so trouble now can be fatal. We must be very alert, always looking over our shoulders.''

They found a small boat marina downriver from Gloucester Point near Achilles. It was on a tributary of the York, mostly frequented by local people. When they told the owner they were looking to rent one of his seldom-used small boats for a week, and offered to pay cash, up front, he greeted them like long-lost cousins. And for an extra twenty dollars, he didn't mind at all if they just left the camper right there and slept in it.

''No problem at all, boys,'' he said. ''This way you can get a head start on the fish, and I've got someone to look after the place at night. Nope, it'll work out just fine for both of us.'' And the twenty dollars didn't hurt much either.

''Just throw the line out every so often,'' Rashid said. ''Try to look like a native.''

''We should have brought some Doctor Pepper and a couple of toothpicks.'' Arazi laughed to break the tension. ''If we really do catch something, maybe we'll find out if a bluefish is really blue. The water is sure cold enough.''

It finally got dark as they passed by the Coast Guard station off to their right. Well into the shadow of the bridge, Rashid steered straight for the third piling.

''We'll tie up here on the side away from the shore. Anchor it at both ends. I want to be sure it's still here when we come back down.''

Arazi found a large iron mooring ring set in the concrete and tied the rope off firmly. Looking around, he saw that most of the base of the piling was shielded by heavy wood beams that went up above the high water mark to protect the bridge from accidental bumps by passing ships.

The large rectangular concrete column stretched high above them into the darkness. It was eery down at water level. They could hear an occasional car pass across the steel panels and its movement vibrated down the piling, amplifying the rattle and hum of the rubber tires. On the water, it was chilly, damp, and very dark.

"All right, Hafez, let's go," Rashid said quietly as he took one last look around. They both slipped out of their coats and hats and slung the light haversacks across their backs. "Be careful of the wood pilings, they are very slippery—careful, but quick."

Once on top of the wood, it was easy to find the steel rungs sunk in the concrete. Their rubber-soled shoes bounced quietly as they scurried up rung after weary rung. Finally, they reached the top of the tall concrete pedestal where the steel legs of the superstructure were anchored.

Rashid pulled himself up onto the broad base, sitting down for a moment in the deep shadow. He could feel the tight ache in his thighs as the muscles complained of the brisk pace he'd set coming up. Closer to the top now, the rattle and hum of the passing cars were much louder. The steel around him came alive each time one went overhead.

As he looked up in the darkness, he could make out the thin gray lacework of steel as it spread upward, arching, connecting, back and forth between the larger vertical columns that went straight up to the platform of the bridge, and straight down to the square, steel base plate beneath his hands.

Rashid carefully pulled off his pack and took out the first of the heavily wrapped packages of plastic explosive. Looking it over, he pushed in the small radio-controlled detonator and turned on its receiver. Reaching up, he pushed the package firmly down into the crotch of the girders. He did the same with the other two. Painted gray, they could only be seen under the most detailed of searches. And if it ever came to that, it wouldn't make much difference anyway, he thought.

His parcels and the ones that Arazi was putting into place were on different frequencies. They'd been carefully checked and tested out to ensure they'd work when they were needed. They were supposed to be delivered to the IRA two months ago, but they didn't mind that the shipment was a little light. With two separate systems and frequencies, it gave him the extra little edge he liked to have. The odds were they'd both work flawlessly, but just in case, the other set was all they needed to get the job done. If only one went off, the bridge would be impassable and

190

would probably come down. But if they both went off, it would come down in a most spectacular fashion! They'd have a great view, he thought, too bad they'd be a little too busy just then to really enjoy it.

Looking over to his right, Rashid gave a soft whistle. A few moments later his answer came back and they both started down.

Moving back down the cold, damp rungs, he could feel the excitement grow within himself. The last of the many preliminary steps was now complete.

The planning phase had been finished a month ago. Now the preparation phase was done. As of this moment, they were in the execution phase.

This was what it was all about, he thought. Going back to his earliest days of training, this was the point you longed to reach. The execution phase meant a whole new set of parameters: maximum alert, a higher acceptable level of risk, combat readiness, guards out, weapons locked and loaded. Until now, they were prepared to walk away if success was not probable. Now they'd go on unless it became impossible. Before, they'd retreat in the face of any opposition. Now they'd eliminate it if they could.

Tomorrow, he thought. Less than eighteen hours. The long wait was almost over.

Tomorrow!

17

Halperin kept staring into the bare refrigerator. Resigned to his fate, he shrugged and pulled out the lone can of Budweiser, popped the top and took a long swallow. With his other hand he pulled out the half-full box of chocolate chip cookies from the bottom shelf and padded into the living room to enjoy his supper. Not exactly gourmet, he thought, but what the hell! Besides, one consolation about living alone was that the last can of beer was always there when you wanted it.

He flopped down on the couch and stretched his legs out on the coffee table, making room by shoving over the tall stack of unread magazines. The last half of the Nine O'Clock Movie was about to start.

Just as he was beginning to nod off, there was a knock at the front door. He got up and went down the long hall to the door. Opening it, he was greeted by a large dark man in an overcoat that he vaguely remembered from somewhere.

"Mr. Halperin. My name is Kamal," he said. "From the Egyptian Embassy. I believe we met a few months ago at a reception."

"Oh, yes, now I do remember. Mouse introduced us, you work for him. Sure." Halperin noticed a second Arab was standing against the far wall, looking at him over Kamal's shoulder. He glanced quickly at each

192

of them and began to get the picture. Kamal had a faint smile, but the other man had none at all.

Halperin asked tersely, ''What's up?''

Kamal replied politely enough, ''We hate to bother you at this late hour, but I would request for you to come downstairs with us for a few moments.''

''Why?'' Halperin asked warily. He didn't need ESP to guess these two had just got off the boat, and weren't the type you wanted to go on late-night walks with. ''Let's make it in the morning when we're all fresh,'' he said with a smile as he began to close the door.

''Mr. Halperin,'' Kamal said firmly as he stepped into the doorway, ''let's just say this is a personal request from our ambassador. He is down in his limousine waiting for us in the street. He just wants to have a few words with you, that's all.''

Halperin paused. He was skeptical, but he couldn't think of any other reason for these two bananas to be at his front door at this hour. ''Uh . . . sure, I guess so. Let me get my coat and a pair of shoes.''

He turned to walk back into the apartment and noticed the Egyptian following right behind him. ''Why not just get your shoes,'' Kamal said with a wooden smile. ''We'll only be a moment, and the car is heated.'' He followed Halperin all the way into the living room while the second man waited in the open doorway. They both had their hands in their pockets.

Spinning around angrily, Halperin snapped, ''What the hell is this?''

''As I said, just a personal request from our ambassador. We just have a certain security routine we go through, as I'm sure your people do. We won't be long. Please put your shoes on.'' The voice was still polite, but now even the phony smile was gone.

Halperin knew there was no sense trying to get away from these two; they had him well boxed in as they walked down to the ground floor. Both of them had the appearance of men who knew their work. And if the ambassador was downstairs, he'd look like an ass if he tried to bash it out with them. If he wasn't, the street was his best chance anyway. One thing was sure, Halperin thought, he wasn't getting into any car unless he saw a face in it that he knew.

Outside, the night air was cool. They walked up the sidewalk about two hundred feet to an unmistakable long, black Mercedes limousine with the small flag of the Egyptian Embassy on the fender and a diplomatic license plate. Well, Halperin thought, if it's a setup, these guys are on one hell of a budget.

Kamal opened the rear door and stood aside. The other man got in and went to the jump seat on the far side. "After you," he said. "The rear seat, please."

Halperin stuck his head in first and saw the familiar figure of the ambassador on the far side of the rear seat. "Come in, Mr. Halperin," he heard. "Don't mind Kamal's rather brusk manner, he's only doing his job. After all, he simply doesn't know what a good friend you are."

As Halperin sat down, he realized too late that there was the faintest undercurrent of distaste in the ambassador's voice, but it was there. Kamal sat down across from him on the other jump seat and Halperin could hear a soft metallic click as an electrically controlled door lock slipped into place. There was no handle on the inside, he noticed, it must be controlled by the driver. The car immediately drove off.

"Mr. Halperin . . . David, I believe Mustapha Khalidi calls you. I hope you'll excuse my disturbing you at this late hour, but it was important that we speak without delay. Anyway, it is a beautiful night for a drive around this lovely city, don't you think?" The voice was warm but precise as the Ambassador continued to stare at him from the window.

As Halperin looked back, he saw the man was small and delicate, like Mouse. By reputation, he had one of the best minds in town. This wasn't the type of guy to sling bullshit at, not if you didn't want to get sliced into very thin ribbons. "The city is very pretty," he conceded. "Now what is this all about?"

"Just a little conversation. Mustapha said you were very witty with conversation, Mr. Halperin. I thought I'd let you amuse me a little," he said as he turned toward the Israeli.

As their eyes locked, Halperin could see a tense anger just behind them that showed itself in the lines around the corners of his eyes and mouth. He stated, "From what Mustapha said about you, I assumed the two of you had become good friends over the past years, even before the peace."

"Yes." Halperin replied, looking directly at him. "Mouse is really top notch, personally and professionally. I like him and I respect him."

The ambassador sat quietly as he pulled out a leather cigar case.

Choosing a slim panatella, he bit off the tip and slowly lit it with a wooden match. The flame was very still, but above it Halperin saw the dark eyes never left him. "Would you tell me, precisely, what the two of you have been working on for the past couple of weeks, and what has developed so far."

"I assumed he'd been keeping you up to date on this Rashid thing?" Halperin said surprised.

"Bits and pieces, but I'd like to hear the whole thing from you." The ambassador put his arm across the rear of the seat and leaned a little closer.

So Halperin shrugged and began. For five minutes the ambassador sat intently listening to every word.

When he finished, the ambassador turned and looked back through the side window. "So..." he said quietly. "As of right now, you've found nothing. Mustapha and Ullman have gone to Los Angeles, they found nothing in Chicago, your people think this Rashid may be in Damascus, and the whole thing is fading away. Is that about where things are right now?" he asked as he turned back toward Halperin.

"Uh, yes," Halperin replied, puzzled.

"A couple of minor points..." the ambassador said wearily. "It was Ullman who told you all these things, correct?" He watched Halperin nod. "And you haven't actually seen or talked to Mustapha since they first arrived in Chicago?" Halperin nodded again. "And it was about two o'clock yesterday afternoon when you last saw Ullman, as he was heading to Dulles to catch a plane to Los Angeles?" Halperin nodded again, but with a noticeable trace of irritation.

"Right on all counts, Mr. Ambassador. Now what's the point of all this?"

The ambassador ignored the question as he inhaled deeply on his cigar. Halperin could see the dark eyes bore into him above its orange glow. "Halperin, that story is preposterous," he said nonchalantly. "Why would they fly here from Chicago, and then turn around and fly right back west to L.A.? If they found nothing in Chicago, wasn't the plan for them to go on to L.A. directly? The only reason for them to come here was if they did find something in Chicago. If they didn't, they'd have just phoned you and had you report on to Mossad. You could have done that, couldn't you?"

Halperin was silent as he replayed the events in his own mind. For the first time they didn't make any sense to him either.

The ambassador went on very slowly, pronouncing each word. "Did Ullman say anything to you about Virginia, or Williamsburg?"

"Williamsburg?" Halperin said, stunned. "No, nothing... What's going on?" he asked irritably. "Because I don't know what you're talking about."

"Well, Halperin, it is really quite simple," the ambassador said as he leaned closer and looked at him gravely. "The story you just told is accurate enough, until they reached Chicago two nights ago. From that point on, it is nothing but lies... nothing but lies!" He repeated harshly with a bold sweep of his hand. "They did get a solid lead on Rashid in Chicago, so solid that your Ullman had to kill an IRA man to shut him up! They were hot on Rashid's trail when they flew back here yesterday. And when Ullman left you he wasn't headed to Dulles Airport, he was headed to Williamsburg to meet Khalidi. That's where Rashid was a few days ago!"

Halperin raised his hands in a helpless, confused gesture. "But... that's crazy. That just couldn't be true.... how...."

"If it isn't true," the ambassador's eyes grew pained and malevolent, "explain to me why Khalidi's body was pulled from the James River at eleven A.M. this morning, weighted down, with three bullet holes in his head!"

Halperin slumped back in the corner and looked up the black ceiling in shocked silence. Now that the last pieces of the puzzle had crashed down into place, the picture they revealed made him sick. It was all too unimaginable, perverse and obscene.

As he looked down, he began to feel a deep personal grief mixed with his own rising anger and hatred. Looking into the face of the ambassador, their eyes locked for a few seconds as the beginning of understanding passed between them.

The ambassador's features softened as he went on quietly. "His body got tangled in some crab lines under a bridge. The police say it had been in the water for twelve to fifteen hours. We know he arrived in Williamsburg about three P.M. yesterday, by car, from Dulles. The police don't know all of this and they don't know who he is yet, either. His papers were for a front business we operate, so they phoned there." He turned to point forward. "Kamal went down there to check it out.

We can track his movements from the charge cards he used when he rented the car at Dulles and checked into the Hilton under one of the code names he uses. By the way,'' he said, turning back to Halperin, "neither one of them had any flights booked to Los Angeles. Khalidi was well on his way to Williamsburg before you even saw Ullman. But I doubt you'll see him again soon, since he flew to Rome at ten thirty this morning.''

Halperin cleared his throat and began in a whisper, "I don't have the slightest idea what happened to him. We were friends, I want you to know that! If you seriously think I had anything to do with his death, then why would I be stupid enough to get into this car with you . . . or even be around to answer the door?'' He looked slowly around at the three of them.

The ambassador lit another match and began to puff on his cigar again. Finally in a low voice he said, "No, I don't believe you had anything to do with it. You would have never told such a stupid story if you didn't think it was the truth.'' His eyes narrowed as he added, "But, for a few moments here I gave thought to having Kamal kill you and throw your body into Rock Creek. You see, there is still one very troubling aspect of this whole episode.''

"Ullman!'' Halperin said sharply.

"Precisely. When we picked you up, I thought Rashid had gotten Khalidi before Ullman arrived, or perhaps gotten both of them. I was mad, because Khalidi isn't that stupid, and I wanted to find out what went wrong and whose mistake got him killed. But now I can see that is not the case. Ullman's story could only have been intended to deceive you. He did not want you to know where he was going, or where Khalidi was, because he wanted to kill him without your knowing about it. But why?'' he screamed in frustration.

The logic was irrefutable and Halperin knew it. "I . . . I just don't know. Something must have . . . happened.'' His voice trailed off slowly as he began to remember his last conversation with Ullman. In the basement. He was just coming out of the conference room. He said he'd just finished talking to Gershon. Gershon! Halperin could feel his face flush in anger. He quickly leaned back against the cushion in the darker shadow of the corner. Gershon, he thought. Gershon! Or was that just another lie, too?

"But,'' Halperin asked, "how do you know all these details about what they were doing in Williamsburg?'' He had to deflect this conversation away, he thought. "You didn't say you spoke with Mouse?"

"Halperin, I've read your file and I know you're fairly new to this line of work, but still . . . we aren't rank amateurs! All of our operatives carry a small wire recorder when they are out in the field. It's built into an electric shaver. It was intended to enable them to keep notes and records as they progressed on an assignment, but it sometimes is useful in more unfortunate circumstances. Kamal retrieved it from Khalidi's room. Because it was under another name, the room had not been disturbed yet. We just had it transcribed before we picked you up. I assure you it was Khalidi's voice. His last message was at six thirty. He expected Ullman shortly." He turned to face Halperin again. "That's how I knew your story was so totally wrong . . . but it was so consistently wrong it became obvious that you were not involved." His eyes flashed for a second as he said. "But if even one detail had been correct after Chicago, you'd be dead right now!"

"What else was on the recorder?" Halperin asked nervously.

"Here's a copy of the transcript; you can study it yourself," the ambassador said as he threw an envelope onto Halperin's lap. He turned to the driver and said in Arabic to go to the Israeli Embassy. "I believe you have some work to do, David. I don't forget for one seond that both you and Ullman work for the Mossad. You find out why he murdered my man!"

As they drove on in silence the ambassador sat back in his seat and said quietly, "One more thing I want you to understand. I had the very painful duty to call Khalidi's father today and tell him of his son's death. He and I are very old friends from university days. Our children often played together and I loved Mustapha like my own son. . . . I had a very special obligation to his father since Mustapha was assigned to my staff. I'm trying to stay professional about this, but I swear to you that someone will pay for this act of extreme treachery. We Arabs don't threaten, we make prophesies!"

When they reached the embassy, Kamal got out and opened the door for Halperin. "Wait one second," the ambassador said. "When you get in touch with Jerusalem, I want you to make it very clear that we believe a representative of your government has murdered a representative of my government. Until they prove otherwise, I will still hold you responsible. I expect you to come to my office within twenty-four hours and give me an explanation. Don't make us come looking for you!"

198

PART
5

WASHINGTON, D.C.
OCTOBER 19, 1981

18

Early Morning

It was after midnight. He sat at his desk reading and rereading the short transcript and getting more confused and angry by the minute. Why? he thought. Why would they do this?

Halperin picked up a red pencil from his desk drawer and began to sift through the pages underlining the key facts. Be rational, he thought.

But he was rational! And in an ice-cold rage at the same time. The words weren't disembodied black type on white paper to him. They were alive. They spoke to him in the voice of a dead friend. That made Halperin mad, madder than he'd been since the Golan in '73. They had no right to do either one, he thought. No right at all!

So he began to read and underline.

... went to Chicago   Murphy set up   Ullman
interrogated him   broke him down   Teraki was
Rashid   met with him in Chicago on Oct. 9
$100,000   stole a 4.2-inch U.S. mortar
24 rounds of ammunition with it   Murphy tailed Rashid
to Williamsburg   there on the 12th   second man

with him   Colonial Motel   car   got camper truck
in Columbia   red and white   Dante's Garage
Ullman killed Murphy   shot him in the head   he's
one savage bastard . . .

Halperin's eyes were fixed on the words like they were an obituary. He nodded slowly as again the conclusion was unmistakable. But why?

. . . I came to Williamsburg   rented a car
Ullman to arrive soon   we'll move in together
I'm checking out the hotels and campgrounds by phone
Ullman's updating Halperin   still don't know
what Rashid's up to . . .   End of report

But why would Ullman lie to me? Why would he kill Mouse? Something happened. Something between the two times Mouse last saw Ullman, and that could only be one thing, Halperin thought. Ullman's conversation with Gershon. If it happened! If that wasn't just part of the con!

Halperin reached over and lifted the phone to his ear. He dialed the number of the communications center.

"This is Halperin. Let me speak to the signals officer. . . . Hi! Say, I'm trying to finish some reports up here and need some backup facts. You know how it is," he laughed. "How about checking the signal log for Saturday. What time did Colonel Ullman call Jerusalem?"

"Just a second," came the reply as he could hear pages being flipped. "Here it is . . . He got on the line at twelve seventeen and off at one thirty-eight."

"What else do you have under the entry?" Halperin asked.

"Kind of a strange call . . . he used the teletype downstairs you had put in, and had the signal routed there, but we placed it. Priority Red, used scramblers, and it was eyes only for a General Gershon."

"Good. Pull out your file copy of the transmission and I'll be up in a minute to take a look at it."

"Uh, that's a problem, sir. . . . There isn't one."

"What do you mean? That's standard procedure, isn't it?"

"When it's sent from here, yes, sir. But when you set up the remote down in the basement, the colonel left strict orders that no hard copy was to be retained here. He had the security clearance for the project to do that. He said you'd be keeping your own files. Sorry."

"Damn," Halperin swore as he slammed down the phone.

He began to feel very much alone. Ullman was one of the Mossad's top operatives. He wasn't the type to do something without orders. Whatever happened to bring about Mouse's death, the answer was in that hour and a quarter of teletype messages. And that wasn't going to be easy to crack, he thought.

He picked up the phone again and dialed the night duty officer. "This is Halperin. I have to reach the ambassador. Is he at home?"

"No, sir. He's out of town until tomorrow evening."

"Where could I reach him? It's important."

"Well, he's in Williamsburg. I . . ."

"Oh, Lord," Halperin broke in. "What's going on down there?"

"It was in the bulletin yesterday, didn't you read it?"

"I've been off. Now what the hell is going on down there?"

"Uh, it's some big American celebration he's been invited to," the duty officer replied. "A big State dinner, and a ceremony tomorrow at Yorktown. Some historical observance; it's been on the news, you know."

"How can I reach the ambassador? It's critical."

"Call the Colonialtown Inn. The State Department has the whole thing booked. Ask for their duty officer. It's the only way to get through to the room. Give him our code for the day, but it better be important at this hour."

It took twenty minutes to get the ambassador on the line, and another fifteen to try to explain the situation to him.

"David, this is all so very hard for me to comprehend. Are you sure of your facts?"

"I'm not sure about anything anymore, sir. It's completely insane, but I've given you all the pieces as I see them. I was hoping you might know what is going on."

"No, I don't! That's what has me worried the most. But this business about the Egyptian and Ullman, and perhaps Gershon—I want to step lightly until we talk to Jerusalem."

"But what if Rashid is down there in Williamsburg with this mortar right now! Shouldn't I contact the FBI or the Secret Service?" Halperin asked.

"If it comes to that, of course; but not yet. What if Ullman killed Rashid and the Egyptian was just an unfortunate casualty? We could be blowing the cover off a very sticky mess. David, I'm a diplomat. I don't like sticking my nose in a Mossad operation without all the facts. But you're right. There are a lot of questions that need answers, and I'm worried."

"I'm a lot more than worried, sir! I'm damned mad."

"I understand. Look, you are at the embassy, I'm not. I want you to get on the wire to Jerusalem . . . but to the Foreign Minister, understand. Use my code, top priority, say you are calling on my personal instructions. Give him the story, and ask him to tell us what to do. And for God's sake, let me know what he says. I'll wait up for your call."

It gave him an eerie feeling to know he was sitting in the very same spot Ullman sat in just thirty-six hours before, doing the same thing he'd done. But the purpose was far different, Halperin thought.

It took him forty-five minutes just to get the Foreign Minister on the line, but the machine had been clattering back and forth with question after question ever since. Questions, but not many answers.

Halperin was bone tired. After all, it was now after 3:45 A.M. He'd given them every shred of information he knew almost an hour ago, seeking some wisdom from the other end of the line; some sign that would suddenly and miraculously part the clouds and reveal the answer.

"Bullshit!" Halperin muttered to the lifeless machine.

He sat there at the console with his elbows on his knees and his chin resting on the palms of his hands. The guessing game had lost its humor a long time ago. What he wanted now was some hard answers.

The machine finally snapped him awake with a sharp chatter.

DAVID, SORRY FOR THE DELAY. I'M HERE WITH THE PRIME
MINISTER. WE HAVE VERIFIED WHAT YOU TOLD US AND HAVE
A MAJOR CRISIS ON OUR HANDS OF IMMENSE GRAVITY TO OUR
GOVERNMENT AND PEOPLE. YOU SHOULD KNOW THAT TOP SECRET
PEACE NEGOTIATIONS HAVE BEEN GOING ON BETWEEN U.S.
GOV AND ISRAELI GOV THIS WEEK. WE FACE SOME VERY DIFFICULT
DECISIONS BEING FORCED UPON US BY PRESIDENT BANNON.

DEF/MIN STRONGLY OPPOSED. WHEN GERSHON TOLD HIM THAT
RASHID'S TARGET WAS BANNON, THEY DECIDED NOT TO STOP
HIM, TO ALLOW RASHID TO CARRY OUT HIS PLOT. HIS TARGET
IS UNDOUBTABLY BANNON, TODAY, AT YORKTOWN SPEECH. RASHID
MUST BE STOPPED! DO YOU COPY? L.

Halperin sat stunned for a second as he stared down at the paper.
"Those idiots!" he screamed. Bending forward, he furiously typed
out,

ROGER! H.
GOOD. WE HAVE QUESTIONED GERSHON AND DEF/MIN. THEY CLAIM
HIGHEST NATIONAL SECURITY AS JUSTIFICATION. WE TOTALLY
REJECT THIS AS COMPLETELY CONTRARY TO POLICY AND BELIEFS
OF THIS COUNTRY. ALL THREE ARE NOW UNDER ARREST. ULLMAN
ADMITS KILLING EGYPTIAN. HE WAS THE ONLY ONE WHO KNEW ALL
THE PIECES. THIS MUST BE PUT RIGHT. WE'LL INFORM U.S.
GOV AND EGYPTIAN GOV. RASHID MUST BE STOPPED! DUE TO OUR
RESPONSIBILITY, WE MUST ENSURE HE IS. YOU ARE THE ONLY MAN
WE HAVE ON THE GROUND. NO TIME TO SEND HELP. GO TO YORK-
TOWN. DO WHAT YOU CAN. WE ARE RELYING UPON YOU, DAVID.
OUT.

The ringing telephone on the bedside table finally stabbed deep
enough into his consciousness to wake him up. "Yeah . . . Daniels . . ."
"Frank, this is David Halperin. I hate to wake you up at this—"
"Oh, no," came the groan. Opening one eye, he tried to focus in on
the luminous dial of the clock. Suddenly incensed, he grabbed it and
pulled it to his face. "It's four fifteen! Four fifteen in the goddamn
morning!" he screamed.
"I know, Frank, I know. Look, I'm sorry, but it's—"
"Sorry! It's the middle of the damn night!"
"Frank, will you listen," he pleaded. "I couldn't think of any-
one . . ."
"Well, not me, that's for damn sure!"
"Rashid's going to kill President Bannon . . . today!" he said, since
it was the only way to get Daniels's attention. "Your President, Bannon.
In Yorktown. Now will you shut up and listen?"

"What? Bannon?" Daniels replied as he sat up in bed. "Are you sure? What's going on? Bannon?"

"I'll fill you in on all the details later. We've just pieced it together, but he's down there in Yorktown, and he's after Bannon."

"Okay, okay. Uh . . . let me call the Secret Service, I'll call you right back."

"They are already being contacted right now, you don't have to."

Daniels was confused. "Then why are you calling me?"

"Because I need your help. I want to go down there. I need someone with me who has some heavy weight IDs whom I can trust. I wouldn't get past first base alone and I need you. It's become very important to me, okay?"

"That's not our league, Dave. What the hell can you or I do that the Secret Service can't? Besides, once they know his description, he'll never get anywhere near Bannon, believe me!"

"He doesn't have to. He's got his hands on a big mortar, one of your Army's four-point-two-inch ones."

"A Four-Deuce! God! Yeah, I've seen them work in Vietnam."

"And he's got two dozen rounds of ammunition to go with it. He can do an awful lot of damage with those things!"

Daniels was silent for a few moments. "Agreed, but what could we do? It's not the FBI's action down there! I'd catch holy hell if I horned in on a Secret Service operation."

"Frank, you've got a perfect excuse. You guys are responsible for foreign subversive groups in the United States, aren't you? Well, let's just say that Israeli intelligence has been working with you to get this guy. You're on his trail and you're in hot pursuit, no time to wait for the red tape. I'll make sure we have more data on Rashid than they have, so we'll just be there to help out. Okay? Surely your bosses would think that was good initiative, wouldn't they?" He paused while Daniels thought it over. "Besides, he's a PLO colonel on a military operation. He's not just taking a potshot at Bannon. It's going to require putting a lot of heads together that the Secret Service doesn't usually work with, and my people know more about PLO tactics than anyone else. The excuse will hold water!"

"It might work . . . but why should I get involved?"

"Because it's your President! If Rashid pulls this off, you'll have a hard time explaining why you did nothing. . . . And where else can I get a helicopter? The sun will be up in a couple of hours, and we must—"

"A what?" came Daniels's loud, astonished reply.

"A helicopter! Look, I've given this a few minutes' thought before I called you. We need to get down there soon, to have time to look around real good once we're there. It's the only way. Can you get one?"

"Jesus . . . not if I go through channels. The Bureau would blow a gasket! We'd have to open the whole thing up, and the Secret Service will raise hell as soon as we ask."

"Remember the target . . . can you get a helicopter?"

"There is a way. . . . I know a guy who's just crazy enough to fly us down there. It would be an army chopper, not one of ours, but they don't care. This guy's got an aviation company out at Fort McNair. His name's Larry Gordon, he's a major. A real maverick. We were in the First Air Cav Division together in Vietnam. The Second Battalion of the Seventh Cav—you know, General Custer and everyone singing the 'Garry Owens.' "

"Sounds like a lot of fun," Halperin said in a limp tone.

"It wasn't! I had an infantry platoon and he flew a gunship. He tried to take care of us and I got to know him real well when we went into the A-Shau Valley in April '68."

"I didn't know you were a war hero," Halperin commented.

"Oh, I wasn't! I was too busy being scared. Westmoreland was probably sitting in his office and saw a map with no dots on it. He hated for us to have nothing to do, so we got handed Operation Delaware. Search and destroy—we searched and they destroyed. Getting in was a snap. It was staying and getting back out that was a problem. I don't know how many medals Larry got, but it must be the only thing that keeps them from firing him. Yeah, if I asked him, he'd take us. Last year he called a 'class reunion' and took some of us up to Pennsylvania to go deer hunting in one of his Hueys. He says they always need a little 'check flight.' Let me give him a call. And David?"

"What?"

"You damn well better be right about this. If you aren't you can help me look for another job."

"Mr. Halperin, on behalf of the Secret Service, we really appreciate your efforts and we want to thank your government for letting us know about this plot against the President. However, you're coming all the way down here from Washington just wasn't necessary at all." As the agent spoke his smile was polite, but firm and confident. But as he turned toward Daniels, it changed to a well-calculated blend of chilled stare and arrogance. "As you know, the Secret Service has the responsibility of protecting the President, and we take that duty very seriously. Naturally we will appreciate whatever thoughts the Bureau can offer, but I assure you we have the situation well under control." He turned his head askew to take a long look at Gordon standing behind the other two in his flight suit, but couldn't decide on anything appropriate to say in his direction.

Halperin wasn't surprised by the less than warm reception. It was what Daniels had warned him to expect, but they had to check in anyway.

The Secret Service established their command post in the historic Moore House on the edge of the battlefield, near a large field they used for their own helicopters. It hadn't been hard to find. As they flew in, they could see the huge crowds pouring in from all directions. Beginning six or seven miles away, they saw the large fringe parking lots, traffic jams, and the road blocks. For the last five miles, the roads were clear of all but official vehicles. Even Halperin began to wonder why they'd come.

Larry Gordon was as crazy as Daniels had said. "Hell, let's go," he said as they talked it over in the car. "I'm bored sick. If you guys don't mind, the general's bird needs a good thorough checkover, and he won't care if we leave his two-star plate on the front. Besides, I like to travel in style." So down they flew.

But it was now nine thirty.

Halperin smiled as he tried again with the Secret Service agent. "Mr. Marchetti, we have no intentions of interfering at all in your operations. We're all professionals. You guys are first class and I wouldn't presume to even suggest how you should do your job." He noticed Marchetti shift a little as he waited for a snow job. "Seriously! We're not here to get in your way, but Daniels and I have been after Rashid for several weeks now. We know a few things about how he and

208

the PLO operate. We just thought it might be wiser if we came and were here in case some question came up.''

"You're going to have to stay out of our way.''

"No problem.'' Halperin said reassuringly. "We thought we'd just walk around and maybe take a look from the air. We'll be out of your hair and you could reach us by radio if there's anything we can do. Okay?''

Marchetti paused. Halperin could tell he was debating the harm they might cause versus the flack he could get from the State Department if he followed his natural inclination to tell them to get the hell out of town.

"Look,'' Halperin added, "since this is an international thing, it's going to make some good press for all of us if we show what great cooperation there is between all our services, don't you think?''

"Well, okay . . . but stay out of our search patterns. We have some aircraft up in the air.''

"Absolutely, whatever you say.'' Halperin said. "Now, could you tell us a little bit about your defenses against Rashid?''

"Mr. Halperin, we just don't discuss presidential security with foreign nationals. I'm sure you can understand that.''

"Completely,'' Daniels broke in. "That's not what we're asking for. We're only interested in Rashid and the mortar. After all, that's theft from an armory, and a foreign subversive. And that is well within FBI's operational charge! You protect the President, as I'm sure you will, but I want to catch Rashid. There's a lot more targets he can go after once you frustrate him here.''

"Okay. Okay . . . I guess we owe you that much. Look, I'm busy right now, but let me have you talk to Major Hastings here. Major!'' he called out to the other room. "He's a weapons specialist we called in from Camp Perry. Counterinsurgency, and all that crap.'' Turning to the tall uniformed officer who joined the group, Marchetti said, "Major, would you fill them in on how we are handling this Rashid thing and the mortar, our search pattern, the cordon, and countermeasures? I've got to run.''

The four of them watched him dart into the other room and close the door. Halperin could see the look of amusement on the major's face. "Why the hell did I have to stay in town this weekend?'' Hastings said.

"Anyway, let's see . . . do you people know much about the weapon itself?"

"Not all that much," Halperin smiled.

"I'm not surprised, it's a unique weapon. Its characteristics, however, will explain to you exactly why we are doing what we are doing to prevent its successful employment here." Hastings continued as if he were giving a class at Benning. "The Four-Deuce has been in the Army's inventory for a number of years now, but it is not all that common in the field. Too heavy. Too hard to move around. Too complicated to be very proficient with. Takes practice and experience. With a well-trained crew it can be both effective and accurate. But two Arabs, out in the woods—I really doubt if they could put a round without a thousand meters of a target."

"Major," Halperin warned, "please don't underestimate these people."

"Oh, I'm not. I've spent my entire career with irregular troops, and they can be excellent. No, it's the weapon I'm talking about. Your man Rashid really blew it. He should have taken an eighty-one millimeter or even a sixty millimeter, but not a Four-Deuce!" Hastings said emphatically.

"Why?" Daniels asked sharply as he saw his early retirement coming.

"It's too damn big and heavy! Assembled it weighs almost seven hundred pounds, and the shells are almost twenty-seven pounds each. It only breaks down into three or four pieces and the tube alone is almost five feet long. Just how far do you think two men can get with all that in rough, wooden terrain like this? They'd have to set up right next to a vehicle or no more than a few hundred meters from a road. And we aren't going to let them do that!"

Hastings paused as he looked at the withering expressions on Halperin and Daniels. "If he had an eighty-one, I'd be scared. It shoots almost as far and he could have taken it anywhere. The shell is a lot smaller, but he could carry a lot more and they make a nice bang! It's a two-man weapon. A Four-Deuce isn't. It's specialized. We use it at battalion level, mostly for defense. It's like a vest pocket howitzer, and one of its rounds has about the same punch as a one-oh-five. But you don't walk around with either. The Four-Deuce has a five-man crew.

210

When we do take it out to the field, we put it in an armored personnel carrier. But we sure don't try to carry it around!''

Halperin saw the man had a point. "But just out of curiosity, what is its range?''

"Maximum, about four miles, but it has its best accuracy at about one to three miles.''

"Wow, that's a lot of ground to cover,'' Daniels whistled.

"Not really,'' Hastings said as he turned to a large wall map which hung behind him. "We've drawn a half-mile and four-mile circle from the core battlefield area. That's our zone of air search and where we have the roads completely cordoned off. All peripheral parking is being closely guarded. That was part of the Bicentennial plan, nicely enough. As of this morning, the bridge over to Gloucester is closed, and we put road blocks out over there too. All campgrounds are patrolled within ten miles. And you can be sure any red and white camper is being stopped and searched. We have our air units up watching the roads and open spots within the belt, but as you can see, most of the land around us is part of a closed military base. There are very few roads coming in here. Even if he gets in, there is no time or place where he can unload or set up. His plan is silly now that he's lost the element of surprise. It just won't work. Do you know what I think has already happened?''

"What?'' asked Halperin.

"I think his plan was made before he saw what this place would be like with the crowds. He came down and hitting all the traffic, got thrown off schedule, saw the line at the first checkpoint, and got the hell out of here. He couldn't be stupid enough to try it now!'' Hastings looked slowly around at three silent faces as much as to say 'class dismissed.'

19

Noon

It was hot and stuffy in the back of the camper. They sat against the front wall with their shirts off, but it didn't help. The perspiration ran down their chests in rivulets. Not that it was hot outside, but the sun had beat down on the poorly ventilated metal box for six hours now with no relief.

They had pulled into the small gravel lot at the north end of the bridge shortly before dawn. Taking the empty back roads from the marina, they slowly wound their way back west to Gloucester Point.

There was a cold early morning chill in the air then, and a ground fog hugged the low-lying areas near the water. Ralshid let the truck idle for a few minutes until the engine ran smooth, wanting very badly to leave, impatient to get to the act; yet realizing this was no time for haste, no time to stall the truck on a lonely road, no time to arouse questions.

The parking lot was already beginning to fill up when they arrived, but they were able to get a good spot near the exit on firm, level ground. Arazi got out to check and make sure they were away from any overhead wires or trees. It was also important that the spot allow a quick departure. With the truck now in place, he knelt down and carefully smoothed out the gravel where the pad of each jack would rest. Once the sun came up, they would not be going outside again. As the first pale pink light of dawn arrived, Rashid sighted in on the white pinnacle of the monument as it reflected back the rays of the sun. He used his surveyor's level several times to ensure the angles were measured precisely.

Their work complete, they locked themselves in. Just one more empty, deserted vehicle sitting in a dusty parking lot. Inside, they sat quietly waiting for the long hours to pass.

As the morning wore on they heard other vehicles arrive and the lot filled up around them. Time after time they could track the path of an unseen car by the crunch of its tires on the brown pea gravel. Engines were turned off, car doors slammed, people laughed, or argued, or said nothing, as their footsteps trailed away up the hill.

Hour after long hour the sun rose and beat down on the dark blue roof. The heavy insulation and padding on the walls covered the small windows and the louvered door. It may have been a tactical necessity, but the small turbine vent in the ceiling was just not enough to help. By late morning under the full rays of the sun, it was hopeless; but they sat and endured, since both of them had experienced far more discomfort and pain for far less important missions. Security came first! They never even considered opening the door or the roof hatch, not even a small crack. They weren't there for comfort.

But alone with his thoughts, the lack of ventilation troubled Rashid. Not physically; that was trivial. What bothered him was that it was a mental error. A mistake! A flaw in an otherwise perfect plan he'd put everything he had into. Was this the first sign it was unraveling! What else had he overlooked?

It was a tense way to pass the hours, sitting alone, quiet, each with his own deep thoughts. Finally the hands of their watches came up to the verticle. Finally it was noon.

The President's long, black Cadillac limousine was the third one in the six-car convoy that quickly wound its way up the Colonial Parkway from Williamsburg to Yorktown. It would only take fifteen or twenty minutes and Bannon savored each of them as he gazed out at the spectacular beauty. He saw the bright autumn foliage unfolding mile after mile as they passed. The trees curved in over the roadway to form a long arch of reds, yellows, and greens.

He only wished he could give it his full concentration and just sit back quietly and enjoy the view, but he couldn't. The short drive offered

213

little enough time to explain his dramatic speech to the other three heads of state accompanying him. Without saying so, they should have seen that he only gave them these fifteen minutes because he was informing, not discussing. He fully expected the usual protests, but they could all go to hell. Diplomatically, of course!

"I'm sure you all realize," he said, "this has been very difficult for us to arrive at, and only in the very last few hours. Had I known more, earlier, we'd have let you know. We could delay no longer in going public. I had no choice except to pull you aside now."

Bannon felt he really didn't owe them even that much. They should be glad someone was finally grabbing hold of the mess they'd created. Besides they couldn't keep a secret, much less be counted on for support.

The convoy finally left the tunnel of trees and broke out into the bright sunlight as it crossed Indian Field Creek. Slowing down, they were waved through the state police roadblock and on for the last leg of the drive. The parkway skirted along the high bluffs of the broad York River, which lay to their right. Bannon looked out on hundreds of sailboats and a long line of modern navy ships that had crowded into the channel for the occasion. It was a beautiful sight, Bannon thought as the conversation droned on.

Despite the agitated rhetoric of the French and German leaders, Bannon knew the British would be with him. They were the only ones who appreciated the issues involved, and they had the good manners not to criticize others for what they themselves couldn't pull off. Even Carter had told him that during the worst days of the Iran crisis Mrs. Thatcher said they'd do what we asked even if it hurt. He'd repaid them by backing her to the hilt in Rhodesia. They had no ax to grind and could be trusted.

Not so with the French or Germans. The French were disturbed because someone else's success diminished their own prestige. Plus, his big surprise hadn't given them the chance to play both sides of the fence in case it didn't work. The Germans were disturbed because it might help the dollar and in turn undercut their own dreams of economic supremacy in Europe, then the Middle East, and eventually, *die Welt*. So to hell with them, he thought.

Once past the Naval Weapons Station with its smartly saluting Marine guards, the convoy again plunged into the deep woods. Nearing Yorktown they crossed above Route 17 and drove on to the entrance of the National Park. They finally came to a halt in the circular driveway of

214

the Visitor's Center and Bannon followed his red-faced guests out of the car. The greetings were warm and friendly from Governor Lane and the long line of dignitaries.

Bannon smiled as he watched the other heads of state pass up the line chatting and pumping hands like any good politicians finding themselves in a crowd.

Halperin sat in the grass in the middle of the huge exhibition area, drinking a Coke from a nearby concession stand. He was too hot, tired, and embarrassed to even look over at Daniels and Gordon. They'd walked everywhere there was to walk and hadn't seen a damn thing, he thought. They even took a close look at the speaker's platform, each of the exhibits, the commercial trucks, and the whole perimeter of the tree line. Nothing but sore feet!

"Somehow, I didn't expect to see this Rashid guy you're looking for out here selling hot dogs with a Groucho Marx mask on," Gordon said breaking the strained silence.

"I hate to admit it," Daniels added, "but Hastings was right. I don't see how the hell they're going to pull this off." Looking over at Halperin he balled up his paper cup and threw it at his head. "I should have know better than to let you talk me into this!"

Halperin nodded and shrugged his shoulders. "I just don't know. I don't see how he could pull it off either, not with all the security and problems he'd have." He sat back and watched several helicopters flying low over the distant trees. The only thing moving on the roads were several shuttle buses and police cars. "It sure does look ridiculous. Everything is wrong—wrong place, wrong weapon, wrong time. But I guess that's what bothers me the most. It is too ridiculous."

"Most military plans I've ever seen are!" Gordon replied.

"True," Halperin said quietly. "But an experienced PLO colonel doesn't make such basic mistakes. The ones this dumb never live past second lieutenant. This is too obvious; he'd have done his homework better. It was too easy to learn about the crowds and the restricted access." Turning up to look at Daniels, he said, "And he knows his weapons—he wouldn't have gone to the trouble of getting a Four-Deuce unless that's exactly what he wants. No, something stinks."

"Okay, genius, what?" Daniels challenged him irritably.

"I don't know, but Hastings is wrong about one thing. There's no tomorrow for Rashid. He's hot property right now with his own people and doesn't have the time to pick out another plan. He has to make this work! And I have a sick feeling he knows how to do it.''

Daniels could think of nothing more to argue about. "Well, we're here. What do you want to do? It's already twelve fifteen.''

Halperin looked around the field again. "Larry,'' he said, "let's go on up and have another look around. Maybe we'll notice something.''

But they didn't. They crisscrossed the woods, flew up the interstate, and back over the battlefield—several times. But each time it was the same: the area was cordoned off and sealed up tight.

Gordon turned toward Daniels and rapped on his fuel gauge. "We need some more juice!'' he shouted over the roar of the engine. "Fort Eustis!'' he said, pointing southwest.

They both nodded in understanding as he banked the Huey off to the left. Up ahead they could see the broad blue expanse of the James River beyond the miles of rolling woodland. As they got closer they could see the runway of Felker Army Airfield at the far corner of the post.

As Gordon set the helicopter down and cut off the engine, he said, "Take me about fifteen minutes—why don't you guys stretch your legs over at the flight shack. I'll start up the engine when I'm ready.''

Walking across the tarmac, Daniels asked, "Okay, champ. What's next?''

"I think we could fly over those woods all week and not get anywhere. But,'' Halperin knit his brows slightly, "I've been thinking . . . we know a lot about Rashid's plan, but what about the camper?''

"What about it? The Secret Service called the garage in Columbia and got the make and model and description. There's an APB out—''

"But one thing that's bothered me is why did he take it there? What was wrong with it? It was supposed to be new, so what did he have done to it?''

"How the hell should I know?'' Daniels asked. "We got a good description of what it looked like when it left. What else do we need?''

"Have you got the phone number of the garage? Let's give them a call.''

"Now my girl says she told you fed guys what you wanted to know

216

this morning,'' Dante fumed. ''Why you botherin' us again? I got an honest business to run here. I got no time to keep foolin' around on the phone. If that guy was up to no good, ain't no fault of mine!''

''Mr. Dante, my job's just to make sure the press release is correct,'' Halperin replied. ''I'm sure all the Richmond papers are going to want to know what a fine job you did helping us out once we catch this guy. Of course, if you don't want the publicity, or the letter from the President that he usually sends whenever a citizen really helps us . . .''

''Now, you should have said that to start with. All us citizens are more than glad to help out when the call goes out.''

''I knew you'd see it that way! Now, how about describing it for me?''

''It was a big new Dodge truck, red and white, with one of them big matching campers on the rear. Like we told ya'll this mornin'.''

''Right, I've got that right here. But the note I got from the agent in charge doesn't mention what the camper was in your garage for. What was wrong with it?''

''Nothin' was wrong with it,'' Dante replied.

''Then why did he bring it in?''

''Cause he wanted some work done on it, that's why. Why'd ya think?''

''Mr. Dante, you aren't helping me much,'' Halperin said, quietly exasperated. ''What work?''

Daniels watched Halperin's eyes grow larger as he listened to Dante's description. ''Why didn't you tell that to the people who called this morning?'' Halperin shouted angrily.

''Cause nobody asked! That's why! Only my girl was here, and she knows better than to go discussin' my client's personal business for no good reason. I figured if they was interested they'd a asked. And they didn't! Everybody's always in a big damn hurry. Never even said thanks!''

Finally, Halperin handed the phone to Daniels. ''You better hear this,'' came his strained voice.

They ran back out to the flight line where Gordon stood watching the big olive-drag Army gasoline truck filling the tanks of the Huey.

"Larry," Daniels screamed. "We've got to get back to Yorktown, quick!"

"Hell, they're only half full. I wish you two would make up your minds."

"We aren't going that far, but every second counts. Get them out of here, we've got to get in the air." Turning to Halperin, Daniels shook his head. "You were right! He's more clever than I thought. Damn!"

Rashid sat on the side bench and said quietly. "It's time. Let's get the equipment set up, it's almost one o'clock."

Unlocking the large storage cabinets that stretched down each side of the interior of the camper, they began the well-drilled routine that would transform it into a tactical fire control center. First out was the heavy, circular base plate, which Arazi held in place while Rashid clamped it down to the floor mounts.

From the back of the cabinet, they untied the five-foot-long mortar tube and rolled it out into the middle of the floor. While Arazi held its lower end in the socket of the base plate, Rashid muscled it upright so Arazi could grasp it firmly. Rashid then attached the verticle elevating support to the tube and the base and quickly checked the traversing and elevating cranks to ensure they functioned smoothly. After making one last check, he looked up and nodded as Arazi released his grip. Taking a deep breath, he turned both cranks again. Broad smiles lit up their faces as it worked, just as it had in countless practices.

It was hard, hot work. Their skin glistened with sweat as they both collapsed back on the benches to rest for a moment. Looking down at the weapon, Rashid laughed to himself. It looked so gangly and awkward, ready to topple over, but he knew it wouldn't. To the trained eye of the soldier it was a thing of beauty; totally efficient. It was designed for a single lethal purpose, not for symmetry. It was like seeing a stork walk along in its ugly fashion versus seeing that same stork soaring high overhead in the sky, doing what it was meant to do.

Rashid stood and resumed his chore of putting the precise elevation and deflection of the aiming mechanism of the tube. Using the tables he'd rechecked hundreds of times, he carefully set the angles.

While he did that, Arazi attended to the heavy ammunition. He pulled out each round and placed it in its position on the cushioned benches. The detonators went toward the outside walls and the stabiliz-

218

ing fins toward the center aisle, half on the left bench and half on the right.

The first time they'd practiced the firing drill, their motions were unskilled and lacked synchronization. Long days later it became sharper, crisp and precise, and in cadence. The Field Manual told them that the maximum rate of fire was supposed to be eighteen rounds per minute, but that was only the goal for an experienced crew. They were out to beat that figure. They had to. One minute, perhaps a few seconds more, was all they'd get to put twenty-four rounds in the air. Plus, they wanted to adjust the settings every six rounds to correct their aim and spread the rounds out. Each change would take five seconds, so they only had forty-five seconds to actually fire.

Instead of using the conventional method with one man firing and the other passing him the rounds, they went to the much more dangerous system where each man stood on opposite sides of the tube and they'd then alternately drop a round down the muzzle. It violated every known safety rule for a mortar, but it was effective, Arazi conceded. It also required careful, precise movements, since it wouldn't do to have one round going down while another was coming up. They'd be killed; but worse still, the mission would come to an abrupt end.

Rashid called out the cadence. "One," Arazi picked up one of the heavy bombs, placing his left hand under its top and his right hand over its thin waist just above the fins. "Two," he lifted it up and pivoted to his right with the bomb at port arms. "Three," he placed the base of the bomb over the muzzle and released it, bringing his hands down and away from the tube. "Four," he would straighten up and pivot back to where the next bomb was waiting. The cadence was precise. He fired on "three" and Rashid fired on "one." They followed the sequence like two bobbing robots.

All of the first six rounds would be in the air before the first one struck. Plenty of time for Arazi to spin around to the bank of TVs fastened to the front wall and watch their effects. Rashid would already be kneeling in front of the mechanism, waiting to crank the corrections onto the tube. Then it was back to work. One. Two. Three times more.

Each round carried over seven and one-half pounds of high explosive. No two rounds could ever have precisely the same ballistics, so the first barrage would bracket the target in a violent firestorm of death and destruction. Subsequent barrages would refine the effect and pinpoint it onto the speaker's platform. Undoubtably, some of the rounds would fall short and some go long, but this would only help the overall outcome.

"Let's get the jacks into place," Rashid said. He went to the right front corner and opened the small control box. Wiping his sweating palms on his slacks, he looked at the four toggle switches. "Well, here goes . . ."

Raising the first switch, he heard a faint hum as the right rear jack slid down into place. He turned it off as soon as the corner of the camper shifted slightly and he heard the base plate crunch into the gravel. With one in place, he then activated each of the others. Ready for the final test, he pushed all four of them up together. Rashid grinned as the floor beneath them slowly rose up about six inches. When it reached the mark on the wall, he turned them all off. Pulling down a long carpenter's level off the wall, he began the slow process of fine tuning the height of each jack until the floor was level and perfectly horizontal.

Arazi jumped up and down on the solid steel platform. He was in ecstasy. "It works! It really does work!" He laughed.

Noticing the time, Rashid turned his attention to connecting the wires for the radio-controlled detonators for the explosives they'd placed under the bridge.

Arazi went back to the side benches and reached far back to pull out two short but deadly MP–5 submachine guns hidden there. They were stubby, with fold-up metal stocks and thick, round silencers. Balancing one lightly in his hand, Arazi knew these put out a quick, quiet stream of bullets.

Finished, Rashid smiled to himself as he looked at his watch. It was 1:35. He reached over and turned on all three battery-powered Hitachi TVs mounted on the front wall.

Twenty-five minutes to go.

They were ready.

As Bannon rose to speak, the room fell silent.

"Ladies and gentlemen, I can't tell you how much we've enjoyed this luncheon and the tremendous Virginia hospitality you've shown me and our official guests yesterday and today. We would all like to stay and enjoy your company for the balance of the afternoon, but I'm afraid the hour grows short. I've been told there's a large crowd outside, and no politician leaves that many voters standing in the hot sun."

When the polite laughter died down, he continued, "I'd be remiss if I didn't take this opportunity to personally thank you, Governor Lane, Mrs. Lane, the officials of colonial Williamsburg, the National Park Service, and the Virginia Independence Bicentennial Committee for the splendid program you've put together here to mark the two hundredth anniversary of the victory at Yorktown. It's an occasion that deserves a commemoration such as this."

Pausing to turn serious, he said, "I hope that each of you will pay particularly close attention to my speech this afternoon. We are here to honor Yorktown, but the speech will deal with an issue that is more contemporary—our foreign policy. I shall be announcing some startling new developments in the Middle East. I hope each of you will consider what I have to say today and be able to support us in the spirit of Yorktown."

Turning to the others seated at the head table, he smiled and said, "I'm afraid we must leave now; it's almost showtime."

20

1:45

As soon as the helicopter set down in the grass next to the Moore House, Halperin and Daniels jumped out and charged across the front lawn.

"Marchetti! Where are you?" Daniels shouted as they ran through the front door. Heading to the large wall map, he added, "Get Hastings, too!"

"What's all this crap over the radio about changing our search patterns because of the camper," Marchetti said as he stormed angrily out of his office. "The President is about to come out and I don't have time to piss around with any of your half-baked theories about—"

"Just shut and listen," Halperin said as he stared back fiercely. "It's the camper. That's the key. The garage is a body shop. He rebuilt it! That's why he took it there." Turning to squarely face Hastings, he raised out both his hands and said, "Don't you see . . . it is just like you said, only a fool would try to use a Four-Deuce around here on foot. He isn't! He's rigged up the camper with special flooring and jacks and a roof hatch. The mortar's inside! Just like you do with an armored personnel carrier."

Marchetti's eyes grew wide as he stammered, "What? Could he do that?"

222

Hastings didn't reply. He stood and looked at the map. "Oh, Lord."

"You said you were combing the woods and the roads for a place he could get off by himself," Halperin said quickly. "Well, that's exactly where he isn't. He'll have it set up in the middle of a bunch of vehicles—in a parking lot, or one of the exhibition areas. Somewhere he can stop for a little while. Don't you see, the search is all wrong!"

Marchetti spun to stare at the map in panic. "Are . . . are you sure?"

"Yes," Daniels replied. "And you can forget about your cordon. If he went to all of this trouble, you can bet he's figured out a way to get the damn thing close enough."

Marchetti ran his hand across the map and said, "God! We've got about ten campgrounds or parking lots inside the four-mile radius."

"Then get your helicopters over as many of them as you can, right now!" Halperin said firmly. "Tell them to watch the roofs. One of them is going to open real soon. Do it! There's no time left."

Marchetti's confused gaze scanned across the map. "But . . . all our plans, and . . ."

Halperin grabbed him by the shoulders and spun him around. Looking directly into his eyes, he saw the panic. "Please!" Halperin pleaded, "before it's too late." Turning to Hastings, Halperin added, "You tell him! He didn't take the wrong weapon, we just didn't understand his plan."

Marchetti looked at him for a brief second and then ran into the other room. They heard him order, "Get the helicopters on the radio, quick!"

As Bannon stepped out the front door of the Visitor's Center into the bright sunlight, the waiting fife and drum corps began to play. The deafening whistle and thump was heightened by the overhanging granite portico of the entryway.

They played a few bars and turned smartly to their right. Marching forward to the amphitheater, the official party fell in behind. It was a short walk over the battlements, across the field, and on to the large speaker's platform. As they walked on, Bannon looked around and noticed the rest of the dignitaries chatting and slowly stringing out far to the rear.

Standing and watching, he also noticed that the Secret Service agents around him were listening intently to their ear pieces. The detail chief walked over to him and said, "Sir, we're getting some information over the radio that there may be a problem. It may be wise for us to return to the building until we have this sorted out."

"Don't be ridiculous," Bannon snapped. "If you have something definite, fine, but I can't delay a thing like this for nothing."

Halperin beat Daniels back to the helicopter, where Gordon had kept the engine idling. They took to the air immediately and gained altitude over the battlefield.

Daniels leaned over to Gordon and shouted, "Get on their frequency and let's monitor the search." Turning around in his seat, he saw Halperin lift a small suitcase he'd brought with him onto the seat. As the top opened back, Daniels looked down at a small arsenal of weapons. "What the hell is all that," he exploded.

"Relax, Frank, it's just a little insurance. A traveling salesman left it behind. You know how to use one of these?" he asked as he handed the shocked FBI agent an Uzi machine gun. "It's simple. Just shove in a magazine and pull the bolt back. Ready to go!" He smiled innocently.

"Are you nuts! That stuff's illegal."

"Suit yourself. If you'd rather go after Rashid with that little thirty-eight-caliber snubnose, be my guest." Daniels wavered, then snatched the Uzi away before Halperin could put it back in the suitcase. "Now, of course you're right, this stuff is illegal, and we'll be real sure to turn it into the proper authorities just as soon as we get back to D.C.," he said with a wry grin. "We wouldn't want anyone to get hurt with them, now would we?" Turning back to the open suitcase, he looked down and said, "I also have some illegal grenades here. Want one?"

Daniels' eyes rolled up in his head, but he bit his tongue and kept quiet. He also kept the Uzi.

Flying at three thousand feet, they looked down on the green woods and fields spread out below, where huge crowds hurried from the exhibit areas to the semicircle around the amphitheater. Tension mounted as they watched the other helicopters darting across or hovering over the nearby campgrounds and parking lots. They watched and listened to the brisk radio traffic, but as the seconds dragged on it was becoming more and more obvious they'd found nothing.

Gordon turned around and looked at both of them. "We have to clear this air space over the battlefield. There's a flyover of F–Fifteens coming right through here in three minutes when the ceremonies start. They're coming right up the peninsula from east to west, so we have to move to one side of the line or the other. North or south, take your pick."

Halperin looked around in frustration, then leaned over to Daniels.

"There's five or six choppers over here already, but I only see one over there on the Gloucester side." Pointing to the north, he said, "Let's try over there."

Daniels nodded and motioned with his hands for Gordon to bank right.

The two Arabs sat nervously turning their eyes from one TV set to the other in rapid succession. It was confusing, like looking at something with three widely separated eyes. Spinning over to glance at the next set, they went through some quick mental gymnastics to remember each camera position on the scene.

The commentators droned on and on. One network was covering the recreated militia units from the Revolutionary War period as they stormed one of the trench lines. A second showed the panorama of the sailing regattas on the York River. The third peered down from the Goodyear blimp high overhead. So it went, minute after agonizing minute.

Finally one, then a second, then all three stations cut away to the door of the Visitor's Center. They watched the door open and heard the fife and drum corps begin to play. At last a familiar face came out the door and stood under the portico.

"Bannon!" Rashid whispered as he stared intently at the picture. His face was calm and expressionless as he observed the narrow scene. The reporter's voice was soon drowned out as the band turned and began to walk past his position. All three sets had the same area of coverage. Panning back, Rashid watched as the band, Bannon, and a long line of dignitaries began to walk out across the grass field. In the line he could see other faces he knew from TV and newspapers: congressmen, senators, governors, and the rest.

Looking at his watch, Rashid said, "Here they come, right on time."

He and Arazi were spellbound as they watched the group get nearer and nearer to the platform. Just as the drum major reached there, the sound of the fifes and drums was swept away by the streaking roar of wave after wave of sleek, supersonic F–15 Eagles passing low overhead. They watched as Bannon and the rest of the party turned their heads upward. Hands were raised to shade out the bright sun as all eyes looked up at the awesome American might passing over. It would be of little use to them today, Rashid thought.

It was 2:00 P.M.

"Open the roof, Hafez," he exulted. Grasping him by the shoulder, their eyes locked. "It is time! It is finally time for our revenge!"

Gordon continued the slow bank to the right until the helicopter came parallel with the bridge. From high overhead, they looked down and saw the shuttle buses traversing its narrow deck. Far ahead, Halperin spotted the other Huey flying low over the highway and its nearby side streets.

Halperin looked at his watch and knew that their time had run out. They had a huge area to cover and no time to do it in.

"Damn!" He swore in frustration. He leaned forward and shouted, "Anything at all on the radio?"

"Zilch," Gordon replied, "but they're still looking."

Scanning ahead through the plexiglass nose bubble, Halperin said, "We're out of time. Let's start at the foot of the bridge there and work north. Those lots," he pointed. "Let's go on down."

"There go the F–Fifteens," Gordon said as he threw his thumb back over his shoulder.

Halperin turned in his seat to catch a glimpse of the gray streaks flashing low over the battlefield.

Gordon took the helicopter up as he hopped over the bridge and shot down toward the parking lot around the boat slip. Coming in low, they saw individual cars and trucks and campers in the left-hand lot.

As they swooped over the land, Halperin's eye was attracted by a flash of movement. Turning his head to the right, he looked underneath the bridge to the lot on the other side. Scanning across the rooftops of the vehicles, he spotted the movement again. The glare of the sun was caught for a split second and reflected back at him from a dark roof. He saw it moving, tilting back, unfolding, opening.

"There!" he shouted. "There! Off to the right, in the other lot, the dark blue roof."

226

Halperin was pitched back in the seat and thrown onto his side as Gordon put the Huey into a violent, banked turn to the right. Using its full power, the machine clawed the air for a second before it shot upward, skimming across the foot of the bridge in a wrenching, looping about-face. While his two passengers grabbed for handholds, Gordon dropped in low over the lot on the other side, swiftly and precisely.

Pulling himself up to look out his side window, Halperin was pressed against the door as the Huey continued the momentum of its banked turn. Out of the blur he was finally able to find the camper coming up quickly under him. The twin blue roof panels stood wide open, gaping. Just as the helicopter shot overhead, he focused his eyes into the opening below.

"That's it!" he screamed. "God! I could see the mortar and two men standing next to it."

"I saw one of them look up as we passed over," Daniels replied. "I'd swear it was Rashid."

"Put this thing down, quick!" Halperin yelled, reaching over to grab his Uzi.

As the helicopter continued its banked turn, Gordon suddenly pulled back on the control stick, raising its nose and halting the machine's charging forward momentum. At the same time he let the rear rotor race on and brought the tail around in a quick 180-degree turn. Like a magnificent bull elephant made to pirouette around on one leg atop a tiny pedestal in the center ring of a circus, the huge helicopter strained, but did Gordon's bidding exactly as he commanded. He cleared some overhead wires and set it down in the center of an open area on the hard-packed gravel road only a few hundred yards downhill from the camper; the Huey's nose pointed directly at its rear door.

A pleased smile crossed Gordon's lips as he said, "Not bad. A little rusty, but not bad." Neither Halperin nor Daniels heard him. They were still bouncing in their seats, watching the cloud of leaves, dirt, and small stones billow out from under the Huey's blades. It had been many years since Gordon had done a combat assault landing into a hot LZ, but a well-skilled hand never forgot.

Regaining his balance, Halperin pulled back hard on the side door latch and slid it open. He and Daniels hit the ground at the same time, but Halperin stopped to reach back inside for one of the grenades. Shoving it into his jacket pocket, he dashed off after the FBI agent.

Gordon watched them come around the nose and run up the road toward the camper. He activated his chin mike and broke into the Secret Service frequency. "Marchetti!" he yelled. "Marchetti, this is the FBI bird. We have the target in sight and confirmed over on Gloucester Point. I say again, confirmed on Gloucester Point. Get some backup over here quick!"

With the roof panels opened all the way up to the vertical, the cool outside air cascaded down into the hot, stuffy compartment. They both stood still for a few seconds and breathed deeply to clear their heads. It reinvigorated them like a cold shower.

Rashid turned back to the TV sets to follow the progress of the presidential party as it got closer and closer to the speaker's platform.

"Come on! Just a little closer!" said Arazi, drumming his fingertips on the first shell.

Rashid was also in agony as he nervously waited, but it had taken too long to get here and he wanted his revenge to be total. He'd wait. Just a few short minutes and the whole group would be in the kill zone. Just a few minutes.

As he stared intently at the screens, his concentration was suddenly broken and he cocked his head to listen. He bolted upright as the first faint sound became the unmistakable thump-thump-thump of a rapidly approaching helicopter.

Arazi also shot his eyes upward and exclaimed, "No . . . No, not now!"

"Quiet!" Rashid snapped back, listening hard. As the sound grew very loud he instinctively turned his face up just as the glare of the sun was blocked out. He saw the olive-drab machine hurtle by, barely fifty feet over their heads. The powerful downdraft of wind from its swirling blades slammed onto his sweat-covered body like a sleet storm, forcing him to blink and turn his face aside from the sharp pain. It passed over and was gone as quickly as it had come.

Arazi looked at him, his mouth open in sudden shock. "They've found us! They've found us!" He screamed. Spinning around, he grabbed for the first mortar shell.

"No!" Rashid called out as he grabbed his arm. "Calm down. They cannot stop us even though they know where we are. So keep to the

228

plan! Bannon and the rest aren't in position yet. This is no time to throw it all away, just wait a few seconds more.''

Turning back to the television sets, he watched the fife and drum corps split into two lines as the official party passed on between them.

"Just a few more moments," he said. "I want them up on the platform where they are exposed and can't scatter." Turning around, he said, "Hafez, look out the back door and see where the helicopter is.''

Arazi tore down the black drape and fumbled with the lock on the rear door. Frustrated and unable to get the small mechanism to work, he took a step back and savagely kicked at the door handle. The lock snapped and the door flew wide open, crashing against the side of the camper.

He leaned out and stared down the road in disbelief. He twisted his head around and shouted. "It landed! Right out there, it landed! There are men running this way.''

Rashid turned his head back to the doorway. "I only see two. We're lucky!'' Reaching over for one of the machine guns lying on the bench, he tossed it to Arazi and said calmly, "You must hold them off for me . . . a minute or two is all. Go! You must not fail.''

By the time Halperin had dashed around the nose of the Huey, he saw Daniels was already fifty feet ahead and racing at full speed up the gravel road. Pounding after him, trying to catch up, he reached back to remember lessons from his basic training. Give the butt of the magazine a good hard slap to make sure it is firmly seated in the receiver. Pull back on the bolt and let it snap forward, solidly ramming a new round in the chamber. Then keep your hands away from the bolt and the barrel. Short bursts, don't rush it! Suppress the return fire. In an assault, fire from the hip and keep moving fast! Panting and running fast up the road, he got the sick feeling he wished he'd paid more attention to a class he never thought he'd need.

Only halfway there, the rear door of the camper came flying open. Seconds later, a dark, bare-chested man leaped to the ground, his legs spread in a crouched firing position. He had a short black object in his hands that he held at waist level as he pivoted around to point it at them. Before Halperin could react, he saw Daniels stagger forward, his toes digging into the gravel. He spun around and began to tumble forward as the stones around him were kicked up by a silent hail of bullets.

Running at full speed, he was past Daniels' limp form before he even thought to fire back. He raised the Uzi in front of him and began to press the trigger inward, while the Arab was trying to sight in on him. Short bursts, hell, he thought, as he held the trigger in on full automatic. That guy's trying to kill me!

For an instant their eyes met in mutual terror. The long strides meant the distance was closing rapidly. It was a split-second dance of death as they each saw that the one who hit his target first would be the one who lived.

The Arab was the more skilled, but Halperin had the advantage of a stationary target. Such was the fine line between living and dying, as the chattering stream from the Uzi hit first. It stitched an exploding red line across the Arab's bare chest and slammed him backward into the camper door. He collapsed in a heap on the ground.

But Halperin never saw his target go down. Just as his bullets struck, a series of lightning-quick hammer blows knocked his own legs out from under him. It was like running full speed into a knee-high brick wall. He flew forward and tumbled through the air, rolling, sprawling, puzzled as to why his body was doing this. How stupid to fall down now, he thought, as he crashed onto the ground and rolled over into a shallow drainage ditch.

Halperin lay face downward in the gravel, dazed. Got to get up, he thought. Got to stop them! Raising his head he saw the camper still fifty or sixty yards away. In its rear door was a second man.

"Rashid," he muttered wearily as he wiped his eyes.

Looking around, Halperin saw his Uzi lying fifteen feet away in the middle of the road. Got to get it, he thought. But the legs wouldn't move! Rolling over onto his side, he looked down and saw a half-dozen red stains on his legs. Blood? There was no pain, but could he have been shot? He lay his head back on the ground and chuckled to himself. Well, that's a lot better than being clumsy.

Looking back at the camper, the haze over his eyes began to clear a little. He could see Rashid moving, moving toward the mortar! Got to stop him, he thought with a new determination. Reaching into his pocket, he got a firm grip on the grenade and brought it out in front of his face.

230

Halperin raised his head and pulled the pin out of the grenade. Rolling over onto his left side, he took a deep breath and hurled it as far as he could with his fading strength.

He saw it fly through the air; a tumbling black dot against the blue sky. It landed on the road and bounced a few times before it rolled to a halt a good ten yards short and off to the right side of the camper.

For a long second he stared helplessly as it just lay there. Suddenly the small black ball erupted in a blinding flash that shook the ground beneath him. Looking up as the smoke cleared away, Halperin saw the blue camper still standing there. Its side was blackened and dented, but it still stood there!

He gave a loud groan, then collapsed back on the ground. As Halperin passed out, it was with the sure knowledge he'd failed. All the weeks of work, the deaths, and now the pain had been for nothing!

In the last brief second before it all went black, he heard a loud thumping noise rush past, pelting him with stones and dirt, but he was far past caring.

From his pilot's seat, Gordon watched the scene unfold through the plexiglass nose bubble. Still holding onto the controls he yelled out in vain as Daniels went down. Suddenly the windscreen of the Huey was shattered as the bullets meant for the running Israeli passed on to punch into the helicopter.

Smacked back into his seat, he shook his head and looked down to see a neat, red hole in his chest. "Damn!" he said in shocked surprise, slowly covering the wound with his hand. Stunned and fascinated, he looked on as blood began to pump between his fingers and flow down his shirt.

"Ain't that a kick in the ass!" Gordon whispered to himself. "All those times I've worn my flak jacket and one never even got close. Figures I'd buy it like this!" he muttered in disgust.

Hearing the grenade explode he looked up. The camper rocked, but it wasn't really damaged. Through the open door, he could see the second Arab stand up.

"Aw, shit! Daniels is down, Halperin's down . . . Looks like I'm it!"

Turning on his microphone he coughed and winced from the pain.

231

"Okay, Marchetti, you dumb bastard . . . Looks like the cavalry's got to come to the rescue—but you better get Bannon the hell out of there!"

He began to whistle and left the mike open. Turning the throttle up to maximum, he let the torque build up a full head before he threw the stick forward. The tail rotor section shot up and the Huey leaped ahead charging with nose down and tail high. Hugging the ground, it raced up the road.

Across the river, Marchetti stormed out of his office in a panic when he heard the first message.

"What was that! What's going on?" he asked, turning from face to face. "Put it on the speaker, quick."

As it clicked on, they all strained to hear a song being softly whistled over a roaring engine. The song was punctuated by several deep coughs.

Turning to Hastings, Marchetti screamed, "What is that? What's going on out there?"

Suddenly the song was cut off by a loud crashing explosion and the speaker fell silent.

Hastings turned and looked out the window across the broad blue river.

"Don't you ever watch any old movies?" he asked Marchetti in a tense, hoarse voice. "That was the 'Garry Owens'—the battle song of the Seventh Cav. . . . Remember *They Died with Their Boots On*, Errol Flynn charging all the Indians at the Little Bighorn?"

"I don't understand." Marchetti threw his arms up.

"You never will," came the sad reply.

Rashid ignored the chatter of gunfire outside as he concentrated on the television screens. Bannon walked up the wooden staircase and onto the wide platform, waving to the crowd. The rest of the dignitaries followed more quickly now, finding their seats along the front row. The band was into its last flourish.

Now! Rashid reached down for the first shell as Bannon took his seat. Now! The time has come!

Lifting the shell with both hands, he turned toward the weapon with his eyes still riveted on the distant scene. Suddenly he was thrown off balance as the camper rocked from a jarring explosion. He was knocked off his feet and sent sprawling backward across the bench. He slipped off and fell heavily to the floor, his head striking the steel base plate.

Dazed, he picked himself up and blinked to clear away the fog. Reaching down, he grabbed another shell from the side bench. Turning around to face the television, he saw men running onto the platform, grabbing the President, pulling him toward the stairs.

"Too late," Rashid laughed out loud. "Too late!" He reached for the muzzle of the mortar.

His eyes involuntarily darted to the open doorway as he saw something large moving toward him. Hearing the rapidly accelerating roar of the turbine engine, he stood for a second, frozen. The Huey was racing at him, nose down, tail high, like a wounded scorpion ready to sting and die. The engine pitch rose to a crescendo as the apparition grew in size to fill the doorway and still more.

Rashid realized too late. His hands groped for the mouth of the tube. Finally he got the base inserted, then the fins. Smiling, he released his grip and let the shell drop downward, out of his hands. The fins, the narrow waist, and then the nose disappeared from his sight.

But too late! The rotor blades of the helicopter slashed through the thin body panels of the camper, disintegrating as they tore open its top and rear end. Propelled forward at over a hundred miles per hour, the nose bubble of the machine crashed through the doorway. Like a big snowplow it folded open the rear wall and top as if they were cardboard. Carried on by its momentum, the heavy aircraft smashed into the mortar, tearing it loose from the mountings on the floor. Rashid looked through the plexiglass nose for an eternal second as he saw the face of the pilot. The onrushing Huey ground him and the mortar into the forward bulkhead, as the shell exploded in his face.

Finally reaching the solid supports of the truck chassis, the force of the helicopter knocked the vehicle thirty feet forward into a long row of parked cars. The four jacks underneath plowed deep furrows in the gravel, marking its path.

With its forward momentum now stopped, the nose section slid to a halt. But the high tail section carried on, upward and over, flipping the long body of the machine onto its back, crashing down on top of the grotesque pile.

The tangled wreckage lay there for a brief second before carcasses of the vehicles were blown apart by a shattering series of explosions culminating in a spectacular orange ball of flaming aviation gas engulfing them and shooting upward above the deck of the bridge.

21

2:25

Returning to the podium, Bannon watched the crowd begin to settle down and look up toward him. Smiling, he concentrated on his speech to try to put the shocking news out of his mind.

"I'm very sorry for the short delay we've had in the beginning of the ceremonies, ladies and gentlemen," he began in a pleased, confident voice. "It seems there was a . . . very serious aircraft accident just across the river, but everything is now in order."

He paused with most of the crowd to watch the oily black smoke still rolling sluggishly above Gloucester Point.

"Under the circumstances, I'm sure you can all understand the delay." His hand trembled slightly as he flipped the cover of his folder. "Turning now to the substance of my remarks this afternoon, I want to discuss a subject that is as critical to our nation's future today in 1981 as the victory here at Yorktown was to our Founding Fathers. . . ."

EPILOGUE

Thursday, October 22

Halperin groaned and turned his head from side to side on the pillow. He licked his lips and frowned. The mind was becoming conscious, but the body fought back. It had grown accustomed to lying here safe and warm and comfortable. Waking up meant remembering. Remembering meant pain.

" . . . Looks like the sedative's wearing off . . . he should be coming out of it now." He heard the words, but they were far away and didn't register. It was just some background noise and had nothing to do with him.

He heard a rustle and the space around him grew bright. One eye opened and squinted closed at the sight of the bright sun coming through the open window.

"Please keep it short," the voice said. "He's out of danger now, but his system's had a rough time. We don't want to tire him out. I'll be back in a few minutes."

Halperin heard steps going away and a door closing quietly. He was gradually becoming aware. The mind kept nudging the body to do something. It was curious and puzzled. It needed to have exercise and be active again. It was hungry and wanted the senses to wake up and feed it.

Slowly the eyes fluttered open. He blinked to try to chase away the white haze. Focusing, he realized it was a white ceiling, with dots, the small dots of acoustical tile.

"Welcome to the land of the living."

He turned his head toward the voice and focused in on the Israeli ambassador sitting calmly in a blue pinstriped suit a few feet away.

Preposterous, he thought. He closed his eyes again, then thought about it and opened them to look slowly around the room. Soft pastel colors, nicely furnished, big, he thought. He realized that he was lying on a high bed under crisp white sheets. Next to him was a night table that held a huge floral bouquet. But it still didn't register.

"Glad to have you back with us, David." He looked up and saw the familiar face of the Israeli ambassador seated on a chair at the foot of the bed. "You had us very worried the past few days."

"Where am I . . . what is this?" Halperin asked in a rasping voice.

"Relax. You're in Walter Reed Hospital, in Washington. The VIP Suite, no less; compliments of the American government."

He reached up and felt the bandages on his head and could feel tight wrappings on his legs and his chest. It just didn't sink in, his visitor could tell from the confused expression on his face.

"Just lay back and take it easy, David," the Israeli said. "It'll all come back sooner than you'd like. You were hurt pretty bad in all the gunfighting and the explosions when the camper blew up."

"I feel like I got run over by a truck," he said, but slowly the images began to flash out of his subconscious. The search, the helicopter, the camper, Daniels, Gordon, Mouse, Gloucester Point. "Rashid!" he said as he raised his head. "What happened?"

"He failed," the ambassador said quietly. "He failed. He never got a shot off. He's dead. Thanks to you . . . and Daniels and Gordon. He failed! You know there was a tremendous explosion, David. You're the only one to make it out, I'm sorry to say. You took a number of bullets in the legs, but the doctors don't think there's any permanent damage. You also have a concussion, a couple of broken ribs, and a lot of bumps, bruises, and burns. But you'll be up and around in a few weeks. Fortunately, you were flat in a ditch and unconscious, so most of it passed over you. Except for one of the roof panels, but it could have been a lot worse."

237

"I'm glad you think so," Halperin replied.

"Once you're well, you're going home for a long rest. You stopped him, David! You stopped him, and it was worth it."

Halperin looked up and saw a small card next to the flowers. He reached over and brought it closer. It had the small seal of the President of the United States and a neat, hand-written note that said, "With deepest gratitude to a very brave friend, Edward Bannon."

"I think you'll want to keep that, David," the Israeli said. "It's about the only public display of recognition you're likely to get. It has been decided by all the parties involved that it is best to place a lid on this whole Rashid affair. The truth would help none of us now. The Americans don't want it known that someone could get that close. We and the Egyptians have agreed that the role of Gershon and Ullman in Khalidi's death was an aberration and knowledge of it would only undermine our close ties. Even the PLO wants very much to have the matter forgotten."

The ambassador looked down and picked at the seams of his trousers. "So it has all been written off as an unfortunate aircraft accident." He paused painfully.

"But what happened and what you did will not be forgotten by those of us who know. Gershon and Ullman have been quietly retired in disgrace. They are finished," said the Israeli ambassador harshly.

The door opened and a nurse leaned in, pointing to her watch.

"I must leave now," the Israeli said as he stood and put on his coat. "By the way," he smiled, "the prime minister promoted you to lieutenant colonel. When he gets you back home, he says he has some medals to pin on you, too. Of course, the official citations will refer to your service in the '73 War, but that's the usual convention. So relax and get well. Many things have happened since the nineteenth and we'll need you up and around as soon as possible."

Halperin lay on the bed and said nothing. There were just no words worth saying.

The ambassador stopped in the doorway and turned back. "Get well, David," he said. Looking down to carefully straighten the band of his hat, he added, "I know . . . but you did all you could."

As the door slowly closed behind him, Halperin turned his head toward the wall. "You did all you could," he thought to himself. He repeated it over and over again, but the words kept coming out hollow and off key.

238